Dear Diary,

It's no secret that my family has had their share of problems lately. Especially where baby Cody is concerned. But I refuse to be glum. Abby's wedding is only days away and the preparations are transforming the mansion into a Christmas wonderland. What a joy it's going to be to see my daughter marrying the man she loves!

And have I mentioned that Jake is coming home? I'm not sure if he's returning to Austin to play Santa Claus or Daddy, but I'll wonder about his reasons later. Right now, the gift of having my son in my arms again is enough for this mother.

Yes, diary, it appears my holiday wishes are beginning to come true. Now if this season of love could also work some sort of miracle and bring Hope and Drake Logan back together again, I would count this a very merry Christmas....

Megan

Dear Reader,

There's never a dull moment at Maitland Maternity! This unique and now world-renowned clinic was founded twenty-five years ago by Megan Maitland, widow of William Maitland, of the prominent Austin, Texas, Maitlands. Megan is also matriarch of an impressive family of seven children, many of whom are active participants in the everyday miracles that bring children into the world.

As our series begins, the family is stunned by the unexpected arrival of an unidentified baby at the clinic— unidentified, except for the claim that the child is a Maitland. Who are the parents of this child? Is the claim legitimate? Will the media's tenacious grip on this news damage the clinic's reputation? Suddenly, rumors and counterclaims abound. Women claiming to be the child's mother materialize out of the woodwork! How will Megan get at the truth? And how will the media circus affect the lives and loves of the Maitland children—Abby, the head of gynecology, Ellie, the hospital administrator, her twin sister, Beth, who runs the day care center, Mitchell, the fertility specialist, R.J., the vice president of operations— even Anna, who has nothing to do with the clinic, and Jake, the black sheep of the family?

Please join us each month over the next year as the mystery of the Maitland baby unravels, bit by enticing bit, and book by captivating book!

Marsha Zinberg
Senior Editor and Editorial Co-ordinator, Special Projects

# STELLA BAGWELL

# Just for Christmas

Published by Silhouette Books

**America's Publisher of Contemporary Romance**

SILHOUETTE BOOKS
300 East 42nd St.,
New York, N. Y. 10017

ISBN 0-373-65065-5

JUST FOR CHRISTMAS

Copyright © 2000 by Harlequin Books S.A.

Stella Bagwell is acknowledged as the author of this work.

Visit Silhouette at www.eHarlequin.com

Printed in U.S.A.

For as long as she can remember, **Stella Bagwell** has loved to read. Add that to being an incurable romantic and she definitely happened onto the perfect job fifteen years ago when she became a full-time romance writer. Now, over forty novels later, she still finds her job a joy and a challenge.

Being married to her high school sweetheart for twenty-nine years has taught Stella much about the staying power of true love. She and her husband live in the beautiful mountains of southeastern Oklahoma and they consider the fifteen mile trip into town a small price to pay for the solitude they enjoy. They have one grown son who lives in Texas, where he teaches high school math and coaches football.

To two of my most faithful fans,
my sisters-in-law, Dorothy and Denise,
with much love.

# CHAPTER ONE

HOPE LOGAN GLANCED at her wristwatch, then out the open door of the gift shop to the main waiting area of Maitland Maternity Clinic. Noon hour had cleared most of the personnel from the building, but she didn't have to wonder if her husband would be in his office. As the vice president of finance, Drake was a busy man who rarely took time to eat a sandwich at his desk, much less leave the building for a leisurely meal.

Hope had to see him today. She couldn't put it off any longer. But she dreaded walking into his office. Since he'd moved out of their home two months ago, she hadn't asked him for anything. And she wasn't at all sure how he'd react to her request. But good or bad, she was soon going to find out.

She glanced over her shoulder at her young assistant, who was arranging a row of teddy bears on a display shelf. "Can you handle things for a few minutes, Tess?"

"Sure, Hope. Take your time."

*Time.* The word stayed with Hope as she left the gift shop and walked across the quiet waiting area to the elevator doors. For the past several months, she'd felt each tick of the clock as it chipped away at her fertile years. At thirty-two, she wasn't getting any younger. Yet she was no closer to having a child of her own than she had been at twenty-two. The miscarriage she'd suffered had risked her life, and Drake refused to consider another pregnancy. Not only had she lost her baby, but her husband, too. She shook the depressing thoughts from her mind. Right now she had a more immediate problem to deal with.

On the second floor Hope headed down a long corridor until she reached a door with a gold nameplate that read Vice President Drake Logan.

Even though she'd walked slowly, her heart was pounding. She breathed deeply and prayed she would appear calm and in control once she was facing her husband. The last thing she wanted was for him to think she was crumbling without him.

When Hope entered the office, Juanita, Drake's longtime secretary, was busy at a computer. She hit several buttons on the keyboard before she glanced up to see who was standing beside her desk.

"Hope! How nice to see you!"

Hope gave the older woman a rueful smile. "How are you, Juanita?"

The secretary folded her hands on top of her desk and gave Hope her full attention. "I'm doing well. I've missed seeing you these past few weeks."

In a nervous gesture, Hope pushed a hand through her hair. "I'm still running the gift shop. I'm here in the clinic every day."

Juanita's smile was full of concession. "That's not the same as you dropping by the office for a visit."

The older woman's keen black eyes took stock of Hope's pale face and loose-fitting clothes. In spite of the brave front Hope tried to present to her friends, everyone in the clinic knew she was grieving over her separation from Drake. Everyone except Drake, she thought sadly.

"You've lost weight," Juanita said gently.

Hope gave a negligible wave of her hand. "I needed

to. My clothes were getting too snug. This way I'll have plenty of room to eat for Christmas."

She glanced across the small room to the closed door leading into Drake's private office. At this moment she'd rather venture into a den of lions. "Is he busy?"

Juanita smiled wryly. "Some things never change. But at least he's alone. Go on in," she urged.

On shaky legs, Hope left the secretary's desk and crossed the expanse of carpet to Drake's office. His deep voice immediately answered her brief knock.

"Come in."

Opening the door, Hope stepped inside the all too familiar room with its comfy leather armchairs and shelves of books and mementos. Drake was behind his desk, and for a moment she said nothing, letting her eyes drink in the precious sight of him.

Even now, after all the pain he'd put her through, she still had to admit he was the most impressive-looking man she'd ever known. Thick, light brown hair lay in unruly waves above his ears, long enough in the back to tease the top of his collar. A wayward hank was always falling forward onto his wide forehead, which was more often wrinkled in a scowl than a smile. Sandy brown brows and long lashes framed a pair of eyes as green as a tropical sea.

His face was lean and angular, his lips full and well defined. The strong lines of his nose and cheekbones belied a trace of Choctaw blood, handed down through his father's side of the family.

Hope had always considered Drake's features a bit too rugged to call him classically handsome. But coupled with an athlete's body and a strong masculine presence, his looks were positively potent. So potent that the sight of him never failed to stir Hope, even after ten years of marriage.

"What is it?" he asked, not bothering to look up from the file he was studying.

"I need to talk to you, Drake."

At the sound of her voice, Drake's head jerked up. As his startled gaze collided with hers, he slowly closed the manila folder and lowered it to the desktop.

"Hello, Hope," he said blandly.

Since Drake had moved out of their home, Hope had barely spoken with him. They'd had to put on a good front at the wedding of their friends, R.J. and Dana, and both had attended the Maitland family's Thanksgiving dinner. Unlike Hope, Drake didn't seem to be suffering any ill effects from their separation. His trim body looked just as fit as ever.

Trying to ignore the painful longing pouring through her, she returned his greeting.

"Hello, Drake."

Leaning forward, he rested his elbows on the desktop. Hope's gaze followed the movement of his broad shoulders beneath his pinstripe dress shirt.

"I'm surprised to see you here," he said frankly.

She pressed her dry lips together and silently prayed once again for her heart to slow its frantic pace. She couldn't imagine anything worse than fainting in front of Drake. He'd think he was the reason. And he'd be right.

"I'm sure you are."

Her short reply put a twist to his lips. "Are you going to keep standing there by the door or are you going to sit down?"

If she had a choice, Hope would rather remain by the door, away from him, but given the purpose of her visit, that would make her look ridiculous.

Taking a seat in one of the cordovan leather armchairs, she forced herself to cross her legs and ease back as though seeing him again was no more unusual than chatting with an old friend.

"So what's brought you up here today?" he asked. "Do you need more money?"

Inwardly she flinched. Drake had always believed money and things were important to her. But *he* was the one who'd been brought up in a wealthy family. *He* was the one accustomed to having most anything he wanted. Not Hope. All she'd ever wanted was a family. Someone to love. Someone to fill the void she'd experienced growing up without anyone except an irresponsible mother.

"I'm not here for financial reasons. We both know you've made sure I have plenty of money," she reminded him, trying to hide the deep resentment she was feeling.

A frown of frustration marred his features. "Then what do you need, Hope? I have a meeting in fifteen minutes with Megan and Ellie. I don't want to keep them waiting."

She wanted to remind him that he'd kept her waiting for months now, but her throat was suddenly so tight she didn't know whether she could continue to breathe, much less speak.

"I need you, Drake."

THE SIMPLE WORDS were not what Drake had been expecting to hear, and for a moment he felt as if someone had whacked him in the middle of the chest.

As he tried to regain his breath, his gaze covertly slid over the luscious sight of her. Hope was just as beautiful now as she had been ten years ago when she'd become his wife. Her honey-blond hair was thick and straight and swished against the top of her shoulders. Her skin was as creamy and luminescent as a pearl. And her lips. He didn't want to think about their sweet fullness, any more than he wanted to think of her long legs wrapped around his, her soft, slender body urgently pressed against him.

"Hope, we've been through this argument so many times we might as well be two voices on a tape recorder saying the same things over and over," he said wearily. "It's senseless to keep beating the issue to death. I haven't changed my mind about us trying to have a child. I'm not going to change it."

Anger flashed briefly in her blue eyes and at the same time her chin lifted with pride and a hint of defiance. "I'm not here to discuss my desire for a child, Drake," she said curtly.

Drake's brows lifted with guarded suspicion. "Oh. Then why are you here? To tell me you've realized the risks of what another pregnancy might do to you?"

His question caused her lips to compress to a grim line. "I *know* what the risks are, Drake. You're the one who can't get past—"

She broke off and quickly glanced away from him. Drake didn't urge her to finish what she'd been about to say. He didn't want to hear it, much less think about it. He'd spent this whole year trying to forget how close she'd come to dying.

Releasing a heavy breath, he picked up a pencil and unwittingly tapped the end against the manila folder lying before him. "So you haven't given up on the idea of being a mother. Have you made any progress with your plans to adopt?"

Her gaze skittered to him, and for a moment, the shadow of pain he glimpsed in her eyes tore at him like the angry whip of a briar bush.

"I still have my name on a list of adoption agencies.

But they all tell me it's a slow process." Determination squared her jaw. "But I'm not giving up, Drake. I won't ever give up wanting a baby."

Drake was careful to keep his disappointment hidden as his senses continued to drink in her classic beauty. After being without her for two long months, having her this near was both precious and painful.

He rose from his chair and moved around to the front of the desk. Folding his arms over his chest, he stared at her. "Okay, so you're not here because you've changed your mind about having a child. And you don't need more money. Maybe you'd better tell me exactly why you are here?"

Drake could see anger simmering beneath the surface of her blue eyes. He wasn't surprised. These past few months, any little thing he said seemed to set her off.

"Don't speak to me as if I'm one of your business associates, Drake. I am still your wife, even if we don't live under the same roof."

His nostrils flared as he skimmed his gaze over her flushed face. "Do you think I've forgotten that?"

"I think you've forgotten a lot of things," she said tightly. "Or maybe you just never knew them to begin with."

"What's that supposed to mean?"

*Dear God, don't let me lose control now,* Hope silently prayed. She was here to help little Stevie, and she couldn't do that by pushing Drake even further away from her.

She drew in a calming breath, then shook her head. "Nothing. Forget that. I didn't come up here to argue with you, Drake. Far from it." Her gaze slipped to the sculpted line of his lips, and yearning instantly sprang up inside her. "I'm here to ask you to come home."

Stunned, Drake stared at her for long moments. Then, muttering an oath, he crossed to the other side of the room, where a wall of plate glass looked over the sweeping drive leading to the clinic. Outside it was a cool winter day in Austin, and the trees were as bare as his heart.

"Hope, I don't know why you're doing this to me. You've already said you haven't changed your mind. And I still feel the same. What could possibly be gained by my coming back home? We'd only wind up hurting each other more than we already have."

Tears stung the back of Hope's eyes, but she fiercely fought them away. Weakness was the last thing Drake needed to see in her. He had to know that nothing he could say or do would break her determination.

"The last thing I want to do is hurt you, Drake. But—"

Her words halted as he suddenly whirled, his face dark with anger.

"Don't try to act as though you've been thinking of my needs or wants these past few months," he rasped. "Because we both know what's been on your mind, and it sure as hell hasn't been me!"

Quickly, Hope rose to her feet and crossed the room to where he stood. "All right," she said quietly. "Blame everything on me if you must. I don't care if you want to paint me the villain. None of that matters right now. I'm not even asking you to come home for my sake."

Drake was trying his best to digest her words, but it was a hard thing to do when his attention kept slipping to the dove-gray sweater clinging to her breasts, the long black skirt slit up her calf. He knew every inch, every sweet curve beneath her clothing, and he was aching to touch her, taste her, bury himself in the warmth of her body.

"Then why?" he asked hoarsely. "Why do you want me to come home? You think us being back together will improve your chances for adoption?"

If adopting a baby was the only choice she had, she would gladly snatch it. But Hope was still fairly young, and she was healthy. Her deepest desire was to have her husband's baby, but if not his, then she had to believe there was some man out there who would be glad to give her the family she wanted.

"Whatever you might think of me, Drake, I would never use you—for any reason."

The trail of his suspicious green eyes was like a red hot torch sliding over her body. She tried to ignore it, but heat was rapidly flushing her cheeks.

"Then why ask me to come back? I don't—"

"For Stevie," she interrupted.

Drake's expression went blank. "Stevie?"

"Yes. Your sister's son. Denise called a few days ago and asked if I'd be willing to keep him from now until the New Year while she and Phillip are in Europe."

"Europe!" he burst out. "What the hell are they doing going there? The last time I talked to her, she was ready to divorce Phillip and move to Houston."

Hope clasped her hands in front of her—mostly to keep from touching him. "Apparently, she's had a change of heart. They've decided to spend some time alone, away from everything, to try to work out their differences."

Drake shook his head with disgust. "Denise doesn't know what the hell she wants! And God knows, she should never have had a child. From the time he was born, she's done nothing but shoulder that little boy off on someone else!"

The last time Hope had seen Stevie, had been a year

ago. He'd been five then. A kindergartner with toffee-brown hair, a smattering of freckles and a frail little body. But it had been his eyes that had stayed with Hope. Somber brown eyes without a flicker of joy or laughter to light them.

Denise and Phillip had come to Austin to attend a blues concert and had dropped the boy off at Hope and Drake's house, expecting, more than asking, them to baby-sit. During his brief stay, Hope had tried her best to make friends with her nephew, but he'd remained a closed book. Since then, the memory of his sad little face still had the power to haunt her.

She nodded in agreement. "That's one of the reasons I couldn't refuse. I don't want Stevie hurt any more than he already has been by his parents' neglect."

He glanced at her sharply. "Then why didn't you insist they take the boy with them? That's where he needs to be. Not with me. Or you."

A sigh escaped her as she pushed one hand through her hair. "I know the boy isn't my responsibility. But it was obvious just by talking to Denise that she's in no better shape to care for Stevie now than she ever was. And as for Phillip, I never considered him to be father material. But then I don't suppose Denise ever pressed him to be a dad to Stevie."

"Why would she?" Drake snorted. "She doesn't want anything interfering with their social life in Dallas."

His voice was full of bitterness, and Hope knew he was thinking about his parents. His father had died three years ago from a sudden stroke, and his mother two years before that from a lingering illness, but even with them gone, Drake was still deeply affected by their lack of love and interest in him. Like Stevie, he'd been raised by nannies and placed in one boarding school after another until he was eighteen and on his own at college. He knew all too well what it was like to be neglected and cast aside, and she could only pray he wouldn't let the same thing happen to his nephew.

"I'm sure Denise and Phillip are both to blame," Hope said. "But right now I'm more concerned about putting some normalcy back in Stevie's life while he's here in Austin."

Drake frowned. "I don't see where you need me to do that. The boy has rarely laid eyes on me."

Hope raised a hand in protest. "He doesn't know me any better than you. We're both going to be strangers to him. And he's going to feel frightened and abandoned. That's why we need to try to give him a sense of security."

Drake wearily wiped a hand over his face. "I agree the boy needs security, Hope. But I can't see us giving it to him. We don't even have our own house in order!"

"Okay, so we don't. But we can pretend. That's all I'm asking, Drake. Just for one month while Stevie is here."

His brows puckered with confusion. "What are we supposed to pretend? That his parents really do love him? A child knows when he's loved and when he isn't. It would be cruel to mislead him."

She glared at him. "Do you have to be so harsh?"

He sighed. "I'm not being harsh, Hope. I'm being realistic. I can't help it if you don't like the truth."

She didn't know why his attitude should hurt her. Drake had never been one to sugarcoat anything for any reason. He expected people to face facts, no matter how painful they were. But these past two months without him had been living hell for Hope. Her emotions were raw, and his words were pouring salt deeper into the wound.

Tears were once again scalding the back of her eyes. She blinked and swallowed, then looked away from him before she could manage to speak.

"I don't want you to—" She stopped, shook her head, then swallowed again. "When I said we could pretend, Drake, I was talking about us. You and me. All I'm asking is that you come home for a month. And make believe you love me."

*Pretend. Make believe.* Dear Lord, Drake thought, he didn't have to do any of that. He loved Hope more than his own life. He always had. She just couldn't believe it. She thought he was a selfish bastard. And maybe he was, Drake admitted. But that didn't mean he loved her any less.

When he didn't say anything, Hope stepped forward and placed her hand on his forearm. It had been too long since she'd touched him, and the feel of her left him trembling inside.

"It's December, Drake. Christmas is coming. You know how important that is to a child."

As a young boy, Drake remembered it being a special time for his friends. But not for him. He'd dreaded the holidays. His parents had never failed to fill the house with people he didn't know. He was relegated to his room upstairs while the parties went on and on. Christmas morning, he and his sister were given a generous hour downstairs to open their gifts, and then the two of them were packed up to their rooms to spend the rest of the day with their nanny. But somehow the worst for Drake had been when he returned to boarding school and heard the stories of his friends' holidays. Their fathers had played football with them, or taken them fishing and horseback riding. Their mothers had let them help bake Christmas cookies and decorate the tree. Drake hadn't known what any of that was like, and he'd felt an outsider.

The bitterness of those memories was reflected in his voice when he spoke. "I'm not the right person for the job, Hope. I'd end up making the kid more miserable than he already is."

Her fingers tightened on his arm as she shook her head. "If I believed that, I wouldn't be up here right now. I wouldn't be asking for your help."

It amazed Drake that even after this separation, she still believed he could be a father. She was like a blue heeler who wouldn't give up until the last cow was penned. And suddenly he wondered if a month with the three of them together was exactly what Hope needed to make her see just what a rotten father he would make. Maybe then she would realize their marriage could and would survive only if she put the idea of having a child behind her.

"If you're worried I'll try to keep you there once Stevie goes back to boarding school, I won't," she hurriedly promised. "You can return to your apartment and everything can go back to the way things are now."

"When is Stevie coming?" Drake asked.

Something in his voice sent hope flickering through her heart. "I have to pick him up at the airport in the morning. Tess is going to run the gift shop for me tomorrow."

Today was Thursday. He had one more day of work before the weekend. But Drake made his own hours, which were usually far more than what the Maitlands expected of him. He could take off long enough to go to the airport with her.

"I'll move my things back tonight. Will you be home?"

Hope was suddenly so weak with relief, her legs threatened to give way. "Yes," she said, then in spite of everything, she had to smile at the small miracle that had just happened. "I'll be home."

The joy on her face stabbed Drake right through the heart. Making his wife happy was all he'd ever wanted to do, and he'd tried hard to see that she'd had everything she needed or wanted. But it hadn't been enough. *He* hadn't been enough. And he'd be a stupid man to believe the smile on her face was because of him.

"I'll be there," he said, then pulling his arm free of her fingers, he stepped around her and headed out the door.

## CHAPTER TWO

LATER THAT EVENING, on her way home, Hope decided at the last minute to stop by Austin Eats Diner. After her meeting with Drake, she'd been too stirred up to eat lunch, and her stomach was gnawing in protest.

Since the diner was on the street corner right next to the clinic, it was often filled with Maitland Maternity staff. Thankfully, Drake wasn't anywhere to be seen, but she quickly spotted a woman with dark hair in a booth by the window.

Hope made her way through the bustling diner and slid into the seat across from her friend Abby Maitland.

"I stopped by your office before I left the building," Hope told her. "I was surprised to find you'd already left."

Abby was the chief ob/gyn at Maitland. It was her mother, Megan, who had founded the clinic twenty-five years ago with her late husband and was still Maitland Maternity's CEO. The same age as Hope, Abby had been her personal physician and dear friend for many years. Recently, she had become engaged to Kyle McDermott, a local businessman, and their wedding was only a week away. Hope was one of Abby's bridesmaids. Along with her mother and twin sisters, Beth and Ellie, Abby had been frantically planning the details of the ceremony, which would no doubt be a major social event. Nothing about the Maitland family went unnoticed in Austin, especially of late.

"I had a couple of last-minute cancellations so my schedule ended up being light today," Abby explained. Then with a bright smile, she asked, "What's up?"

Hope's expression turned sly. "Maybe I should ask you that. I heard through the clinic grapevine today that your younger brother Jake was on his way home. Is his return to Austin for your wedding? Or do you think he really might be Cody's father?"

Groaning, Abby rolled her eyes. "I honestly don't know what to think anymore. With all the women who've shown up at the clinic swearing to be the baby's mother, you'd think the Maitland men had made love to half the female population of Texas." She shook her head with disgust. "But as for Jake, none of us really know where he's been or what he's been doing. I guess it's possible he might be the father. I just wish the whole thing would get resolved. The publicity is really wearing on Mother."

Almost four months ago, Abby, her mother, Megan, brother R.J., and sister Ellie had discovered an abandoned baby boy in a basket at the back of Maitland Maternity. The only clue to the infant's identity was a note pinned to his diaper, which read, "Dear Megan Maitland, This baby is a Maitland. Please take care of him until I can again."

"Your mother is a strong woman, Abby. Otherwise, she would have cracked under the pressure she's had piled on her these past few months."

The corners of Abby's lips turned downward and concern shadowed her blue eyes. "That's true, Hope. But everybody has a breaking point. Every day I wonder just how close my mother is to reaching hers."

Hope shook her head. "Something will happen to resolve this thing soon. It has to. And in the meantime, Megan has your wedding to look forward to. I know that seeing you married to the man you love is going to make her very happy.''

Appreciation warmed Abby's eyes. "I needed to hear that, dear friend. Thanks for saying it.''

Before Hope could make any sort of reply, a waitress stopped beside their booth. Everyone called the young, blue-eyed blonde Sara, but no one knew her real name. She'd wandered into a local shelter a few months ago, suffering from amnesia, and still hadn't regained her memory. Nor had anyone recognized her.

"Hi, Ms. Logan. Can I get you something this evening?''

"A Reuben sandwich and coffee will be fine, Sara. Thanks.''

The pretty waitress scratched the order on her pad, then hurried away. Hope turned her attention to Abby, who was staring thoughtfully after the young woman.

"Has anyone figured out who she is?''

Abby shook her head. "I don't think so. There wasn't much information for the authorities to go on. I guess the only thing anyone can do now is pray her memory returns.''

Hope glanced across the room to where the young waitress was serving coffee. "Isn't there something medically that could be done for her? Some sort of drug or psychoanalysis?''

"Generally doctors like to let amnesiacs heal on their own. It's not good to try to force a memory.''

The same way it wasn't good for Hope to try to force Drake into trying for another baby. That was why she hadn't fought him when he'd announced he wanted to move out of the house. She didn't want to beg or cajole or demand anything from him. If he ever decided to give her another chance to have a child, she wanted him to do it willingly. A baby should be something they both longed for, not something he felt obligated to give Hope. But so far, his mind was closed to the idea.

"How are things going with you?"

Abby's question interrupted Hope's bleak thoughts. Her gaze drifted to her friend. "I asked Drake to come home today. And he agreed."

Surprise, then joy lit Abby's face. "That's wonderful, Hope! I'm so glad to hear it."

Before Abby could get too excited, Hope held up her hand. "It's not what you're thinking, Abby. He's not moving back because he wants to. He's doing it for his nephew, Stevie."

Abby's brows lifted. "His sister's child?"

Hope nodded grimly. "Stevie's parents are going to be gone for a month, and Drake has agreed to move back in to help me with him."

"Oh." Abby thoughtfully sipped her coffee. After a moment, she asked, "Are you sure you're doing the right thing, Hope?"

It was no secret to Abby how much Hope wanted to try to get pregnant again. As her doctor, Abby had assured her the problems with her first pregnancy were highly unlikely to recur. Miscarriages were painful and heartbreaking, but they were also common. Most women went on to deliver healthy, normal babies. Abby was fairly certain Hope would fall into that category, and Hope had every confidence Abby was right. Drake, however, could not be convinced.

"What do you mean, mistake? Do you think I shouldn't have asked Drake to come home?"

Before Abby could answer, Sara returned with Hope's

sandwich. After filling both their coffee cups, the waitress moved on to the next table.

Hope picked up her sandwich and tried not to let the doubtful frown on Abby's face ruin her appetite.

"Maybe I shouldn't have said that, Hope. But—" She shrugged as she carefully considered her next words. "I was just thinking that Drake has been telling you over and over he doesn't want a child. He even made that clear before the two of you were married. And then when he did finally relent and you got pregnant—well, we won't go into that right now—I don't have to tell you how devastated he was when you lost the baby. I'm just wondering if having Stevie around might be a reminder of all that pain."

Hope glanced out the window of the Austin Eats Diner. The streets were growing dark, and she needed to head home as soon as she finished her sandwich. Drake would show up before too long, and she needed to be ready for his arrival. In more ways than one.

"That's a chance I have to take, Abby."

Abby glanced at her sharply. "Is this child that important to you? I wasn't aware that you were close to Denise, much less her son."

"We're not close," Hope admitted. "It's been almost a year since I've seen Stevie. But that last time was enough—" She broke off as her throat tightened at the memory. "I can't remember ever seeing such a sad, troubled child, Abby. And when Denise started whining about leaving him at boarding school if Drake and I couldn't keep him, well…"

Abby nodded knowingly. "Your soft heart caved in."

Hope made a palms-up gesture. "Guilty as charged. And I know it seems foolish, offering to spend my whole holiday taking care of someone else's child, but—"

A knowing smile tilted Abby's lips. "You want to try to give the kid at least one memorable Christmas."

"How can I expect to be the mother of an adopted child if I can't even bother to see that my own nephew is nurtured for one month?"

"I see your point."

Hope's gaze searched Abby's face. "But you're still not convinced I'm doing the right thing."

Her friend's features wrinkled into a scowl. "I didn't say that."

"You didn't have to. I can see it all over your face."

"Forget about Stevie for a moment and consider this," Abby said. "Your marriage hasn't ended yet. There's still a chance to save it."

"How?" Hope groaned. "By giving up everything I've ever wanted? I don't know that I could be happy that way, Abby. I love Drake, but I want to be a mother."

Abby reached across the table and gave Hope's hand an encouraging squeeze. "Believe me, I understand how you feel," she said gently. "Year after year, I've helped bring scores of babies into the world. But delivering a new life is not the same as creating one yourself. I've stopped counting the times I've asked myself when it will be my turn to take one of those bundles of joy home with me."

Hope nodded glumly. "That's true. We've both been in the same boat for a long time. Except I had a husband and you didn't. But now you're about to be married and you're going to get the child you want. I don't even know if I'm going to continue to be Drake's wife, much less have a baby with him. And as for the idea of adopting— well, as long as Drake and I are separated, I realize my chances are reduced somewhat."

"Well, if Drake is so determined not to be a father,

it's obvious to me you'd have to cross the idea of adopting off your list if you hope to get back together," Abby pointed out. "That's why I'm wondering if this thing with Stevie will only cause more problems."

Hope gave her friend a worried glance. "What kind of problems? I've been thinking—and hoping—that having Stevie around will help change Drake's attitude about children."

"Or make it worse," Abby said, then quickly shook her head. "Oh, I don't mean to sound pessimistic, Hope. But from what you've said, this child might have problems that a real parent would find hard to deal with, much less a man who doesn't want to be a father."

"That thought has run through my mind, too, Abby. But I can't turn my back on the little boy. And deep down, I can't believe Drake would be coldhearted enough to turn away from him, either. If he is, then…I've wasted all these years loving him."

After that Hope carefully changed the subject to Abby's wedding plans, and once she'd finished her sandwich, she said goodbye to her friend, then stopped by the counter to pay her bill.

Shelby Lord, the owner of the diner and a longtime acquaintance of Hope's, stood behind the cash register.

"Hi, Hope. How are things going today?" Not waiting for an answer, the hardworking redhead leaned forward and lowered her voice for Hope's ears only. "Have you made any headway with that husband of yours?"

Shelby was well-meaning, and Hope liked the other woman very much, but it was a known fact she was a bit of a busybody. Hope decided to keep the news of Drake's moving back home to herself. Shelby would find out soon enough. Here in the diner, no news escaped her. And anyway, nothing had really changed between her and Drake. The only difference was that they'd be sleeping under the same roof.

"Not really, Shelby. Have you been busy today?"

The young woman wearily pushed a stray curl from her forehead as she searched through a stack of tickets jabbed on a spike. "Horribly. The place has been full all day. But that's what I like to see."

With the matching ticket finally in hand, she turned to Hope and the register. "You've probably already heard about Jake Maitland coming home."

Hope nodded. "Everyone is saying he's coming back because of baby Cody. But I'm not so sure. He might just be coming back for Abby's wedding and to see his mother. You're a friend of the family, Shelby. Surely you know him enough to have some ideas."

Shelby's green eyes twinkled, and a shrewd grin spread over her face. "Growing up, I thought he was the best-looking guy I'd ever met. But because I was a girl, I didn't have the chance to know him like my brothers did—especially Garrett."

"So you haven't talked to him lately? Abby just told me she didn't have a clue why her brother was coming home."

Shelby shook her head. "I can't remember the last time I talked to Jake. But I do think the timing of his return looks a mite suspicious. And since Jake moved away from Austin, no one seems to know what he's been doing. Not even his own family."

Hope handed her a bill large enough to cover the sandwich and coffee. "Well, just because he's a private person doesn't necessarily make him a prime suspect as the baby's father."

Shelby's laugh was deep and rich as she counted

Hope's change to her. "You're no fun at all, Hope. You're just too darn logical."

On the drive home, Hope thought about Shelby's comment. Maybe she had become too objective. Maybe she was looking at this baby issue between her and Drake in terms that were only black and white.

But what other terms were there? she wondered grimly. She wanted to try to have a baby again. He didn't. As things stood, they were at a bitter stalemate. And she was beginning to doubt Stevie or anything else could break it.

Drake and Hope's two-story brick home was located in a quiet, well-to-do neighborhood just a street over from Abby's Western-style stucco.

Not too many months ago, Drake had hired a crew of carpenters and painters to give each room a facelift. The results had been beautiful, but Hope had liked the house just as well before. Deep down, she knew Drake's motive for undertaking the expensive renovation had been to dim their memories and make it harder for both of them to remember the rooms as they'd been before they'd lost the baby. And their dreams for the future.

With a weary sigh, she headed the car onto the wide circular drive. At one end of the four-car garage, she stopped long enough to push the remote to lift the door. Not until she'd pulled inside did she notice the dark green car parked at the far end.

It was Drake's! He was already here!

Snatching her keys and purse, she quickly went inside the house. The kitchen was dark and quiet, so she hurried to the living room, only to find it empty, also. Drake was not to be seen in the den or the study, either. That meant he had to be upstairs in one of the bedrooms.

Her footsteps were soundless on the carpeted stairs and

along the dimly lit landing. Ahead, she could see a long shaft of light coming from an open door. Hope walked steadily toward it, a mix of emotions swirling through her.

It wasn't until she had taken two steps inside the room that Drake sensed her presence. He looked away from the dresser drawer where he'd been placing his underwear.

"I see you finally made it home."

Letting his remark slide, she took another step toward him. "What are you doing here, Drake?"

He straightened to his full height, one corner of his mouth cocking upward in the semblance of a grin. "What does it look like? I'm moving back in. That *is* what you asked me to do."

Confusion wrinkled her forehead. "Yes. But—" She made a sweeping gesture with her arm. "This is *my* bedroom."

Slowly his thumb and forefinger rubbed the arrogant jut of his chin. "No. You've got it wrong, Hope. This is *our* bedroom. And if you want me to stay in this house for the next four weeks, then that's the way it's going to be."

Hope felt her slender body quiver with outrage. "You can't be serious!"

"Have you ever seen me when I wasn't?"

No, she thought. Drake was a man who rarely joked. He'd often been accused by his friends of being as sober as a judge. And oddly, his lack of frivolity had been the very thing that had first drawn Hope to him. After living with a mother who considered life one big joke, Drake's seriousness had comforted her. After ten years of marriage, his inflexibility had driven a wedge between them.

Quick, angry steps carried her across the room to

where he stood by the dresser. "Why are you doing this?" she asked tightly.

One brow lifted questioningly as he looked at her. "You asked me to come home. To make believe we still love each other. Didn't you?"

"Yes! For Stevie's sake! But that doesn't mean—" She vigorously shook her head. "He's only six and a half years old. He doesn't know a husband and wife normally sleep together!"

Drake couldn't stop a bitter sneer from spreading across his lips. Apparently Hope hadn't considered that it would take more than just having him under the same roof to convince Stevie they were a happy family. As for himself, he hadn't thought of their sleeping arrangements until the moment he'd stepped into the house.

"That's where you're mistaken, Hope. When I was his age I knew something was wrong because my friends' parents had one bedroom, and mine had two. So if you want this little farce with Stevie to work, then you're just going to have to endure me being in the same bed."

Her hands began to tremble. "I can't!"

He turned to the dresser drawer and picked up a stack of underwear. He could have told her it wasn't going to be easy for him, either. Just the thought of her being that close was enough to cause his stomach to tighten and his palms to sweat.

"Then maybe we'd better forget this whole thing right now," he muttered tightly. "I thought it was a stupid idea, anyway."

Hope had never had the urge to do bodily harm to anyone in her life. But at this very moment she would have taken great pleasure in kicking him right in the shins.

"You're doing this on purpose," she accused. "To spite me."

Did he want to spite her? Drake asked himself. For making demands on him that he couldn't keep? For ruining everything precious and dear about their marriage? He didn't like to think so. Nor did he want to believe he was simply trying to see if she still wanted him in a physical way. As far as he was concerned, their sleeping together was just another part of the make believe.

He looked at her over his shoulder. "Sleeping with your husband is that abhorrent to you? I can remember a time when you never wanted to be out of my arms."

She suddenly had to swallow as the truth of his words brought sweet memories rushing through her mind. "I'm not the one who called a halt to our sex life. You did that, Drake." She turned away from him and stared at the floor as pain threatened to swamp her. "Obviously your distaste for having a child with me is far greater than your desire to make love to me."

Bitter anger rose in him, and he forced himself to bite back several curse words. She didn't want to understand or see that the mere thought of her getting pregnant again filled him with desperate fear. And not just fear of losing the tiny life they would create. It was the thought of losing Hope he couldn't bear to even contemplate. No. She didn't want to acknowledge his feelings in the matter. It was easier for her to simply paint him the selfish villain.

"You don't want to admit that you gave me no choice in the matter," he accused her. "It was either sex without birth control or no sex at all."

His words so infuriated Hope that she whirled on him. "For years you gave *me* no choice. Sex with absolutely no hope of ever having a baby! Don't talk to me about choice or manipulation!''

Drake released a deep breath, then wearily pinched the bridge of his nose. "This is exactly the reason I moved out, Hope. You and I both know that. Ten minutes haven't passed since I've come back, and it's starting all over again.''

He was right, she thought sadly. But what had he expected her to do when she'd found him moving into her bedroom as though he had a right to? *He is still your husband, Hope,* a little voice reminded.

She sighed. "I'm sorry, Drake. I just…didn't expect this." She gestured to his personal things scattered around the bedroom. "I had planned on you using one of the guest rooms.''

His face like stone, he moved away from her and began to search through a leather duffel bag on the end of the bed. "But I'm not here as a guest, Hope. If we're going to give the appearance of a real husband and wife, this is the way it needs to be." He glanced at her, his green eyes unyielding. "Or would you rather I leave and we'll call the whole thing off?''

It was too late to call it off. Stevie would be here in the morning. The boy needed all the male guidance he could get.

"No," she said quietly. "I don't want you to leave.''

He straightened away from the duffel bag and faced her. "If you're worried about me wanting to resume our sexual relationship, that's not what any of this is about. From what you told me earlier today, this is all for Stevie. Isn't that right?''

She nodded as an empty ache began to fill her heart. Of course he wasn't moving into their bedroom for sex. She'd been crazy to think, even for a second, that he'd changed his mind and wanted to make love to her again. This was his way of torturing her. He wanted to remind her over and over what she was giving up, what she was missing night after night. And there was nothing she could do about it until Stevie's stay was over.

"You're right," she said, then raised her chin to a determined angle. "And it's not as if we've never slept together before. I can manage, if you can."

His gaze raked her slender curves. "I wouldn't be here if I thought I couldn't."

She really ought to hate him, Hope thought. She really should want to walk out and never look back. But she'd never been able to kill the love she felt for this man. It had run too deep and for too long to die a quick death. There was still a part of her that wasn't ready to give up on him or their marriage. Not yet.

"Good," she said with forced ease. "Then neither of us should have a problem."

He turned his attention to the duffel bag. "No problem at all."

Not for him, at least, she thought ruefully. "Well, I'll let you get back to your unpacking. Have you had anything to eat? There's fresh bread and cold cuts."

"I've already eaten. I'm fine."

He didn't want to be here. She had forced him into it. The fact shouldn't be crushing her heart. After all, he'd chosen to live away from her for many weeks now. But she couldn't help wishing things between them were so very different.

"I'll be in the den," she said, then hurried toward the door.

Before she could pass through it, he called her name and she glanced at him, an ache in her heart and a painful lump in her throat.

"I wanted to—" He stopped, then with a rueful shake of his head said, "Nothing. Forget it."

Whatever had been on his mind, he wasn't going to share it with her, Hope realized. Which wasn't surprising. He'd quit sharing himself with her a long time ago.

"I understand this isn't easy for you, Drake. But I do thank you for coming home. Very much."

For a moment it looked as if Drake wanted to reach out to her, to draw her closer to him. But when he spoke, his voice was cool, almost businesslike.

"At the end of this month, we'll see how much you really thank me, Hope."

# CHAPTER THREE

WHEN THE ALARM CLOCK sounded the next morning, Hope opened her eyes to find she was the sole occupant of the bed. But she didn't need to see the indentation of the pillow next to her to know Drake had slept there. All through the night she'd been desperately aware of his hard, masculine body stretched out only inches away from her.

For hours she'd lain there staring into the darkness, remembering when their love had been full of fiery passion. He would have automatically reached for her or she for him. Hope had always been eager to give him pleasure, and she had to admit Drake had been more than a generous lover. Now he refused to touch her for fear of making her pregnant.

The thought renewed the deep ache that was always inside her these days, and she sighed as she reached out and touched his side of the bed. Last night she'd been afraid to sleep, afraid she would unconsciously creep into his arms. As a result, she'd dozed fitfully until the alarm clock had buzzed on the nightstand beside her.

Across the bedroom, to her right, the door to the bathroom was shut. The sound of the shower told her Drake was already getting ready for the day ahead. In the past, he would have lingered in bed, using what little time they had before work to be close to her. But that part of their life was over. She had to forget it and move on.

With a tired groan, she shoved her hair off her face and reached for her robe. She couldn't survive a month of this, she thought as she groggily tied the sash at her waist. It would kill her.

In the kitchen, she discovered Drake had already made coffee. She quickly filled a mug, and after a heavy dollop of half-and-half took a grateful sip. Caffeine would have to sustain her through the day. And tonight…well, she would just have to forget her husband was lying beside her.

Hope was finishing her coffee when Drake entered the kitchen dressed in a dark suit, a white shirt checked with tiny black windowpanes and black Western boots. His light brown hair waved damply away from his broad forehead and his strong jaw shone with freshly applied aftershave. As he crossed to the coffeepot, the musky scent trailed to where she sat at the table.

She hadn't realized having him back in the house was going to be so tempting. Or so painful.

"You're early," she said to him. "Stevie's flight isn't scheduled to arrive until nine-fifteen."

He poured a mug full of coffee, then turned to her. As her eyes scanned his face, she decided he looked disgustingly rested. Obviously sleeping next to her hadn't been the least bit distracting for him.

"I have some work in the study that I want to go over before we leave."

"Oh." She should have known he hadn't put aside this morning exclusively for her or his little nephew.

He made a point of glancing at his wristwatch. "Will you be ready by eight-thirty?"

She nodded, then forced her attention to the bay window across one wall of the kitchen, which gave a view of the backyard. "I'll come to the study when I finish dressing."

"Fine," he said, then left the room and Hope without a clue to what he was really thinking.

Upstairs, she made a point of dressing casually in jeans and a bright red sweater with a rhinestone candy cane pinned to one side. She didn't want Stevie to view her as a starched and staid aunt whom he couldn't get near for fear of ruining her clothing.

As for Drake, she supposed his tall, stern demeanor would seem formidable to most any child. But Hope knew that beneath his outward cool was a man capable of warmth and love. She could only wonder whether he would show Stevie that part of himself. As for ever showing any tender feelings toward her again, she'd given up on that months ago.

Less than an hour later they left the house with a minimum of conversation. The residential area was behind them and the morning rush-hour traffic buzzing on either side of them before Drake decided to break the somber silence.

"You've been very quiet this morning. Did you sleep last night?"

Hope glanced across the car seat to where his lanky body sat comfortably behind the wheel. His gaze was on the traffic ahead, yet even if she could have seen his eyes, she doubted she would have known what was on his mind. Drake had always been a man to keep his feelings hidden. Now that trouble had come to their marriage, he was even more of a closed book.

"Yes, I slept." Drake didn't need to know the sum total of her sleep had probably been less than an hour and that he'd been the sole reason for her miserable night. "I've been thinking. About Stevie."

"What about him?"

Hope sighed, wishing her heart felt as bright as the morning. The gray clouds had cleared and sunshine spilled over the busy city streets of Austin. Maybe the sudden break in the weather was a good omen. She certainly needed one.

"I just wonder what he'll think about us," she answered. "The last time we saw him was nearly a year ago. Do you think he'll remember us?"

Drake shrugged one shoulder. "Kids remember more than you think. It probably won't matter much if he remembers us or not. I figure the boy is constantly being thrown on strangers. We'll just be two more in his life."

She grimaced as her gaze slid over his hard profile. "How can you be so callous? None of this means anything to you, does it?"

Even though they were traveling a busy thoroughfare, Drake shot her a look of disbelief. It wouldn't do any good to explain to her that his comments had come from personal experience. That if he'd sounded callous, it was because he knew what it was like as a child to be dumped by your parents. Hope only wanted to believe that he disliked children. Even the thought of them in general. Nothing could have been further from the truth.

Biting back a sigh, he asked, "Then why am I driving you to the airport to meet Stevie? The clinic has been thrown into turmoil lately. All the bad publicity surrounding baby Cody has begun to hurt Maitland's finances, and I'm the man responsible for the money that keeps everything running. It's made hell out of my job. At this very moment I have urgent work waiting on my desk."

Hope looked away from him before he could see the disappointment in her eyes. Work and money. She, more than anyone, understood how important those two things were. As a child, it had only been Hope and her mother. And Georgia had never understood the word *responsibility*. What little money her mother had made at waitressing or cleaning houses, she'd spent frivolously. And the men she'd married after Hope's father had skipped out weren't any better.

"I'm aware of all the trouble going on at the clinic."

He cast her a sharp glance. "But that doesn't mean anything to you?"

Hope bit her lower lip, wondering how things between them had gotten to this point. Their marriage had always been special. As the years passed, the two of them had grown closer rather than apart. They had rarely argued over anything. She realized the miscarriage had been as traumatic for Drake as it had been for her. But she'd managed to get past it. Drake, however, couldn't seem to let go and move forward with her. The gap it had created between them had grown to mammoth proportions. He seemed to misinterpret her feelings, along with everything she said.

"Of course it means something to me," she replied. "I understand you're a busy man and that you made an extra effort to come with me this morning. And I'm grateful that you did. But I—get the feeling your heart isn't in this."

What heart? Drake wanted to ask her. The little that had survived losing the baby had been crushed by their separation. It amazed him that she thought he ought to be able to love and laugh and live as the two of them had before she'd talked him into the notion of having a child.

Long moments continued to pass as he negotiated the car through a lane of heavy traffic. Eventually, he said, "To hear you tell it, I don't even have a heart."

He was baiting her. Just as he'd been baiting her last night about their sleeping arrangement, and it suddenly dawned on Hope that he was doing it on purpose. He wanted to rile her to the point where she would send him packing. But she wasn't about to let him off the hook that easily.

"For Stevie's sake, I hope I'm wrong," she murmured.

Drake didn't know what the hell was wrong with him. He knew he was behaving like a jackass, but he couldn't seem to stop himself. From the moment Hope had come to his office yesterday, he hadn't been able to think about anything but her and this month ahead of them. It might be the last chance, the last time in his life to live with her. He had to make it right or he was going to lose her forever.

Last night in bed, Drake had lain there pretending to sleep while Hope had clung to her side of the bed, desperate to keep her distance from him. He'd never undergone so much agony, knowing her body was inches from his, yet her heart was far away. Drake could only wonder how many more nights he could continue like this before he cracked and reached for her. Or was forced to leave the bed entirely.

From the corner of his eye, he could see her face was still turned toward the passenger window. This morning her hair was brushed loose. The color of the silky strands reminded him of a jar of honey lit with warm sunlight. If he were closer, he knew it would smell like lilac or lily of the valley. She only wore the fragrance of a single flower, and he'd often told her he liked her best when she was wearing nothing but the scent of a rose.

Drake cleared his throat and tried to shake the erotic vision from his thoughts. After a moment he said, "Whatever you might be thinking, Hope, I don't want my sister's kid to be hurt any more than he already has been. But for all we know he might have turned into a little tyrant since we last saw him. I could hardly blame the boy if he has.''

Surprised by his admission, she turned her gaze to him. ''From what you've told me about your growing-up years, your parents weren't any better than Denise and Phillip. Did you behave like a little tyrant?''

A dry laugh escaped from him. ''No. But I wish I had. I should have dealt them as much misery as they dealt me.''

Her eyes scanned his face, and the bitterness she saw there was like a cold hand clamped around her throat. Drake had never tried to hide the resentment he'd felt for his parents. Even before she and Drake were married, Hope had realized he wasn't close to either his mother or father. In fact, she didn't meet the Logans at all until it was nearly time for the wedding. And then she hadn't been impressed. Harris and Lilah had both been pompous and self-absorbed. The couple had made it easy for Hope to see that Drake had grown up feeling unloved and unwanted.

After the meeting with her in-laws, Hope had vowed to make up for Drake's parents' lack of affection. And throughout the years of her marriage, she'd tried to show her love in a million different ways. But it had obviously not been enough to take away his bitterness.

''You can't forgive them, can you?''

His brows lifted ever so slightly as he glanced at her. ''No. And I doubt I ever will.''

ONCE INSIDE the busy Robert Mueller Airport, the two of them located the correct airline gate and took a seat to wait for the flight from Dallas to arrive. Drake said very little and Hope didn't push him for conversation. As each minute ticked away she was becoming increasingly nervous about meeting Stevie. What if he had become a little tyrant as Drake had suggested? She might not be able to handle him and then the whole household would be in an uproar. Drake would be only too happy to point out another reason they shouldn't try again for a child of their own, and this whole thing would backfire in her face.

But the moment the passengers began to come through the gate and she spotted Stevie, escorted by a flight attendant, her worries were instantly forgotten.

"There he is, Drake!" Jumping to her feet, she unconsciously reached for his hand, then, as though realizing she shouldn't be touching him, her hand fell to her side and she stepped back. "We'd better let the flight attendant know we're here," she added soberly.

Rising from the chair, Drake deliberately curled his arm around the back of her waist and gave her a brief smile. "We're supposed to be a loving married couple meeting our little nephew, remember?"

Hope wasn't sure if he was being sarcastic or sincere, but at this moment she didn't care. She desperately needed the extra support his touch lent her.

It took them a few moments to weave their way through the dispersing passengers to the information desk where the flight attendant and Stevie stood waiting. After a brief exchange of necessary information, the woman smiled at Stevie, who continued to cling to her hand. "Well, it looks like everything is in order, so I'm going to put my little passenger in your care now."

The attendant said her goodbyes to all three of them, then turned to head through the terminal gate. Seeing the lost look on Stevie's face, Hope quickly kneeled to the boy's level.

He was pretty much as she remembered. A bit taller, but she couldn't see that he'd picked up any weight. He was thin and frail, and his complexion reminded her of a child who'd been convalescing from a long illness. Toffee-brown hair fell in a straight bang onto his forehead and freckles dotted his nose. **Big brown** woeful eyes glanced cautiously from one **adult** to the other.

"I'm your aunt Hope, Stevie. Do you remember me?"

His eyes were suspicious as they traveled over Hope's face for long moments. Eventually, he nodded in reply.

Hope smiled with relief. "I'm happy you've come to stay with us for a few days. Do you remember Uncle Drake?"

Beside her, Drake reached down and shook the child's hand as though he were a business associate. "Hello, young man."

Tilting his head way back, Stevie looked up at Drake, and much to Hope's surprise, a glimmer of trust replaced the doubt in the child's eyes.

"Hello, sir."

Drake's chest grew suddenly tight as he looked at Stevie's solemn face. "I guess you're a little bit scared right now," he said.

Stevie nodded awkwardly and his gaze vacillated between Hope and Drake.

"Well, I don't blame you," Drake told him. "I would be, too."

Hope darted a frantic look at Drake. What was he trying to do, scare the child even more? But before she could worry, Stevie stepped forward and slipped his hand into Drake's.

"Can we go now?" he asked.

With a faint lift to his brows, Drake glanced at Hope. From his expression she could see he was just as surprised by Stevie's reaction to him as she was.

"First we have to get your baggage and then we'll go home," Drake promised the child.

By the time the three of them made their way to the baggage area, Stevie's luggage was already on the carousel. Drake picked up the large suitcase, then once again reached for Stevie's hand.

As they headed toward an exit, Hope said to Drake, "You might need to slow down just a bit. Stevie's legs aren't quite as long as yours."

He glanced down to see Stevie trotting alongside to keep up with his pace. "Oh. I wasn't thinking," he said.

Hope smiled to herself as she watched her husband slow his gait to match the child's. Maybe the good weather this morning was an omen, she thought brightly. Right now, seeing Drake holding on to Stevie's little hand was far more than she'd expected.

In the parking lot, Hope buckled the child into the back seat while Drake stowed the luggage in the trunk. On the drive home, Stevie sat straight and rigid and spoke only when Hope or Drake directed a question at him. Otherwise, his brown eyes stared unblinkingly at the view beyond the passenger window.

Once they arrived home, Hope took Stevie to the bedroom directly across the hall from hers and Drake's. Over the past week, she'd worked at night to change the room into something more suitable for a child. The spread and curtains were printed with cowboys and horses. At the foot of the bed, a wooden crate painted bright red and yellow was filled with various toys that were inexpensive, but favorites of most children. On the wall, she'd pinned

Looney Tunes posters and several glossy pictures of kittens and puppies.

"This is going to be your room while you're here," she told Stevie. "Does it look okay?"

The boy's head jerked up and down before turning to watch Drake enter with his suitcase. Once again, Hope noticed Stevie's dark eyes flicker with interest. Maybe Denise had been right when she'd said the boy was starved for male attention. He was certainly drawn to Drake for some reason.

Drake deposited the suitcase on the bed, then glanced with interest at the change in the room. As his features grew rock smooth, Hope knew the decor was taking him back to the bright colorful nursery the two of them had prepared in the bedroom next to this one. As her pregnancy had advanced, Drake had added more and more to the room until it was stuffed with teddy bears, baseball caps and gloves, stacks of little books and a chest of Tonka toys. Once he'd finally gotten used to the idea of her being pregnant, he'd wanted a son so badly. But then so had she.

"When did you do this?"

Swallowing the tightness in her throat, she said, "The past few nights I've been working on it. I wanted Stevie to feel comfortable." She turned her gaze on the child, who was clearly absorbed by the sight of the bedspread. Apparently he'd never seen anything like it. "Stevie, would you like to change clothes now?"

He looked at her with a hint of defiance. "Do I have to go to bed?"

Hope darted Drake a puzzled glance before she knelt in front of the boy. "Why, no, Stevie. You're not feeling sick, are you?"

Glumly, Stevie's head swung back and forth. "No. But sometimes my mommy makes me go to bed."

Drake stepped forward to join the two of them, and even though he didn't appear outwardly angry, Hope could tell from the tight clamp of his jaw that he was furious at the information Stevie had just given them.

"Stevie, no one around here goes to bed unless it's bedtime. So while you're here you forget about what your mommy made you do at home. Do you understand?"

The boy looked at Drake as though he couldn't quite believe him. Yet he nodded in compliance.

Hope straightened to her full height and zipped open the suitcase Drake had placed on the bed. "Let's find you some jeans and a sweatshirt to change into and then you can come down to the kitchen and I'll make us some cocoa. How does that sound?" she asked the boy.

Ducking his little chin, he mumbled, "I don't have jeans or a sweatshirt. Can I come to the kitchen anyway?"

"Dear God," Drake muttered, clearly unable to keep from expressing his anger. "Right now it would give me a great measure of joy to ring my sister's neck."

Hope turned from her husband's disgusted face to Stevie's lost one. She wanted to take the child in her arms and hold him tightly. She wanted to kiss his pale cheek and tug at his chin. But it was too early to try to smother him with physical affection, and she somehow doubted a hug was enough to make this troubled child smile.

Instead, she said, "Of course you may come to the kitchen. I'll see what I can find you to wear, and then later on today, the two of us will go shopping."

"Will he go with us?" Stevie asked about Drake.

Hope didn't bother to ask Drake if he wanted to join

the shopping excursion. He'd already made it clear he was losing valuable work time.

Shaking her head, she said to Stevie, "Drake won't be going with us. He has to work. But he might drink hot chocolate with us before he leaves."

She glanced at Drake, who'd gone to stand near the window. Grim-faced, he pulled his attention away from his nephew long enough to give her a nod, then quickly left the room.

With Drake downstairs, Hope turned her attention to unpacking Stevie's suitcase. There were stacks of dress trousers and crisply ironed shirts, but nothing close to jeans or any sort of play wear. Apparently the child was always dressed like a little businessman.

Eventually, at the very bottom of the case, she discovered a pair of khaki trousers and a navy blue lambswool sweater. She placed the clothing on the bed.

"Change into these, Stevie. I'll be back up to get you in just a few minutes."

The only response the boy gave her was one wary nod. Deciding it was far too early to try for more conversation, Hope left the room and headed downstairs to the kitchen.

She found Drake already there, standing in front of the bay window. He appeared to be watching the cardinals and blue jays vie for the bird feeder that was nestled in the crook of a twisted juniper branch. Yet Hope seriously doubted his mind was on the birds. Stevie's arrival had disturbed him. That much was obvious. What she didn't know was whether it had been in a good or bad way.

"I managed to find a pair of khakis and a sweater for Stevie to change into. I'll go get him in a few minutes."

Drake glanced over his shoulder at her. "What do you think about Stevie?"

His question surprised Hope. She didn't think her opinion mattered much to him anymore. Especially her opinion of a child.

"I—to be honest with you, I've never been around a child quite like him. He's so serious. He hasn't once smiled since we picked him up at the airport."

"I don't expect smiling comes easy for the boy," Drake said. Looking at Stevie was like seeing himself thirty years ago, and it was more than a little unsettling. He hadn't expected to feel much toward the child. After all, he could count on one hand the times he'd seen him since he was born. Stevie was Denise's offspring. Not his own. And yet it troubled him to think the boy was being raised in the same isolated way he had.

"Do you think he's been ill?" Hope asked.

Drake's brow puckered into a frown. "I don't know. Why? Do you think he's sick?"

Hope shook her head as she placed a saucepan on the gas range. "No. But I wonder if he has been ill in the past. He's so pale and thin. He looks as though he rarely eats."

Drake grimaced. "I doubt anyone is ever around to see that the child eats properly."

"Aren't there people at the boarding school to see to things like that?" Hope asked. "I mean, children have other needs besides academics."

He walked across the room and leaned against the cabinet counter a few small steps away from her. "Now you can see what it does to children when adults can't be parents. Denise is a poor excuse for a parent. And I'm her brother. Hell, I must have been crazy to ever think I could be different from her—from our own parents. Maybe that's why—"

She glanced at him sharply. His face was tight, his eyes dark with shadows. "Why what?" she prompted.

Jamming his fists into his trouser pockets, he looked away from her. "Maybe that's why...you had the miscarriage. Fate was trying to tell me I wasn't emotionally set up for the job."

So Abby had been right on one score, Hope thought. Having Stevie in the house was reminding Drake of their lost child. But there would always be reminders. She couldn't shield him from them any more than she could protect herself from all those painful memories.

Pulling a jug of milk from the refrigerator, she poured a hefty amount into the saucepan. "That's what you want to think." She spoke quietly as she worked. "It makes it easier for you to justify your decision not to try for another child."

Drake didn't want to argue with her. Far from it. This was the first time in weeks he could remember them being together like this, and it brought back all the things about their marriage that he'd held dear. She had always gone out of her way to do little things for him. Like cooking his favorite meals, wearing a dress he especially liked on her, playing the music he enjoyed and making sure the remote to the TV was where it should be. And the hell of it was, he'd never taken her devotion to him for granted. In his own way, he'd tried to do equally for her.

But once Drake had refused to try to have another baby, everything good and special between them had dwindled. Until finally they had become two people married in name only.

His gaze was faintly accusing when he turned it to her. "You've always wanted to ignore my family and pretend that part of my life doesn't matter."

Hope had heard this argument from him before, but for some reason this morning, it grated on her more than ever. "What is that supposed to mean? I've never ignored your family. Remember *I'm* the one who offered to help your sister out by keeping Stevie."

"I'm not talking about that sort of ignoring. I'm talking about the fact that Denise and I aren't cut out to be parents. We never had any ourselves! But you want to think I can just skip over all that and become father of the year without any sort of background training."

A weary sigh slipped past her lips. "You're hardly an ignorant man, Drake. No one is born knowing how to be a parent. Everyone has to learn."

Groaning, he lifted his face toward the ceiling. "That's true. But you have to have someone to learn from. And I've decided it's just not in me, Hope. A person has to be special inside to be a parent. It's pretty obvious that Denise sure as hell doesn't have what it takes. And I'm not about to risk a child's happiness by trying to find out whether I do!"

That he would choose this morning to cut into her, when she needed him more than ever, caused something inside Hope to snap.

With slow deliberation, she turned away from the heating milk to face him. "All right, Drake," she said, careful to keep her voice low. "You win. You're not ever going to be a father. You don't want to try to have a child with me. I read you loud and clear and I accept your decision. So you don't have to keep pointing that out. While you're here this month, I won't bring up the subject to you anymore. And I hope you'll have the decency to do the same."

The fierce resolution in her voice stunned Drake. Since he'd moved out of the house, he'd almost resigned himself to the fact that he was losing her. But to hear her speak the words sent a chill right through to his bones.

"And what about after this month is over and Stevie is gone?" he asked stiffly.

Hope couldn't let him know there were tears clawing at the back of her eyes. She was through letting him see just how much pain he was causing. She was finished with the arguing and cajoling.

"I'm going to move on with my life, Drake. With or without you."

# CHAPTER FOUR

"HOPE! IS THAT YOU?"

Hope turned to find a young woman with short, curly red-blond hair and a wide smile standing directly behind her in the checkout aisle. Katie Topper was a pediatric nurse at Maitland Maternity and one of Hope's best friends. Since Katie had been staying in Houston while taking a medical course, she hadn't had an opportunity to talk to the other woman except for a few brief phone conversations. Katie was going to be shocked when Hope gave her the news that Drake had moved home.

"Katie! How wonderful to see you! Are you home early for the weekend?"

Grinning happily, Katie pointed at her jeans and T-shirt. "I got lucky and finished classes yesterday. I'm on my way to the farm to see Papa. I just stopped in here to pick up a pair of new work shoes."

"How are things going in Houston? Are you about to wrap things up? We've really been missing you around here."

"I'll be finished by the end of the month. What about you? How are things going?"

Suddenly remembering Stevie, Hope glanced down to check that he was still standing close by her side.

Katie followed her line of vision and spotted the boy standing quietly next to Hope. Tilting her head in Stevie's direction, Katie asked, "Who's your little friend?"

Hope's hand instinctively came to rest on Stevie's small shoulder. "This is my nephew, Stevie. We picked him up at the airport this morning. Tess is kindly handling things in the gift shop for me today." Then, noticing the man in front of her was finished at the checkout counter, she pushed forward. As she began to place the items from her cart in front of the cashier, she glanced at Katie. "Stevie's going to be staying all through Christmas. His parents have gone to Europe."

Katie was clearly surprised by Hope's news, but didn't say anything. Instead she quickly glanced at her wristwatch. "How about stopping by the diner for a cup of coffee? I have a few minutes before I head out of town and I'd love to catch up on the news around here."

Hope darted another glance at Stevie. So far the boy hadn't given her any sort of trouble. In fact, he was so quiet it worried her. Most children loved to chatter about anything and everything. But Stevie didn't seem to be interested in making conversation or taking notice of anything around him. He had chosen a few pieces of clothing for himself, but only because Hope had practically forced him to. Maybe having him in a casual social setting like the diner would be good for him.

"I'd love to. We'll meet you there," Hope told her.

A few minutes later Hope parked outside the Austin Eats Diner. By the time they were out of the car, Katie had joined them.

"Now do I get to meet this new guy in your life?" she asked Hope, while slanting Stevie a teasing smile.

Stevie sidled closer to Hope's leg as he warily eyed the stranger with bouncy red hair, cowboy boots and jeans.

"This is Stevie," Hope said to Katie. "His mother is Drake's sister, Denise."

Katie's brows flew up with speculation, but instead of expressing any questions, she gave the stern-faced child an impish grin.

"Hello, Stevie. My name is Katie."

Stevie's dark eyes took their time assessing Katie's face. Then finally, as though he'd decided she was an ally rather than a foe, he politely extended his hand to her.

"How do you do?"

Katie was quick to shake his hand, but Hope could see the other woman was a little taken aback by the formal greeting. And Hope could understand why. Katie had grown up with her father and two brothers in a loving but rowdy household where kids sometimes forgot their manners unless an adult was around to remind them.

"It's nice to meet you, Stevie," Katie told him, then glanced at Hope. "Ready to go in?"

Hope nodded and gently nudged Stevie's shoulder toward the entrance of the diner.

Inside the busy restaurant place, Katie suggested, "Let's sit at the counter. I'll bet Stevie would rather sit on a stool."

The child didn't voice his preference one way or the other. Under her breath, Hope said to Katie, "I doubt he's ever been in a place like this."

Katie glanced around at the odd mixture of people sitting in the booths and at the long curved counter. Along with the Maitland Maternity staff who frequented the diner, there were usually a few cowboys, truck drivers, businessmen and manual laborers who drifted in and out during the day. To an isolated child like Stevie, Hope thought, it must seem like a wild, noisy place.

"Why?" Katie asked, her features wrinkling with bewilderment. "What's the matter with the diner? The food is good and so is the company."

Hope chuckled softly. "It is to you and me. Stevie's parents would have other ideas. People of their money and social standing don't frequent diners. You understand."

Katie's lips formed a perfect O. "Only too well."

Like Hope, Katie had not come from a wealthy background. At twenty-nine, the nurse was still single, but Hope considered her friend blessed to have a loving father and brothers living close by. It was far more than she had. Especially now that Drake was more like a stranger than a husband.

Hope helped Stevie onto a stool between her and Katie. He seemed shocked that the seats would turn, but he didn't test them out the way most kids his age would enjoy doing. Instead, he sat rigid and still, his hands folded primly in his lap.

Sara came to take their orders. The two women quickly opted for coffee. Stevie didn't seem to realize he could order anything he wanted on the menu until Hope assured him he could. Eventually he chose orange juice, and as they waited for the pretty blond waitress to return with the drinks, Katie said to him, "I have some friends who have kids just about your age. Maybe you'd like to get together with them while you're here and play soccer or something."

The boy's dull expression didn't change as he lifted his brown gaze to Katie. "I don't know how to play soccer," he mumbled.

With arched brows Katie glanced over Stevie's head to Hope. Then to Stevie, she said, "Oh. Well, that's okay. I'm sure they would teach you. Or you could play army.

Bet you like that," she added with a wink that included both Hope and Stevie. "All little boys do."

He frowned with a mixture of curiosity and defiance. "I don't know how to play army, either."

This time Katie couldn't hold back her disbelief. She groaned loudly. "Where has this kid been, Hope? Mars?" To Stevie, she said, "Sure you do. That's where you act like you're a soldier and you fight the enemy and save the world. Doesn't that sound like fun?"

Stevie obstinately shook his head, and the two women exchanged wary glances.

Deciding it was her turn to try with the boy, Hope asked, "What do you like to do, Stevie?"

"Read books."

"Well, that's great!" Katie praised him.

Sara appeared with their drinks, and while the waitress placed them on the counter, Hope pressed him further. "Reading is wonderful, Stevie. But what do you like to do outside?"

One frail shoulder rose and fell as though he couldn't be more bored with the two women or life in general. "I don't go outside much. Only when the teachers at the boarding school make me."

"Why is that?" Katie prodded.

His bottom lip inched ever so slightly forward. "I don't like it. The other boys push me and call me a sissy."

Katie decided she'd better leave things at that, and Stevie turned his attention to the glass of juice in front of him.

To Hope she asked in a low voice, "So what about Drake? Does he know his nephew is with you?"

Slowly Hope stirred cream into her coffee. "Yes. Actually, he's home now."

"Really!" Katie's dark green eyes popped wide. "Is he—did you two get things straightened out?"

Hope's head swung briefly back and forth as she glanced at Stevie. She didn't want the child to hear too much. "No. And I'm not holding my breath that we will."

Katie groaned with frustration. "Hope, you're an idiot if you don't fight for the man. I know you still love him. This thing with him not wanting a baby might change."

Hope looked grimly past the tables of diners to the busy street beyond. "I'm not as young as you, Katie. I don't have time to sit around waiting for Drake to change his mind. I'm sick of waiting and hoping."

"You must really want a baby," Katie suggested cautiously. "More than anything."

Before Hope could respond to her friend's remark, Shelby stopped by their spot at the counter, her eyes zeroing in on Katie.

"Hello, stranger! Home for good now?"

Katie shook her head. "No. Three or four more weeks."

"The diner isn't the same without you popping in."

Katie laughed. "There's no diner this good in Houston, Shelby. I promise."

Shelby's face glowed with the compliment, then leaning closer, she asked in a lowered voice, "Have you two heard the latest news?"

Katie and Hope exchanged blank glances.

"What news?" Katie asked.

"About the Maitlands."

Clearly, Shelby had heard another round of gossip she couldn't wait to share with her friends.

Hope said drearily, "Don't tell me. *Tattle Today TV* has reported baby Cody was dropped at the clinic by a spaceship and one of the Maitland men was having a relationship with an alien.''

Shelby laughed and her eyes twinkled with excitement. "No! It's much better than that! Just about everyone has heard how Jake is coming back to Austin, right? Well, guess what? He's back and he's brought a pregnant woman home with him.''

Stunned, Katie and Hope stared at her, then at each other.

"A pregnant woman!" Katie exclaimed in a hushed tone. "Who told you this? Or is this something Chelsea Markum reported on *Tattle Today?* If it is, you know it's probably not true.''

"No, no! I doubt even Chelsea Markum has come up with this scoop yet. Beth and Ellie told me about it this morning when they stopped by for breakfast.''

Finding the news difficult to digest, Hope shook her head. "Are you sure about this, Shelby? Abby hasn't mentioned anything about Jake getting married or becoming a father.''

Shelby glanced toward the cash register to make sure no one was waiting to pay, then turned to her friends. "There wasn't any mention of Jake being married. As for Abby not saying anything, she probably just found out. From what Beth and Ellie said, they don't know much about her.''

Clearly caught up with this new development, Katie leaned forward and propped her chin on her fist. "Since last week, I haven't heard much about the baby scandal or anything about Jake. Did Beth and Ellie say why he was back in Austin?''

Shelby shook her head. "Things got busy in here so I had to move on to another table. But they were concerned about what the media would do once they got hold of the news.''

Hope had to agree. She didn't really know Abby's brother all that well, but his showing up with a pregnant woman when there was one Maitland baby already causing a scandal was surely going to add fuel to the fire. ''Do you think this woman is carrying Jake's child?''

Shelby tapped a thoughtful finger against her chin. ''Who knows. He rarely returns to Austin. And when he does, he's pretty much of a closed book.''

''That's the way Abby describes him,'' Hope agreed.

Shelby nodded. ''I know he's always been close to Megan. But I doubt there's a son alive who tells his mother everything.''

Katie considered Shelby's words. ''What about your brothers? Aren't they supposed to be friends with Jake?''

Once again Shelby nodded. ''They do see him from time to time, but from what they say he doesn't speak of his personal life to them, either.''

''Hmm. Well, that rules out Jake being the father of Cody,'' Katie mused as she straightened in her chair and reached for her coffee.

Hope darted a curious glance at her. ''How can you be certain of that?''

Katie shrugged, then chuckled. ''Me, certain? I just think it's unlikely he would have a newborn with one woman and another woman pregnant.''

Shelby's quiet laugh had both her friends turning their attention to her. ''Girls, you've got to remember Jake is a Maitland. And they're not exactly known for living like monks.''

A sly smile curved Katie's lips. ''You're right about that, Shelby. And I'll go a step further and say thank God for the Maitland family. Otherwise Austin might not have

Maitland Maternity Clinic and a lot of babies and children wouldn't get the wonderful care they need.''

"And I might not have a busy diner,'' Shelby agreed with a little laugh, then, spying a customer headed to the cash register, she waved at her friends. "I'll see you two later.''

As Shelby hurried away, Katie reached for her purse. "I hate to leave good company, Hope, but Papa will be calling out the hounds if I don't get there soon.''

"I need to get home, too,'' Hope assured her friend. "We'll have a nice long visit when you get back from Houston.''

Katie slanted her a smile that was both grateful and needy. "I can't wait. Until then, I guess I'll see you at Abby's wedding.''

She gave Hope a brief hug and ruffled the top of Stevie's head, then with a little wave hurried away.

Stevie glanced nervously at Hope. "Are we going, too?''

Every word the boy said was spoken cautiously, as though he feared anything he might say would get him into trouble. Hope could hardly bear to think his parents had intimidated him to such a point.

"As soon as you finish your juice. But you don't have to hurry, Stevie. Everything is fine,'' she assured him. To herself Hope acknowledged the lie and wondered how much worse things could possibly get. This morning, she'd finally lost control and given Drake an ultimatum. Now there wasn't much left to do but wait for the month to end. Along with their marriage.

WHEN JUANITA BUZZED the intercom on Drake's desk, he was jamming papers into his briefcase. Five o'clock was only a few minutes away, and though he normally worked far past office hours, this evening he'd decided to head home early. Though God only knew why. The only reason Hope wanted him there was because of Stevie.

"What is it?" he barked at the machine.

"R.J. is here. Do you have time to see him?"

Besides being one of Drake's few good friends, R. J. Maitland was the president of Maitland Maternity. For both reasons, Drake would always have time to meet with the other man.

"R.J. knows he doesn't have to ask. Send him in."

Seconds later, a tall man with light brown hair entered the office and took a seat in the same chair Hope had sat in—had it only been yesterday? Drake wondered. In his mind, it felt as though weeks had passed. Weeks of torture.

Drake leaned back in his chair and tried to return his friend's smile. "I was about to ask if something was wrong, but from the grin on your face, I can see it isn't," Drake said to him.

At thirty-nine, R.J. had married his secretary, Dana, less than a month ago. Since then Drake had never seen his friend so happy. Which was quite a switch from the workaholic who had kept himself distant from most everyone, including his family.

"It's sickening, isn't it?" R.J. said with a smug chuckle. "But I can't seem to wipe the damn thing off my face."

"I'm glad," Drake said, and meant it. If anyone deserved some joy in his life, it was his longtime friend. R.J. had been only three years old when his mother was killed and his father abandoned him. Drake was one of the few people who understood his friend had spent most of his life trying to make up for his father's sorry behavior.

"Looks like you were getting ready to leave," R.J. said, inclining his head toward the open briefcase on top of Drake's desk. "Can't wait to get back to the empty apartment, huh?"

Drake frowned. "I thought this place was a gossip mill. Somebody must be slipping or you would have already heard."

R.J. cocked one brow at him, then a dark scowl wrinkled his forehead. "Heard what? Damn it, don't tell me Chelsea Markum has come up with another lie about the family!"

Drake quickly waved his hand to stop the direction of R.J.'s thoughts. "For once the gossip isn't about you Maitlands. I thought you might have already heard that I've…moved back home."

The dark look on R.J.'s face suddenly disappeared and a wide smile took its place, making Drake feel even worse than before his friend had walked through the door.

"Well, now, this is good news, Drake. And it's about time, too. I knew you'd come to your senses about this thing with Hope."

Drake wiped a hand over his weary face. "Before you start celebrating, R.J., this isn't what you're thinking. I've only moved back temporarily."

R.J. shoved his tall frame to the edge of the seat. "What the hell's going on!"

Drake turned an annoyed glare on his friend. "It's not as crazy as it sounds. My six-year-old nephew is here for the month. I'm only home to help Hope look after him. Later—well, I'll be moving back to my apartment."

R.J. drew in a long breath, then let it out slowly as he

studied his friend's miserable expression. "And what does Hope think about all this?"

Drake thrust a hand through his wavy hair. "She's the one who asked me to come back home."

"Oh." R.J.'s smile returned. "So you're doing it for her."

Was he? Drake asked himself. He'd told himself he couldn't, in all good conscience, let his little nephew down. He had to go home for Stevie's sake. But he'd be lying if he said Hope hadn't entered into his decision. In spite of their differences, she still had a grip on his heart. It was tearing his insides out to give her up. He didn't know if he could. But it looked as though he no longer had a choice.

He picked a pen up from his desk and rolled it between his palms. "I suppose. In a way."

His friend studied him thoughtfully. "Oh, come on, Drake. You're not a man who can be maneuvered into doing something you don't want to do. Even by Hope."

"That's true," he said grimly. "She hasn't manipulated me into getting her pregnant again. And she damn well isn't going to."

R.J. sighed, then shook his head slowly. "Listening to you is like hearing a recording of myself two months ago. And I'm glad I changed. If you—"

"Look, R.J.," Drake interrupted, "I'd be the first man to say Dana is the best thing that could have happened to you. I'm happy you realize there's more to life than work, but—"

"Drake, I think I know you better than anyone. We're two birds of the same feather. We had no-account fathers. But that doesn't mean you're marked for life. And I know that deep down you don't want to spend the rest of your life without Hope."

The mere thought of living without Hope was like being sentenced to terminal pain. But she was asking too much of him. Each time he thought about her being pregnant again, flashes of her miscarriage gripped him with cold fear. For as long as he lived he would never forget her deathly white face, the pool of blood where she'd fainted on the floor, the frantic dash to the hospital, where the doctors fought to stop her hemorrhaging. Dear God, how could any man be asked to go through such a thing a second time.

"I'm about to decide I'm just not the man she needs to make her happy, R.J."

The other man studied Drake for long moments, then rose to his feet. "You might surprise yourself, Drake. I did."

"Are you leaving?" Drake asked as he watched his friend head toward the door. "You've hardly been here more than five minutes."

R.J. glanced at him. "I didn't have any business matters to talk about and I can see you need to get home. Just think about what I told you. And forget the briefcase. You've got more important things to do tonight than worry about the clinic."

Drake stared at the door his friend had closed behind him. R.J. *really* had changed. The clinic had once been the man's sole focus, his whole purpose for being. Now he was telling Drake there were more important things, meaning the love of his wife.

But after this morning, Drake was fairly certain he'd already lost Hope's love. Now he could do little more than wait until the month ended and Hope presented him with divorce papers.

A FEW MINUTES LATER Drake was mildly surprised to find the house empty. When he'd parked his car in the garage, Hope's vehicle had been sitting at the far end, so he'd naturally expected her and Stevie to be home.

There wasn't a note on the refrigerator saying where she was, so he stepped outside in the backyard on the off chance of finding the two of them there. It was nearly dark. He couldn't imagine Hope staying out for very much longer.

He was on the verge of heading inside when he spotted his wife and nephew walking up the slope of hill that led down to the street bordering the back of their house. Hope was holding on to the boy's hand and glancing at him every few moments as she talked. The child appeared to be listening intently, and Drake figured this was probably the most personal attention he'd ever received from an adult. Especially a relative.

Jamming his hands in his trouser pockets, Drake stepped forward to wait for their arrival. As he did, Hope spotted him and gave a little wave. The greeting both warmed and surprised him. After her ultimatum this morning, he'd expected her to be as cool as the night air.

And then he remembered. For Hope, this was all make-believe. The two of them were supposed to pretend to be a happy, loving couple. For Stevie's sake. Later, after Christmas, she'd be moving on to another life.

The reminder was like a gore in the ribs by an angry bull. If Hope wanted pretense, he'd do his part and then some.

When the two of them drew near, Drake reached out and snared a hold around Hope's shoulders. Surprise instantly lifted her face to his, and he took the opportunity to drop a kiss on her cheek.

"Hello, darling. Been visiting over at Abby's?" he asked.

Even though her eyes were warily studying his face, she smiled at him. "No. Stevie and I went for a walk around the block. To try out his new tennis shoes."

Drake turned his attention to the child. The crisply ironed pleated trousers and shirt had been replaced with blue jeans and a dark green sweatshirt sporting a picture of a bronc rider on the front. Sturdy white tennis shoes had taken the place of polished oxfords. If it hadn't been for the stony, brooding expression on his face, Stevie would have looked like any ordinary kid.

"Well, you look quite a bit different from the boy I saw this morning," Drake said to him. "Your aunt Hope took you shopping?"

Peeping at him through long lashes, Stevie nodded jerkily.

"Did you get to pick out your new clothes?"

Stevie nodded again.

"Do you like them?" Drake prodded.

"They feel good," Stevie answered, then dropped his head and mumbled with a hint of accusation, "but I won't get to keep 'em."

Drake glanced at Hope. She looked at him with quiet despair.

"Why not, Stevie?" Drake asked the child.

Stevie's brown eyes were full of pain as they met Drake's. "Because my mommy and daddy won't let me wear stuff like this."

Drake gritted his teeth to keep from cursing out loud. His own parents had refused to let him dress like other children. Instead, he'd had to give the appearance of a miniature adult. And a businessman at that. No jeans or boots or tennis shoes. He'd felt like a freak, and no doubt Stevie did, too.

"Well, stuff like you have on now is what kids around

here wear all the time. And while you're here you're going to be like everyone else, okay?''

Stevie didn't smile, but Hope could see Drake's words had put a flicker of light in his dark eyes. She was grateful for that much.

''Why don't we all go in,'' she suggested, ''and I'll fix our supper.''

The three of them entered the house through a door leading into the kitchen. Once inside Stevie quickly said, ''I wanta go to my room.''

''That's fine,'' Hope told him. ''I'll call you when supper is ready.''

The boy nodded then made a quiet exit from the kitchen. Once he was totally out of sight, Hope sighed and shook her head.

''What's the matter?'' Drake asked. ''Are you finding out having Stevie here is going to be too much for you?''

With her hand on the refrigerator door, she paused to answer. ''No. It isn't that at all. I just…it makes me so sad that he—well, he doesn't know how to be like other kids.''

Drake grimaced as he moved to a row of oak cabinets. ''That isn't hard to understand. Denise and Phillip haven't let him be like other kids.''

She opened the door and fetched a package of ground round from the meat bin. ''I can see that,'' she said wearily.

Hope left the package on the gas range, then went to the sink to wash her hands. A few steps away, Drake pulled a glass from the cabinet, then moved closer.

''Did you have any trouble with Stevie today?''

Drying her hands on a dish towel, Hope turned to face him. ''I almost wish I had,'' she admitted. ''A little rowdiness would have been better than seeing his sad face all day. The child never smiles. I'm not sure he knows how.''

Drake was hardly surprised. He knew firsthand how tough it was for a kid to smile when he felt unwanted. "I never smiled much. Expect when I was with my buddies.''

No, Drake never had been one to express much pleasure, either with actions or words. But when he did, it had the power to make Hope's heart soar. And it quietly dawned on her that having Stevie here was showing her a side of her husband that she'd hadn't really thought that much about before.

Her gaze suddenly fell to the center of his chest as the warm scent of his cologne drifted to her nostrils and her senses reacted to his nearness. Try as she might, she couldn't stop the pull of attraction she felt every time he came near.

"I wasn't expecting you to be home early this evening.''

He gave a little shrug. "It was after five when I left the clinic.''

"That's early for you.''

"I made an extra effort to be here for Stevie.''

A pent-up breath softly whooshed past her lips as she looked up at him. "Then I guess that little kiss in the backyard was for Stevie's benefit, too?''

To her amazement, one corner of his lips lifted in a cocky grin. At one time she would have been overjoyed to see such a look on his face. But not tonight. She wasn't in the mood for teasing of any sort.

"You couldn't tell?''

"Please, Drake, don't play games with me. I—can't take it,'' she murmured fiercely.

His gaze riveted on her moist lips, he said, "You're

the one who wants to play games, Hope. So what does it matter if I'm pretending or not?''

"You're deliberately being an ass—''

"No!'' he swiftly interrupted, then before she could guess his intentions, he pulled her into his arms. With his thumbs beneath her jaw, he pushed her face to his. "I'm being your husband. Whether you like it or not!''

Even if Hope could have responded, Drake didn't give her time. His lips swooped down and hungrily covered hers.

For a moment Hope was too shocked to resist. And then she didn't want to. Too many long, lonely weeks had passed without the warmth of his arms around her, the feel of his lips making sweet magic with hers. No matter how hard she tried, she couldn't stop wanting this man. Or needing him.

His hands tightened on her back, crushing her breasts and thighs against the hard length of him. Hope's mouth opened to the thrust of his tongue, and as it mated warmly with hers, the room around them became a dim swirl of colors. Heat filled her breasts and belly and loins and had her hands gripping his broad shoulders.

Her thick blond hair slid through Drake's fingers as he pressed them against her scalp and held her fast while he continued to feast at her lips.

She was panting and her knees were threatening to buckle by the time he finally lifted his head and whispered hoarsely against her ear, "If Stevie wasn't in the house, I'd make love to you right here! Right now!''

Just hearing him say the words sent a hot coil of desire spiraling through her. He wanted her. The urgency she'd tasted on his lips hadn't been pretense any more than hers had been. But she knew he wasn't thinking about the one thing that had stood between them for weeks now.

"Have you forgotten I'm not on birth control anymore?"

The question was like a sluice of ice water to his face. His body went rigid, then slowly he eased her away from him. As though she had a contagious disease, Hope thought achingly.

"Yeah, I guess I had forgotten," he muttered.

He turned away from her and started out of the kitchen. Before she could stop herself, she asked, "Where are you going?"

"Upstairs. To cool off."

She swallowed as pain and anger began to engulf her.

"What am I supposed to do?"

He glanced over his shoulder at her, and she inwardly cringed at the mocking twist to his lips and the accusation in his green eyes. "Pretend this never happened."

# CHAPTER FIVE

HE SHOULD HAVE listened to R.J. and left his briefcase at the office. The numbers on the paper in his hand were nothing more than a jumble of black marks blurred across the page. He couldn't work here. There were too many memories surrounding him to let his mind focus on anything except Hope and the fact that he was losing her.

With a muttered curse, Drake tossed the report of expenditures onto the desktop and slumped wearily against the back of his chair. It was Saturday morning and the house was quiet. Unnaturally quiet for a place that housed two adults and a child. But Hope had left with Stevie more than an hour ago, and the two of them had still not returned. She hadn't told him exactly where she was going, only that she needed to run some errands, and Drake hadn't pressed her to explain. He'd never been one to dictate her movements. Still, in the past she would have shared her plans with him, no matter how trivial they were.

The corners of his mouth turned down as he scraped both hands over his wavy hair. He'd been crazy to come back to this house for any length of time. That scene last night in the kitchen had proved just how crazy.

Once he'd had Hope in his arms, he'd lost all control of his senses. Looking back on it now, he didn't know how he'd found the strength to pull away from her. And if that hadn't been enough torture to endure, he'd been forced to lie in bed, waiting in the darkness for her to slip between the sheets beside him.

Her warm, tempting body had remained inches away from him and he could have reached for her. That's all it would have taken for Drake to have had his wife in his arms. He didn't much doubt she would have come to him willingly. She would do anything for a baby, he thought sickly. Even make love to a husband who'd made her anything but happy.

With another silent curse of disgust, Drake rose from the chair and left the study. There wasn't any point in pretending to work.

Outside the house, he headed across the backyard to a small building he'd once used as a workshop. Months had passed since he'd stepped foot in the place. When Hope had begun to pressure him to let her get pregnant again, the urge to create anything had left him.

The door creaked as he pushed it open. A shaft of sunlight moved across the floor, and dust particles floated through the air. He flipped a light switch and two fluorescent bulbs flickered at the back of the small room where a work counter ran adjacent to the wall.

A quick glance assured him everything was just as he'd left it. Vises, drills, jigsaws, table saws, lathes, any kind of tool a person would need to work with wood. Once the hobby had been a pleasurable pastime. Now he wondered if making something with his hands might be therapeutic. God knew, he had to get Hope off his mind or he was soon going to be a babbling idiot.

ACROSS TOWN, in Abby's old bedroom at the Maitland mansion, Hope looked at herself in the mirror. The bridesmaid's dress was made of red velvet. The neckline was cut square and low enough to be just short of shocking, making her wonder if she had the nerve to stand up in front of several hundred people wearing such a garment.

Behind her, Abby pressed her hands together and beamed with pleasure. "Oh, it looks beautiful on you, Hope! Do you like it?"

Hope's short laugh was full of doubt as she experimentally twisted her blond hair up at the back of her head. "The dress is gorgeous. I love the simple, clean lines."

Abby stepped forward, her soft laugh laced with amazement. "Things have been in such a whirlwind here lately, I'm surprised I chose anything right for this wedding. But I remember thinking I had to have red for Christmas. And with such a bright color, I didn't want the style to be fussy with bows or lace or puffed sleeves."

Hope turned to study herself at a different angle in the cheval glass. "You've always had excellent taste, Abby. Even when we were teenagers, you never wore the wrong thing. But don't you think...well, I'm showing quite a bit of cleavage. If it was altered just to here—" she pressed a finger to a spot above her breasts "—it might be more appropriate for me."

Abby shook her dark head emphatically. "We're the same age, Hope, so I know you're not as old as you're making yourself out to be. The dress is supposed to be romantic, not dowdy. Besides," she added with a sly grin, "once Drake sees you in this, his temperature is definitely going to go up several notches."

For those few moments in the kitchen last night, Drake's temperature had been hot enough to scorch her. But the heat of his desire hadn't lasted long. When she'd

reminded him about her lack of birth control, he'd turned
to a block of ice.

The memory sent a fresh burst of anger through her,
but she tried her best to bite it back. Abby already knew
enough about her broken marriage. She didn't need to
hear more. Especially in the midst of preparations for her
own wedding.

Combing her fingers through her mussed hair, she said,
"Actually, I wasn't thinking about Drake's opinion of
the dress, Abby."

Abby's lips twisted mockingly. "So what he thinks of
you doesn't matter anymore."

Hope wished she had progressed to the point where
nothing about Drake mattered anymore. But so far, she
hadn't been successful in putting him out of her heart.
Straightening, she turned to Abby. "I'm determined to
get on with my life. Even if Drake—doesn't want to be
in it."

Moving closer, Abby placed a gentle hand on Hope's
shoulder. "It troubles me to see any marriage breaking
up, Hope. But when I see it happening to my friends, it's
downright scary."

Hope lifted her hand to Abby's in a gesture of reassurance. "You have nothing to be worried about, Abby.
You and Kyle will be in love until you're old and gray."

Abby carefully studied Hope's solemn features.
"Something tells me you and Drake will be, too."

It was too painful for Hope to correct Abby, so she
made no reply. Instead, she moved behind a dressing
screen and stepped out of the bridesmaid's dress.

"We've been back here in the bedroom longer than I
expected. Stevie's probably wondering what's taking me
so long."

Across the room, Abby picked up a framed photograph

of her mother, Megan, on her wedding day, and traced a finger lovingly across the captured memory. "I'm sure Dora and Jessie have kept Stevie busy eating cookies and drinking milk."

It didn't matter to Hope how much food the Maitlands' cook and housekeeper gave the boy. He desperately needed to gain weight. "I hope you're right. He's practically bone thin."

Thoughtfully, Abby placed the photo on the dressing table and glanced in the direction of the screen. "Have you talked to the child's parents since he's come to stay with you? "

"No. And I'd be greatly surprised if they bothered to call."

Abby made a sound of disapproval. "Being a doctor has allowed me to see human nature at its best and worst. But it never fails to amaze me when I see a parent who doesn't care about his or her child."

Fastening the top button of her cashmere sweater, Hope stepped from behind the screen. "Stevie only arrived yesterday, but so far Drake hasn't been indifferent to the boy. At least, not yet."

Abby moved away from the dressing table. "And I can't imagine he will be. Drake isn't that sort of man."

Hope hadn't thought Drake was the sort to refuse to give her another chance to bear them a child. But it turned out she'd thought wrong. Forcing a smile to her face, she looked at her friend. "For Stevie's sake, I hope you're right. Now, as for the dress—"

"The dress stays as is," Abby insisted, wagging a finger at her before she had a chance to make any protests. "You look sexy and beautiful in it. Katie and Dana will be hard put to look as good."

Hope had to laugh. "I promise not to tell them you

said that." She crossed the elaborate bedroom and picked up her purse from a polished bureau.

"Are you leaving?" Abby asked.

Hope nodded. "You're busy with all these wedding preparations. And I need to get Stevie home."

Abby made a disappointed face. "I'm not that busy. Unless one of my patients decides to go into labor before Monday morning."

At the door, Hope paused and looked thoughtfully at Abby. "Speaking of Monday morning, I've been trying to decide what to do about Stevie when I go back to work. Initially, I considered taking time off, but since then I've been thinking that might not be such a good idea. Stevie is going to be here for a whole month. Tess can't run the gift shop by herself for that long."

Abby's brows furrowed in contemplation. "I'm sure a temp could fill in for you if you feel you need to take the time off."

Hope shook her head at Abby's suggestion. "There's already been enough upheaval at the clinic without me causing more. And I had the idea that it might be better for Stevie to go to day care, where he could mix with other children rather than be at home with me all day long."

"You're absolutely right, Hope," Abby said, tapping a thoughtful finger against her chin. "From what I've seen of the child when you first arrived this morning, he needs some good old-fashioned play. And Beth makes sure the older children get plenty of that."

Abby's younger sister was wonderful with all the children in the clinic day care. Hope wouldn't have to worry about him being neglected.

She sighed with relief. "I'm glad you agree. This

mothering stuff is all new to me. And Stevie desperately needs the right choices made for him.''

With a look of gentle understanding, Abby quickly walked to where Hope stood by the door. ''I've brought a lot of babies into this world, Hope. But so far none of them have been mine. I don't know any more about mothering than you. But you know what,'' she added with an impish grin, ''I think we'll both learn. And we'll both be great at it.''

Right now Abby was looking at the world through rose-colored glasses, Hope thought. She was in love and about to be married. And someday, probably soon, she would have a child of her own to mother. But it was different for Hope. Her marriage to Drake was sliding down a canyon so steep it looked as though saving it was impossible. And without Drake, her chances of having a child the natural way would be cut off. She wasn't about to marry a man simply to get pregnant. If she married again, it would be for love and nothing else. No, it appeared her best and only hope right now was adoption.

But she couldn't allow herself to dwell on any of that. The child she was caring for at present had to be her main concern.

WHEN HOPE AND STEVIE returned home, Drake wasn't anywhere around to greet them, and she stopped herself from looking through the entire house for him. Once Stevie had left the breakfast table this morning, the man had barely been civil to her. She wasn't going to break her neck to see if he wanted lunch. Or anything else from her.

After putting the bridesmaid's dress away in her closet, she went to the kitchen to prepare lunch. As she worked at the counter, she slowly became aware of Stevie standing in the doorway, watching her. His face was expressionless. Like a robot waiting for someone to direct his every move.

The idea troubled Hope and made the smile she directed at the child even more gentle. "Are you hungry, Stevie?"

"No. I ate cake at the big house."

Hope wondered if the Maitland employees had gotten any conversation from the boy. She very much doubted it. He still didn't appear to want to talk or even be talked to. But Hope couldn't be satisfied with the boy's silence. It wasn't normal.

"So Jessie and Dora fed you well, did they?"

"They said you wouldn't care if I ate cake."

There was a defensive note to his voice, as if he were daring her to scold him. Hope wanted to think it was simply his way to vie for her attention.

She smiled at him again. "Jessie and Dora told you right. I'm glad you ate cake. Did you like going to the Maitland mansion?"

Sensing he wasn't going to get any sort of reprimand from her, he shrugged and mumbled, "It was okay. But I like this house better."

The boy's simple admission pleased her and she laughed as she placed frankfurters onto a grilling pan. "Hmm. Well, this house is not nearly as formidable."

Intrigued by the word, Stevie cocked his head to one side. "Formidable. What's that?"

"It means this house is not so big and fancy."

Stevie nodded as though he understood, and Hope couldn't help wondering about the town house his parents lived in. She and Drake had never visited the couple in Dallas. The few times they had met with Denise and Phillip it had been here in Austin, at their suggestion. But then Hope had to remember Stevie spent most of his life at boarding school, not at home with his parents.

"I'm making hot dogs for lunch," she told the boy. "You can bring some of your toys downstairs to the kitchen, if you like. Or Saturday morning cartoons are probably still on. Do you like to watch cartoons?"

He shrugged again as though he found her question boring. "I don't know."

Carefully Hope hid the frown from her face. The more she tried to connect with this child, the more she learned that his life, so far, had been void of most normal childhood activities. While he was here, she was going to do her best to change that much for him.

"Then maybe we should find out." She wiped her hands on a dish towel and motioned for him to follow her.

In the living room, Hope turned on the television set and found the right channel. Tom and Jerry were in a mad, comical race across the screen.

"My favorite cat and mouse," Hope said as she handed him the remote. "When you get tired of it, just push the button and make it go off."

He looked at the gadget in his hand as though he couldn't believe she was giving him free rein with the television.

"Don't worry," she assured him. "You can't break anything."

"Can I find cowboys on here?"

His question tilted her lips into another smile. "You can try. Just push the channel button up or down."

Back in the kitchen, she opened a can of chili and poured corn chips into a basket lined with a paper towel. Drake entered the back door just as she was chopping red onion.

Rather than turn and look at him, she listened to his footsteps as they approached her from behind. The sound seemed to match the hollow beats of her heart.

"You finished your errands?"

She tried not to let the sound of his voice or his nearness get to her, but that was like asking herself to quit breathing. "Yes. I went over to the Maitlands' to try on my bridesmaid's dress for Abby's wedding. Since the wedding is going to take place at her mother's house, she's keeping all the preparations there instead of at her place."

Drake hadn't realized Hope was going to be in the wedding party, but since Abby was one of her best friends, he should have guessed. "It's nice that the Maitlands have at least one good thing to focus on. Maybe that's why Jake has come home. For Abby's wedding."

"Everyone seemed to have the idea he was coming back to Austin because of baby Cody," Hope said. "But that may not be the half of it. Shelby was telling Katie and I yesterday at the diner that Jake brought a pregnant woman back with him."

"A pregnant woman," Drake repeated with disbelief. "Are you sure Shelby had her information right?"

She scraped the bits of onion into a small bowl. "I'm positive. It came straight from Beth and Ellie."

Drake groaned. "Good Lord, I wonder what this is going to mean to the Maitlands? Is the woman his wife?"

Without looking at him, Hope shook her head. "Shelby doesn't think so. Maybe she has some connection to Cody. What do you think?"

Hope missed the worried frown on Drake's face as she plopped the cutting board into a sink of sudsy water.

"I think as soon as this news gets out, everyone will

be speculating. I just wish the hell this whole fiasco was over with. It would certainly simplify my job.''

Wiping her hands on a dish towel, Hope turned to look at her husband. He was dressed in an old pair of jeans and a faded flannel shirt. Fine sawdust clung to the fuzzy fabric, telling her he'd been in his workshop.

The realization shocked Hope. He hadn't built anything with his hands since she'd lost the baby. Before that, he'd had all sorts of ideas for the nursery and had just started the frame for a baby crib when she'd miscarried. Since then, he hadn't stepped foot in the workshop, much less touched the crib.

''You've been out in your workshop,'' she said, unable to keep the surprise from her voice.

He shrugged as though her observation was no big deal. ''Just sweeping the place out and cleaning a few tools. I'm—I was surprised to find all my things just the way I'd left them. I figured you'd probably had them moved.''

She frowned. ''Moved? Where? This is your home, too.''

It didn't feel like his home, Drake thought. That was one of the reasons he'd moved to an apartment complex. The loss of the baby and Hope's subsequent pressure to try again had put such a strain on him, he hadn't been able to think straight, much less relax and enjoy this home that had once been filled with love and joy.

''You could've had everything put in storage so the building would be empty for some other use.''

''I'd never do anything like that without consulting you first. Just because I want a baby doesn't mean I'm a bitch, Drake.''

He grimaced. No, but she was too damn bewitching. And if he didn't keep a tight grip on himself, she'd have him under a spell and promising to give her a dozen kids. He'd already given in to her once. And his weakness had nearly killed her. He couldn't let it happen a second time.

"No, but you're a different woman from…the wife I used to know."

The disappointment in his eyes lanced her with pain, followed by a short stab of guilt. Was she the one being selfish? she asked herself. Was she the one ruining their marriage? Damn the man for making her question herself!

"Not *that* different." She turned to the counter and began to shred a hunk of longhorn cheese.

Drake could sense her anger in the rigid lines of her shoulders and the quick snap of her wrist as she brought the cheese down against the metal grater. What had brought the mood on, he didn't know. But he was certain of one thing. *He* wasn't what she wanted. It was as simple as that.

"Where's Stevie?" he asked.

"In the living room, watching cartoons," she said crisply. "For the first time in his life, I think."

Muttering a curse under his breath, Drake went to the refrigerator and filled a glass with water. "Denise is a real peach of a mother," he said with sarcasm.

Hope sighed inwardly. "You know, I almost feel sorry for the woman."

He drank half the glass before he replied. "Denise doesn't deserve sympathy. She ought to be…kicked in the rear for what she's done to that boy. She and that good-for-nothing husband of hers."

At least Drake could see the child needed real parenting, Hope thought. That in itself told her he had the instincts to be a good father. But she knew it would do no good to point that out to him now. He didn't want to believe he could be a father. That made it easier for him to refuse to try again.

"Drake, your sister just doesn't understand what a blessing Stevie is."

"Blessing!" he repeated with a mocking snort. "Denise has always seen her son as a nuisance to be avoided at any cost."

When it came to children of his own, maybe Drake was more like Denise than she wanted to believe, Hope thought sadly.

"Speaking of Stevie," she said, "I've been thinking about Monday and what to do about going back to work. I've decided taking him to the day care in the clinic would be the best thing all around. I talked to Abby about it this morning and she agreed."

Long moments passed without a response from Drake. Finally she felt more than saw him come to stand by her shoulder. "What the hell am I doing here, Hope?"

The softly spoken question was threaded with such resentment, Hope turned her head to him and stared open-mouthed. "What do you mean?"

"Exactly what I said. What the hell am I doing here? I thought you wanted me to come back home to help you with Stevie. I thought I was supposed to be a temporary father of sorts." A sneer pulled his lips away from his teeth. "But I guess you're already seeing what I've been trying to tell you all along. I'm just not cut out for the job."

Fury sent hot color to her cheeks and pounding blood to her temples. "I didn't say anything of the sort!"

"You didn't have to! It's obvious. You consulted your friend about Stevie's needs, rather than me. What I have to say in the matter obviously means nothing to you."

"You're being—" She broke off, then quickly glanced

over her shoulder at the open doorway leading out of the kitchen. The last thing she wanted was for Stevie to hear the two of them arguing.

Seeing where her thoughts had headed, Drake went over and closed the door, then walked back to stand a few scant inches away from her. The scent of his hair and skin mingled with the faint odor of cedar wood, and suddenly, in spite of everything, she found herself quivering with the urge to touch him, to replay their heated scene of last night.

With an effort Hope tried her best to shake away the erotic image. "Do you object to Stevie going to day care? Is that what this is all about?"

Drake knew he was overreacting, but he couldn't help it. For months—no, years—she'd been insisting he had all the makings of a good father. In spite of his own misgivings, she had no doubt he would raise a child in the best way possible. But now that they actually had a child in their care, she'd run to her friend for advice rather than him.

"No. As far as that goes, I happen to think the day-care will be good for him. What I don't like is being treated as though I'm just a fixture around here. Maybe you think I'm here solely to make things look nice and proper. But that's not the way I see it. I'm here to see to Stevie's welfare just as much as you are."

He was more than angry over this whole thing, Hope quickly decided. He was also hurt. And that gave her the tiniest measure of hope. If he was hurt, that could only mean he cared. At least a little. But that was better than nothing.

She sighed as her anger drained away. "I'm sorry, Drake. I agree I should have consulted you first. I just happened to be with Abby and the subject came up."

She was sorry. That should have been enough to pacify Drake. But it wasn't. The damage had already been done. She was clearly cutting him out of her life, and he didn't know how the hell to stop her.

LATER THAT EVENING, Hope made a point of asking Drake to help her explain to Stevie about the plans for Monday. Thankfully, he'd put his anger behind him and didn't refuse. Together, they climbed the stairs to Stevie's room, where the child had spent most of the afternoon with an art pad and a huge box of crayons.

When Hope and Drake reached the open doorway to the boy's room, he was still at the desk, drawing. His head was tilted to one side with deep concentration. The tip of his tongue stuck out one corner of his little mouth. Hope couldn't help thinking that it was the first purely childish expression she'd seen on the boy.

"Stevie, can we talk to you for a few minutes?" Hope asked.

When he saw the two adults entering his room, Stevie's expression turned instantly wary. Hope wondered what could possibly be going through his little mind. From bits and pieces she'd gathered from Denise the few times they had talked, the boy had already been shuffled around too much in his young life. The last thing she or Drake wanted was for him to think he was being shoved aside one more time.

"Do I have to go back to Dallas?" he asked without preamble.

Stevie's reaction brought a flicker of understanding to Drake's eyes. During most of his childhood, he'd been shuttled back and forth between home and boarding school. After a while, he knew better than to expect to ever stay in one place for an extended length of time.

Drake stepped toward the boy, and as he did, the hard lines of his face softened. The corners of his lips tilted into a faint smile that invited the child to trust him.

"No, Stevie," he said gently but firmly, "You're going to be here with us for many more days. We want to talk to you about what you're going to be doing while Hope and I are at work during the day."

Hope took a seat on the side of the bed next to Stevie's desk. Deciding he needed to be more at the boy's level, too, Drake eased down beside her.

Stevie's skeptical glance swept back and forth from one adult to the other. Eventually the brown eyes settled on Drake. "You mean a baby-sitter is gonna come here and stay with me?"

There was a belligerent note in his voice, and Hope wondered if she and Drake were about to see their first explosion from the boy.

"No," Hope answered carefully. "That's not what we had in mind, Stevie. You see, the place where Drake and I work is a place where lots of babies are born. There's a big day care there."

His eyes were stony and his chin jutted ever so slightly forward. "But I'm not a baby."

Hope cautiously measured her next words. A child of any age resented being treated as though he were younger.

"Of course you're not a baby. You're far more grown up. But this day care isn't just for babies. It's for kids of all ages. Some of them just like you. And they play games and do all sorts of fun things. Drake and I will be in the same building with you and we can check on you throughout the day. How does that sound?"

Disappointment washed over the faint defiance on his

face, then his chin dropped against his chest and he mumbled to the floor, "Okay—I guess."

Drake and Hope exchanged concerned glances.

Turning his attention to the boy, Drake said, "You don't sound as if you like our idea."

Stevie's voice held a hint of reprimand as he looked at Drake to ask, "Do you have to work? I'd rather stay here."

Feeling the boy needed reassurance more than anything, Drake reached over and lifted the child out of the chair and settled him on his knee.

"Sometimes we'd rather stay here, too, Stevie. But when you're grown up, like Hope and I, you have jobs to do."

Stevie's bottom lip quivered ever so slightly. Seeing it, Drake wanted to hug the boy tightly to him, ruffle his hair and promise him he didn't have to be scared of being left alone. Not now. Not ever again.

"Mommy and Daddy don't have jobs," Stevie reasoned innocently.

Drake bit his tongue to keep from cursing in front of Stevie. During college and all the years since, he'd worked like a demon to be independent of his family's wealth. But Denise had had no such concerns. She'd done nothing but live on her inheritance.

He tossed Hope a sardonic glance before shaking his head at Stevie. "That's because we're not like your mommy and daddy," Drake explained to him. "There's lots of people who depend on me and Hope to help them. We don't want to let them down. And we don't want to let you down, either. So I want to make a deal with you, Stevie. If you don't like staying at the day care, all you have to do is tell me or Hope and you won't have to go anymore. We'll work out the problem some other way. Okay?''

Hope could see Stevie's brown eyes skeptically searching Drake's face as though he couldn't believe he was being given an option in the matter. She supposed with Denise or Phillip it was a case of do what we say whether you like it or not.

Seconds continued to tick past. Hope held her breath, uncertain what the boy was going to say next. But suddenly a tiny hint of a smile spread across Stevie's face, and then he did the most unexpected thing. He flung his arms around Drake's neck and held on tightly.

Over Stevie's head, Drake turned a shocked, quizzical smile on Hope. ''I take it this means okay?''

Along with the bewilderment on Drake's face, there was a vulnerableness, an openness about him that Hope hadn't seen in a long, long time. Clearly, Stevie's display of affection had touched him in a way he hadn't expected.

''I definitely think it means okay,'' Hope murmured huskily. Then without warning, tears were burning her eyes. She desperately tried to blink them away before Stevie or Drake caught sight of them. But they threatened to spill onto her cheeks anyway.

She sprang to her feet so hurriedly, the bed bounced with the departure of her weight. Drake stared confoundedly at her departing back.

''Hope, where are you going?'' he called after her.

''I—have to go check on something.'' She forced the words through her tight throat. ''I'll be back in a few minutes.''

Drake didn't wait for the few minutes to pass. After making an excuse to Stevie, he went in search of Hope.

He found her in their bedroom across the hall, sitting at the dressing table, dabbing her eyes with a tissue.

"Why did you run away?"

Her body shook as she half sobbed, "I didn't run away."

He moved closer, then frowned as he studied her blotchy face. "Are you crying?"

He sounded disgusted, but that was nothing new. Drake never did like emotional displays of any sort. Through the years of their marriage she could hardly think of a time she'd cried in front of him. Even when she'd lost the baby, she'd been careful to keep her tears hidden when he was around. She wondered if it had been a mistake to hide her grief from him. Sharing it with her might have helped him get past the tragedy.

"Not anymore."

His face like a rock, he jammed his hands in the pockets of his jeans.

"What's the matter? Is this whole thing with Stevie too much for you? And you're worried that I'll be an ass and tell you so?"

"No! I'm very glad Stevie is here." She couldn't admit to him the real reason for her sudden surge of tearful emotions. She couldn't tell him that when she'd seen him hugging Stevie, it had reminded her she'd probably never see him holding a child of their own. The idea had simply been too painful to bear.

"Then it has to be me," he said curtly. "You want me out of here."

For the past year or more, she'd wanted many things from him. Consideration. Understanding. And mostly love. Instead she'd gotten exactly the opposite as Drake had continued to turn his back on her.

"If I wanted you out of here, I wouldn't have bothered asking you to come back for this month, Drake."

With a rough sigh, Drake ran a hand across the back of his neck. He supposed it would be a contradiction for her to ask him here, then just as quickly want him to go. But he wasn't totally blind. He could see how much he upset her.

"Okay, I'll accept that much. But you're not a woman to cry without reason." His probing eyes caught the reflection of her gaze in the mirror. "If you want to call this whole thing off, I—"

Seeing where his words were headed, she whirled to face him. "I don't want to call anything off!" Then softly, she added, "A woman just gets weepy on occasion and I left the room because I didn't want to upset Stevie."

Drake had to accept her explanation even if he didn't think it was entirely true. The way things stood between them, he was reluctant to question Hope further and stir up unresolved issues.

At least not while Stevie was here.

"He was fine when I left him, Drake said."

Glancing away from him, Hope drew a deep breath in an effort to collect herself. "Actually, I was thrilled he showed some affection toward you. I think it's a major step in the right direction."

One corner of Drake's lips curved sheepishly upward. "Yeah, the kid surprised me. I...well, it's almost like he's taken to me—a little. But I'm damned if I know why. I haven't been coddling him since he's been here."

At times Drake wasn't an easy man to love, or even like, Hope silently conceded. But there was a strong, steadying presence about him that Stevie needed and had instinctively recognized in his uncle.

"Denise says Phillip has always ignored his son."

With a cynical snort, Drake turned and walked to the window overlooking the quiet cul-de-sac. Peering through the slatted blinds, he said, "She spoke the truth there, but I'm sure she failed to mention she's done a pretty good job of neglecting him, too."

As she studied the rigid lines of his back, it dawned on Hope that it had been months—no, even longer— since she'd seen him relaxed. She didn't know when or if he ever let himself forget all that they had lost.

"I have no doubts that Stevie has been neglected by both his parents. But he does seem to have a particular need for male attention. I'm sure you can remember how it felt to want guidance and support from your father."

Bitterness shadowed his features as he glanced over his shoulder at her. "Yeah. I remember exactly how it felt to want the old man's respect and concern. And how it felt to never get more than a few sharp words instead."

Hope swallowed and tried not to think of the hurt her husband had endured as a child. It was a pain that had followed him into adulthood and was, in its own way, playing a role in keeping them apart.

"If you remember so well, then you should understand that the only thing Stevie really wants is to know you're here for him and that you care."

And he did care, Drake inwardly admitted. He would be lying to himself if he tried to pretend that little boy across the hall meant nothing to him. The feel of Stevie's arms tightly gripping his neck had filled him with a fierce need to protect the fragile child. He had to do his best not to let him down these next few weeks. And afterward, when the month was over, could he simply hand the boy to Denise without a second thought or worry? Somehow, he doubted it.

Turning away from the window, Drake walked to the dressing bench where Hope still sat. As he looked at the sweet, familiar lines of her face, he tried not to think about all the hopes and dreams they'd once shared. Or the fact that their marriage was slowly and bitterly dying with those dreams.

"I'll be here until Stevie leaves," he told her quietly. *Until he leaves.* Those three words told Hope everything.

Fearful that another bout of tears would roll down her cheeks, she bent her head and swallowed hard.

"I won't ask any more from you than that," she promised.

## CHAPTER SIX

WHEN HOPE ARRIVED at Maitland Maternity Clinic Monday morning, she was appalled to see a news truck already sitting in the parking lot. Apparently something had happened over the weekend with Cody, or else Chelsea Markum was getting a head start on the new week.

As she led Stevie into the building, she was relieved there were no cameramen lurking behind doors or shouting reporters clustered on the steps. That wasn't exactly the sort of thing Stevie needed to see on his first day.

The day care was located on the first floor of the building, close to the nursery and delivery rooms. It was a large, airy room with brightly colored toy chests and mats for nap time. At one end there was an arts and crafts area complete with easels, children's watercolors and blackboards for writing and drawing. At the other, behind a partition, was a room for infants. And outside was a small, bricked-in garden that could only be reached from inside the day care.

At the moment the place was filled with parents dropping their children off as they went to work. Hope stood at the edge of the room with Stevie in hand, waiting for Beth or one of her assistants to notice them.

Only moments passed before a young woman with a mass of dark curls cascading down her back made her way through the orderly chaos of energetic children to greet them.

"Hi, Hope!" Her bubbly smile encompassed both Hope and Stevie. "Is this Stevie?"

Hope smiled gratefully at Beth Maitland. "This is Stevie. He doesn't know anything about day care, so he's a little nervous this morning."

Beth instantly knelt to Stevie's level and introduced herself. While Hope watched the exchange, she couldn't imagine any child being able to resist Beth's warm, playful nature. Abby's younger sister adored children, and it showed in the way she handled each little personality in her special way.

In less than two minutes, Stevie was putting his hand trustingly into Beth's. "Don't worry about him," Beth assured Hope. "I'll keep an extra watch until he gets acquainted with the other kids."

Yesterday on the telephone, Hope had explained to Beth that Stevie wasn't one to socialize and that he might not bond with any of the other children. Beth had assured her he would, given time.

"Thank you, Beth." She gave the young woman a lost, but grateful look, then glanced one last time at Stevie. Was this how most mothers felt when they sent their firstborn off to kindergarten? she wondered.

"I'll check on you later, Stevie. Have fun." Unable to help herself, she bent and kissed his pale cheek. Surprise flickered in his brown eyes, but he said nothing. A brief tilt forward with his head was all the response he gave her.

As she made a quick exit of the day care and walked back to the gift shop, she kept telling herself Stevie would be fine. It would be foolish of her to worry about him all day. Beth was a certified preschool teacher. She knew all about child development. He couldn't be in better hands.

Tess, her assistant, had already opened the shop. Hope gave the young woman a bright smile as she stepped into the room and quickly surveyed the shelves and racks of assorted gifts ranging from clothing and toys to fine chocolates, fragrances and silk bouquets.

"Good morning. All ready to start another week?"

Tess smiled. "Looks like we might be in for another wild one. Chelsea Markum and her crew have already come through and headed onto the elevator. To the second floor, I suppose."

"I saw the news truck in the parking lot. Have you heard or seen anything going on down here?"

Tess shook her head. "No. I got here before most of the clinic's patients started arriving. I saw your husband and R.J. pass through to the elevator, but none of the other Maitlands."

A scowl furrowed Hope's brow. "Well, I just imagine R.J. or Megan herself is throwing the woman out about now."

"You'd think Chelsea would get the message and realize she isn't wanted around here," Tess commented as she ran a dust cloth over a glass display shelf.

Hope stashed her purse beneath the counter, then opened the cash register. Tess had already stocked it with bills and coins, which wasn't a surprise. The young woman was the most efficient worker Hope had ever had.

Tess had come to work for Hope a little more than six months ago. She was a lovely young woman with fair skin and thick chestnut curls that tumbled all the way to her shoulders. At first she would hardly say a word unless Hope spoke to her first. But over the months, she'd opened up and the two of them had become close.

Hope's heart broke every time she thought of all the young woman had been through in the past year. While going to college at the University at Austin, she'd fallen in love with a graduate student. She'd become pregnant, and just when the baby's father was about to marry her, she'd miscarried and lost the baby. Not too long afterward, the young man had called off the wedding and ended their engagement. Tess had been forced to accept the fact that he hadn't loved her. He'd only been about to marry her because his parents were forcing him to accept his responsibilities.

Whenever Tess grew discouraged, Hope would remind her that she was young and beautiful and one day would find a man who'd really love her. But Tess didn't believe her. And Hope could hardly blame her. How could she convince a woman that a miscarriage wasn't the end of the world, when it had seemingly ended her own?

Focusing her thoughts back on their conversation, she said to Tess, "Chelsea Markum doesn't care if she's wanted or not. All she's concerned about is getting her story."

Tess shook her head. "I couldn't stand that. Badgering and pushing my way into other people's lives. I don't want to be where I'm not wanted."

Neither did Hope. She couldn't bear to be Drake's wife if he didn't want her in his life.

She glanced at the main lobby to see a tall, rumpled-looking young man heading straight for the gift shop door.

"Looks like we've got a customer coming our way, and from the big grin on his face, he must have just become a daddy."

Tess tossed the dust rag aside and muttered, "I must have been crazy to take a job here. All these happy daddies remind me what a snake Robert was. If only he'd been a Billy Bob, driven a pickup and chewed tobacco.

But no, he was rich and cultured. I tell you, Hope, I'll never look at another rich man as long as I live.''

Hope didn't have the opportunity to explain to Tess that money or the lack of it had nothing to do with true love. The customer entered the shop, and Tess had already stepped forward to offer him assistance in finding his wife and new baby the perfect gift.

More than two hours later a commotion in the lobby had Hope looking up from a stack of invoices. Chelsea Markum and her crew were stepping off the elevator along with several security guards. It didn't take but a few moments to figure out that the star of *Tattle Today* was being escorted from the building. And by the sound of things, against her wishes.

Hope hated to think what this sort of scene was doing to the clients sitting around the normally quiet waiting area. If baby Cody's real mother or father didn't materialize soon, the media was going to turn this place into a circus.

LATER THAT MORNING, just before her lunch break, Hope gathered up her purse and told Tess she was going to the day care to check on Stevie.

For safety precautions, the door to the day care was locked. Hope tapped lightly, and after a moment, Cheryl, one of Beth's assistants, opened the door and ushered her in.

"Just in time," she said to Hope. "Your husband arrived only a couple of minutes ago."

Hope's eyes flew across the room to the man talking with Beth. His back was to Hope, but she couldn't mistake his sandy hair and tall, lean body.

At the same time, she noticed Stevie. He was sitting on the floor, a few feet away from Drake, rolling a ball back and forth to another little boy about the same age. The sight was a relief to Hope. Over the weekend, she'd worried Stevie would be too shy to connect with the other kids. Or that he might be so resentful about being in day care he would deliberately keep to himself. Thankfully neither of her fears had come true.

Her gaze swung to Drake. He was the last person she'd expected to find here. At breakfast this morning, he hadn't so much as hinted he would check on Stevie. It also niggled that he hadn't bothered to stop at the gift shop and invite her to come along with him, even though it was on the way.

The man clearly didn't want to include her in any part of his life, it seemed. Hope only wished that realization didn't hurt so much.

When she continued to stand just inside the door, Cheryl prompted her. "You can join them if you like, Mrs. Logan."

Forcing a smile on her face, she glanced at the assistant. "That's okay, Cheryl. There's no need to disturb them. I just wanted to make sure Stevie was okay."

The day-care assistant assured her Stevie was doing fine, and Hope decided the best thing she could do was make a quick exit to the gift shop before Drake spotted her and suspected she'd followed him here.

She'd almost gotten past the nursery window when a hand caught her from behind. Gasping, she whirled to see Drake towering over her.

She stared at him, her lips parted, her eyes wide. "Drake! You startled me!"

He grimaced. "Sorry. I was trying to catch up to you. I saw you leaving the day care. Why did you go without saying a word?"

Hope had gone to the day care with the intention of

speaking with Stevie, but the moment she'd seen Drake there, she'd felt superfluous.

With a hint of defiance she answered, "To check on Stevie, of course."

His brows rose mockingly and his gaze traveled from her face down the sleek lines of her red dress. The sweaterlike fabric was soft and clung to her breasts and hips in a very subtle, but most seductive, way.

Throughout their marriage, Hope had grown even more desirable to Drake, and he was not surprised that his body instantly responded to the sight of her. Now that he was in danger of losing her, her beauty had seemed to magnify. He couldn't imagine a future in which he lost the right to look at her, to touch her and know that her heart and her body belonged to him. Obviously such wistful thoughts were not on her mind.

"Must have been a short check," he muttered.

"You were taking care of things."

The curt tone of her voice caused his brows to arch even higher. "Surely you don't resent that?"

"No. I'm very glad you cared enough about Stevie to make a trip to the day care."

"But?"

She sighed impatiently. Her behavior was childish, Hope chided herself. It shouldn't matter that he hadn't cared enough to invite her to join him. "But nothing," she answered. "I—need to get back to the gift shop and eat my sandwich before Tess takes her lunch break."

Not waiting for a reply, Hope turned and walked away from him. Yet three steps was all she took before his hand was once again on her upper arm. The feel of it sent a rush of unwanted longing to the pit of her stomach.

"You're angry," he said with a measure of disbelief. "I want to know why."

Her shoulders sagged with resignation. "I'm not angry. Stevie is settling in. That's all that matters."

Maybe to her. But not to Drake. He despised seeing her this way. Cross. Defensive. Unwilling to share the tiniest part of her feelings with him. This was not the woman he'd married and loved for ten years. This woman hadn't existed until they'd lost their child. And maybe that was his fault, he thought sickly. Maybe he hadn't been man enough to help her get over the loss.

Oblivious to the people coming and going around them, he tightened his grip on her arm and pulled her to one side of the corridor.

"Look, Hope, I don't know what your problem is, but this is not the way I wanted to start the week with you—"

"My problem is that you walked right by the gift shop, but couldn't bother yourself to stop and tell me you were going to see Stevie. Or invite me to come along with you. I understand I'm not exactly your favorite person these days, Drake, but I am still your wife—"

"In name only." He cut in with the reminder.

Her blue eyes were suddenly snapping with fire. "And who's decision was that?" she demanded.

Seeing he'd definitely taken the wrong tack, Drake shook his head, then glanced around to see if any of the people passing by were taking notice of them. "Hope, this is not the time or place for another one of our arguments."

Her spine stiffened to board straight. "You're right about that much."

"I think—"

When he paused, Hope glanced at his face and was instantly surprised to see his expression softening. Slowly she became aware that his fingers had loosened their punishing grip and were sliding temptingly up and down her upper arm.

"What?" she asked, hating herself for sounding as though she'd just run a mile.

"I think we should go to lunch. Together."

That took her by surprise. "Why? So we can continue arguing?"

Drake studied her flushed face, and for a moment he wanted to forget where they were. He wanted to pull her into his arms and ease the hunger inside him with the taste of her lips. "No. So we can stop it. And it does have to stop, Hope. If you want this thing with Stevie to work, we can't continue to harp at each other."

He was right. And even if he wasn't, she couldn't resist his company. In spite of the fact he'd moved out, in spite of his refusal to have a child, her heart was still a slave to the man. Love was a spell, she decided. A sick spell that couldn't be broken.

"All right," she agreed. "Do you want to eat in my office or yours?"

He shook his head and slid his hand possessively against her back, urging her down the corridor. "I thought we might go to the diner."

"Do you have time?"

He didn't. But he was going to make time. "I have a meeting in forty minutes. If lunch runs over, Juanita will stall until I get back."

After a brief stop to explain to Tess that she'd be out of the building for lunch, Hope left the clinic with Drake. In silence, they walked the short distance to the diner.

Along the way, Hope noticed the sky had become overcast since she'd driven to work this morning, but the temperature was still warm enough to be comfortable without a sweater or jacket.

Hope had always loved Austin's mild climate. The only time she wished for cold weather or snow was at Christmas. But snow in Austin was a rare thing. The chances for a white Christmas around here would be about the same as Drake suddenly changing his mind and saying he wanted a baby. And that was poor to none.

As usual, Austin Eats was filled to near capacity. She and Drake stood inside the door, trying to locate an empty booth or table, when Shelby spotted them. Waving a hand, she hurried forward to greet them.

"Georgette is cleaning off a booth in the far corner right now. You two go on back and she'll fix you up."

It wasn't exactly a romantic lunch for two, Hope thought, as she and Drake slid into the vinyl-padded booth, but at least they were out of the main hustle and bustle of the diner's noonday traffic.

A brassy blond waitress in her mid-thirties was rapidly swiping a wet dishcloth over the tabletop. "What can I get you two? Or do you need to see menus?"

"Coffee and chef salad will do me," Hope told her.

Georgette pulled a pencil from its resting place above her ear and a pad from a pocket on her uniform and began to jot down Hope's order.

"What's on special today?" Drake asked her.

The voluptuous waitress shot him an appreciative smile. "Pinto beans and corn bread. Or chili and corn bread. Or you can mix 'em up and have chili beans and corn bread."

"I'll take the chili beans and coffee."

Georgette scratched his request underneath Hope's, then hurried away to fetch their drinks.

Once their coffee arrived, Hope stirred cream into the black brew, then glanced across the table at Drake.

He immediately caught her gaze with his, and for a

moment Hope thought how crazy everything seemed. This was her husband, the man who'd lain next to her all through the night. How could he feel so very far away? Worse than that, how could she still want him so much?

His forearms resting on the edge of the tabletop, Drake leaned toward her. "I wasn't deliberately trying to avoid you this morning, Hope. To tell you the truth, I went down to the day care on the spur of the moment."

In his own way, he was trying to apologize, and Hope felt her resistance to him weaken even more.

"You don't have to explain your every move to me. I'm just—" Sighing, she reached for her coffee. She couldn't tell him that her every waking moment was shadowed by the thought of losing him. Her nerves were like exposed wires. All it took was a word or touch from him to set off sparks. "Leaving Stevie this morning was a hard thing to do. I can't help worrying about him. He's such…a sad little thing."

And so was she, Drake thought ruefully. And he was the reason. It seemed all his life he'd done nothing but disappoint the people he'd tried to love.

"I get the sense that he's angry and afraid and sad," Drake agreed. "But I think the day care is a good thing for him. I doubt he's ever been in such a relaxed setting before. Beth says he's already talking and mingling with the other kids."

"Yes, I noticed he was playing ball with another little boy. And that is what he needs," Hope replied. "To have fun. To be a kid, too."

Without his gaze ever leaving her face, Drake picked up his coffee. "And that's why we're going to have to make an extra effort to put our differences aside, Hope.

Otherwise, Stevie is going to feel the strain between us and think he's the cause.''

His probing gaze disturbed her with too many pleasurable memories. She glanced away from him, then to the tabletop. "You're right, Drake. And that's the last thing I want. It would be better for Stevie to be in Dallas with a hired baby-sitter than to hear us fighting.''

Like his own parents, he thought. His mother and father had bickered over trivial material things. The color of their next new car was a far more important issue than their children's emotional needs. He'd felt like a household fixture that was in the way, but couldn't be thrown out.

"I want us to call a truce, Hope. At least while Stevie is here.''

And afterwards? she wanted to ask. Would he still want them to try to get along, or would he be in a big hurry to pack his things and head out the door? Hope desperately wanted to ask him which it would be. But she stopped herself. The issue of a baby and their marriage was too flammable. To keep the peace, she was going to have to shelve the questions and try to put their differences out of her mind until Stevie went back to Dallas. After all, the little boy was the reason Drake was home. The best thing she could do was remember that.

Looking at him, she said, "You're right, Drake. And I'll try my best.''

To her surprise, a little grin teased the corners of his mouth. The sight warmed her and made her forget, just for a moment, that anything was wrong between them.

"Good," he said softly. "I'll keep my white flag up, if you will.''

It was becoming clear that he cared about Stevie. And Hope was very glad about that. But the foolish part of her, the part that hadn't quite let go of him, wanted to believe this lunch, this effort for a truce, had something to do with their marriage.

"I will," she murmured. "I promise."

The smile slowly faded from his face, and his expression turned unexpectedly tender. "We used to—"

"Here's your orders," Georgette interrupted. "Chef salad and chili beans. Can I get you two anything else?"

Dishes and silverware rattled as the waitress placed their food on the table. Hope waited impatiently for the woman to finish the task and be on her way.

"Nothing for me," Drake told her, then glanced at Hope. "What about you? Will you be wanting dessert?"

"Joe's made some good pecan pie today," Georgette interjected as she tilted her steaming coffeepot over their mugs. "How 'bout a slice with ice cream?"

Hope cast her an apologetic smile. "No, thanks, Georgette. This will be plenty."

The waitress left, and Hope expected Drake to begin where he'd left off. When he didn't, she said, "You were about to say something before Georgette brought our food. What was it?"

He crushed a fist of crackers into his chili beans, then picked up a spoon. "Nothing, really."

He glanced at her, and she could see regret clouding his eyes. "I was just about to say we used to...make a pretty good team."

Her heart squeezed at his use of the past tense. Apparently he believed there was no hope of them being a good team in the future. He already considered their marriage over. The idea left her cold in spite of the diner's overheated interior.

"We can be a good team again," she murmured. "For Stevie's sake."

He appeared to be on the verge of saying something else, but suddenly his attention was distracted.

When he continued to stare beyond her shoulder toward the front of the room, Hope frowned at him. "What are you looking at?" she asked curiously.

"The diner has just been invaded by Chelsea Markum and one of her cameramen."

"Didn't she do enough damage at the clinic this morning?" Hope twisted her head and quickly scanned the faces of the lunch crowd. "I don't see any of the Maitlands in here. I wonder who she's after now?"

"I don't know. But I'm sure we're about to find out."

Hope told herself not to look or listen, but the woman was akin to a coiled copperhead. You had to watch her every move to avoid being bitten by her.

"Miss Lord! Miss Shelby Lord, can I have a word with you?" Chelsea spoke over the loud din of rattling dishes and chatting diners.

Behind the long curved counter, Shelby pushed a hand through her tousled red hair and surveyed the TV reporter with wary eyes.

"Sorry. Not now."

After pushing her way between two men sitting at the counter, Chelsea thrust a tiny microphone at Shelby.

"Just a few words, that's all, Miss Lord," she entreated.

"About what?" Shelby asked with a clueless shrug of her shoulders. "I don't have anything interesting to tell you. Other than it's lunchtime and I'm very busy."

Like a predator on the prowl, the reporter smiled at Shelby. "But this will only take a minute, Miss Lord, and I'm sure you know far more than you think you do."

The sugary note in the Chelsea's voice made Shelby's green eyes narrow.

With one hand, Shelby gestured at the busy tables and booths filled with lunchtime diners. "Like I said, Miss Markum, I'm very busy."

"I can see that. So I'll get to the point. I'd like to ask you about your brother, Garrett—"

Surprise arched Shelby's brows, then with a shake of her head, she said, "My brother is a rancher. That can't be news for your TV show."

Chelsea smiled, but there was a wealth of impatience in her steely eyes. "It's who's staying at your brother's ranch that's news to Austin."

Shelby's expression went purposely blank. "I'm not aware that anyone is staying with him. But then, I haven't been out for a visit myself."

Ignoring the fact that every eye in the diner was focused on her, Chelsea leaned forward impatiently. "It's rumored that Jake Maitland and his pregnant companion are staying with him. You don't know anything about that?"

The two men on either side of Chelsea were staring at the reporter with their mouths gaping. Hope glanced at Drake, who, like the rest of the patrons, was waiting to see what the aggressive reporter would ask next.

Frowning, Shelby stalked to the checkout counter.

Naturally Chelsea followed her every step of the way.

As she stabbed a pair of bills on a spike, Shelby said, "I'm sorry, but I don't. The guests he has at his ranch are his business. I don't ask my brother who stays at his ranch, the same way he doesn't ask me who comes in my diner. We have better things to do with our time."

Seeing she was getting the runaround, Chelsea made a motion to the cameraman to wrap up and leave. As they hurried out the door of the diner, Hope turned her attention to Drake.

"Did you know she and her crew were at the clinic again this morning?"

Drake frowned with disgust. "Juanita told me she'd encountered them in the hallway on the second floor."

He swallowed a bite of the chili beans, then went on, "I tell you, Hope, some of Maitland's backers aren't convinced that one of the Maitland men didn't father Cody and leave him and the mother to fend for themselves. This thing with Jake is going to cause an even bigger explosion if something doesn't happen soon."

"I agree, Drake. But the poor woman with Jake can't be blamed for all that's gone on here in Austin before she came to town. And anyway, no one really knows much about her. It might not be Jake's child she's carrying."

Scowling, Drake shoveled another spoonful of beans into his mouth. "I'm not so sure that matters one way or the other. The way I see things shaping up, the truth, when it finally does comes out, might be too late."

Hope's gaze flew to his face. "What do you mean, 'too late'?"

Even though the two of them were more or less secluded, he leaned forward and lowered his voice.

"If this mess isn't cleared up soon, I'm not sure what the effect on the clinic's financial status will be. Backers may start dropping out like flies. And when that happens...well, it's not going to be a pretty sight. At least, not in the clinic's ledgers. My job is to direct the clinic's money. But if there isn't enough money to meet the needs, well, you get the picture."

Hope did get the picture, and it was a bleak one. She didn't want to think that her job or Drake's might ultimately be affected by this thing. But both of them would be blind not to consider the possibility.

The Maitlands were a rich family. There was no question about that. For years the mansion and the family itself had been a symbol of wealth and grandeur in Austin. But Maitland Maternity Clinic wasn't run entirely on family money. When Megan had started the clinic, she'd envisioned it as belonging to the citizens of Austin, not just her. And because she and the family were so well respected, she hadn't had trouble finding backers for her project. That support had been strong through the entire twenty-five years the clinic had been in existence. Now that foundation had been shaken when baby Cody was left on the clinic's steps three months ago. Since then all hell had broken loose.

"Oh, Drake," Hope murmured anxiously, "does Megan know the severity of the problem?"

Drake nodded grimly. "She does. But she hasn't said much about any of it—at least not to me. I get the feeling—" He broke off with a shake of his head. "I don't know, but the woman seems to be preoccupied lately."

Hope cast him an incredulous look. "Well, is it any wonder?"

"No." He shook his head thoughtfully. "I don't mean just with the gossip about her family. I don't know—it's as if she's holding something back."

Drake had never been one to gossip about anything or anyone, so it only underscored for Hope how worried he was about the clinic and the Maitlands. "You think she knows who the baby belongs to and isn't telling? Why would she do something like that? She, more than anyone, must want this all resolved."

"Maybe not," Drake observed coolly, "if the baby belongs to one of her sons."

Emphatically Hope shook her head. "No. I don't believe that. Megan's a smart woman. She understands a person in her social and business position can't hide the truth. If she did, it would only come back to haunt her.''

Drake's expression was skeptical. ''I'm beginning to wonder if it already has.''

persuade her would be the wisest course. With all of the turmoil the media coverage of her courtroom testi—

*Jonas's suggestion seemed to make sense.* "I'll... I'm beginning to consider it already... but...

# *CHAPTER SEVEN*

To AVOID an invasion by the press, Abby Maitland's eleven o'clock wedding was taking place at the Maitland mansion rather than a downtown church.

Saturday morning dawned clear and beautiful. After a late breakfast, Hope did her hair and makeup, then, garment bag in tow, drove across town to the mansion where Abby and the rest of the bridesmaids would be dressing for the event. Drake and Stevie were planning to drive over later, just before the ceremony started.

As for the red dress, she hadn't made a point of showing it to Drake. In spite of what Abby had suggested, Hope knew her husband wasn't interested in such things. This past week had more than proved that.

Although the two of them had managed to hold on to their truce, Hope could see that underneath the fragile peace, his feelings toward her hadn't changed. Each night when she climbed into bed, Drake never even whispered a word to her, much less touched her.

Over and over she'd been asking herself when her husband had stopped wanting her. And each time she had to accept the fact that his desire for her had ended the day she'd lost their child. It was as if all the passion he'd had for her died along with that tiny life.

Even after more than a year, Hope still couldn't understand why the loss had affected him so deeply, so permanently. He hadn't wanted a baby to begin with. It had taken her years to finally change his mind.

Warm, sweet memories tilted her lips into a smile as she drove down the quiet residential street toward the Maitland mansion. For a man who'd insisted he didn't want to be a daddy, Drake had made an instant change once Hope had become pregnant. She'd never seen anyone so excited. He'd coddled her in every way imaginable and brought little gifts for the baby nearly every day of the week.

The smile disappeared as those happy times faded from her mind. She understood Drake didn't want to face that sort of loss again. Neither did she. But one miscarriage didn't have to be the end of the world. Or the end of their marriage. Somehow Drake couldn't see that. Or he simply didn't want to.

The entrance leading up to the Maitland estate consisted of tall, electronic black gates. Once Hope was allowed to enter, she drove slowly up the winding drive toward the white, four-story structure. As she drew nearer, she could see a flurry of activity in and around the stately home. Luxury cars were parked all around the curved drive and in every other available space.

Florists carried huge pots of pink, red and white poinsettias through the front entrance. Behind them, musicians were lugging in guitars, drums, violins, violas and cellos. Off to one side of the house, near the entryway serving the kitchen, caterers were unloading giant trays of food from a large van.

None of the bustle surprised Hope. When the Maitlands put on a social event, they did it Texas style. And Abby's wedding was truly a happy occasion for the family to celebrate.

At the massive front door, she followed yet another

musician lugging a bass fiddle into the house. Inside the huge foyer, she could see that the doors to the living room had been thrown open and people were rushing to and fro as they attended to last-minute preparations.

The enormous room had been emptied of furniture, and in one corner, an elevated platform had been set up for the musicians. Workers were making the final adjustments to the rows of padded folding chairs that would seat the wedding guests.

Not certain where she might find Abby or the rest of the women in the wedding party, she stood to one side, waiting to catch a glimpse of someone from the Maitland family. Thankfully, only a moment or two passed before Hope spotted Harold, the Maitlands' white-haired butler, coming from a hallway that led to the back of the house. He greeted Hope with a warm smile.

"Hello, Mrs. Logan. Fine day for a wedding, isn't it?"

Hope smiled at his enthusiasm. Usually Harold was a man of few words. His calm demeanor rarely changed, even during times of chaos. He'd worked for the Maitlands so long that he was like a member of the family, and in spite of his stern features, Hope had always had the suspicion that Harold harbored a soft spot for Abby. No doubt it pleased the old man to see her finally getting married to the man she loved.

"It's like spring out today," Hope agreed. "We could almost dance in the garden."

"If you want to dance in the garden, Mrs. Logan, you go right ahead. The roses are still in full bloom. You'll make one more."

Laughing, Hope patted his hand. "I don't know how you've stayed single all these years, Harold."

Harold's sober expression didn't change, but his wink

said volumes. "I've had to work very hard at it, Mrs. Logan."

"Is Abby upstairs?" she asked.

"Yes, ma'am. She and her entourage are on the second floor in the first and second bedrooms on the right. You may go right on up."

Hope thanked the butler, then headed up the wide staircase. The polished balustrade was beautifully draped with evergreens, holly and red velvet bows. At the top of the landing, clusters of poinsettias formed a sea of red petals. Down the hallway leading to the rest of the bedrooms, Hope could glimpse a sparkling wreath hanging on each door.

She found Abby in the first bedroom, surrounded by her twin sisters, Beth and Ellie, and her sister-in-law, Dana. The bride was already wearing her wedding dress, a sleek white satin sheath that draped across her breasts and flared slightly at her ankles. The sleeves were long and fitted, narrowing to points just above her knuckles.

She spotted Hope's reflection in the mirror and turned frantically to her friend.

"Oh, Lord, Hope, what do you think about this dress? I look like Carole Lombard in *My Man Godfrey* or something! What am I going to do?"

Hope laughed. Abby was an excellent ob/gyn. She'd faced many life-and-death crises in the delivery room at Maitland Maternity and no one doubted her ability to remain cool under pressure. But obviously she was finding her own wedding a bit more unsettling than delivering a baby.

Hope hurried over to Abby and gave her an encouraging hug. "You're not going to do anything, Abby. You look stunning. The dress is very tasteful. Sleek and lovely, just like you."

"That's what we've been trying to tell her, Hope," Ellie said. "Maybe she'll listen to you."

Beth slung her arm affectionately around her twin's shoulder and added playfully, "She'll have to listen to Hope. We don't have any extra wedding dresses in the closet around here and it's rather late in the morning to go buy one off the rack at Neiman Marcus."

Abby sent her younger sisters a withering look. "You two aren't really helping matters."

Beth laughed while Ellie, who was always the more serious of the two, simply shrugged.

"Abby," Hope gently scolded, "there's nothing to be nervous about. You're going to make a ravishing bride. Kyle will take one look at you and forget there's anyone else in the room."

Abby took one more doubtful look at herself in the mirror, then turned and squeezed Hope's hands. "If you say so."

"I do. So quit worrying and do your hair. The house is going to be filling up with guests soon."

Beth giggled. "She's already done her hair, Hope. I told her that orange plastic clamp didn't go with her dress. But she wouldn't believe me about that, either."

Abby whirled on her teasing sister. "Beth! Will you please get out of here? Go see if Mother needs help."

Laughing, Beth picked up her long skirt and scurried out of the room. Abby sank weakly onto a chair.

Reaching up to take the clamp from her dark hair, she said, "I didn't know I was going to be so nervous, Hope. My hands are shaking, my stomach feels like a bowl full of bees. I thought getting married to the man I loved would be easy. This is—terrifying."

Hope smiled with gentle reassurance. "Marrying the man you love is easy, Abby. Trust me."

*The years that come afterward are the scary part. When your husband quits loving you.* Hope kept the black thought to herself. Not for anything would she dampen Abby's wedding day. Instead, she prayed her friend would never know a moment of heartache.

Two hours later, the first notes of a Strauss waltz drifted sweetly upward, announcing to the bride and her attendants that the guests were filing through the doors of the Maitland mansion.

When Hope, along with the other attendants, marched into the huge room, she couldn't believe the transformation that had taken place while she'd been upstairs.

Poinsettias, boughs of evergreen and blooming Christmas cactus filled the room with color and the scent of the holy holiday. At the head of the room, an archway trimmed with white poinsettias was flanked by twin candelabra. On either side, a magnificent Christmas tree loaded with elaborate red and gold decorations towered at least twenty feet toward the ceiling.

The truly stunning sight, though, was the bride. As Abby walked down the aisle flanked by family and friends, all eyes were on her. And when she took her position beside Kyle and placed her hand in his, Hope could see an expression of serene rapture come over her beautiful face.

The ceremony was filled with prayers and vows written by both Abby and Kyle. As Hope listened to the words of love and promise being exchanged, her heart cried with joy for her friend. And it was weeping, too. Mourning all that she and Drake were slowly and surely losing.

When Kyle took his new bride into his arms and sealed their vows with a long, tender kiss, Hope couldn't stop the lump forming in her throat or the tears burning the back of her eyes. Drake had once kissed her in the same way; he'd vowed to love her forever. But forever hadn't lasted that long.

Finally, the minister officially introduced the couple to the wedding guests as man and wife. Immediately, friends and well-wishers rushed forward, squeezing around the newlyweds to offer hugs and kisses and handshakes.

Hope moved discreetly to one side to avoid the crush. There would be plenty of time for her to congratulate Abby. Besides, for some damned reason, she still felt too weepy to talk to anyone, much less fight her way through a happy, laughing crowd.

She was dabbing at her watery eyes when a warm masculine hand suddenly closed over her bare shoulder. Without having to look around, she knew it was Drake who'd come up behind her. The familiar touch of his fingers sent little bolts of awareness sizzling through her.

"This is quite a wedding."

His raspy voice was close to her ear, making the urge to turn to him impossible to resist. He was dressed for the occasion in a charcoal-colored suit and maroon tie. The colors were a perfect backdrop for his tanned rugged features and sandy hair. Looking at him, Hope knew that he would catch the attention of many of the female guests, young or old.

"Everything is spectacular," she agreed.

Drake's green eyes slowly scanned her face, then swept downward to where the red velvet stopped and her cleavage began. Over the past months he'd tried to forget the pleasures of her shapely body, tried to forget what he no longer had. But seeing her like this was a torturous reminder.

"Very beautiful," he murmured. "I don't think I've

ever seen you dressed like this. At least, not for anyone else but me.''

His words and the intimate track of his eyes caused a blush to steal across Hope's cheeks. ''It was Abby's choice. She didn't want her bridesmaids looking old-maidish.''

As Drake assessed his wife's attire, he didn't know what he wanted most—to cover her up or drag her off to some secluded place and seduce her. The latter urge was winning ground when they were joined by R.J. and his wife, Dana.

''Bridesmaids are meant to be kissed, too, aren't they, Drake?'' R.J. asked, but didn't wait for permission. Leaning forward, he kissed Hope's blushing cheek.

Drake cast a wry smile at his old friend. ''You're certainly feeling good.''

With a grin, R.J. hugged Dana close to his side. ''Never better. Abby has given the family something to celebrate.''

Dana, who'd deliberately made herself a plain Jane for years, had blossomed since her marriage to R.J., and Hope thought her friend had never looked lovelier. Dana's delicate features were glowing with happiness. Her long, dark blond hair draped her shoulders like a satin cape while sparkling jewels adorned her slender neck and wrist. Gifts from her loving husband, no doubt.

Dana and R.J. deserved each other, Hope thought generously. They would be lovers until their dying days. As for herself—she glanced at Drake, then wished she hadn't. The sight of his handsome face filled her with such regret, she wanted to burst into another round of tears.

''It's wonderful to see Abby so happy,'' Dana said.

"For a long time we'd given up on her ever looking at another man. Isn't that right, Hope?"

Hope nodded at Dana as she recalled the deep hurt Abby had endured at the hands of a man who'd pretended to love her as a way to get to the Maitland fortune. It had taken years for Abby to get over the deception. But at least she'd survived to love again, Hope thought. As for herself, she was obviously going to have to learn to love again, too. Otherwise, she was going to be spending the rest of her life alone.

"Abby was pretty scarred," Hope murmured. "But she's definitely happy now."

"And I think Kyle's just the man to keep her that way," R.J. added with an intimate little smile for his wife.

If this wedding had been for anyone but Abby, Drake would not have attended. Not that he minded social events, but weddings were another matter. He didn't want to think about love or hear people discussing the silly notion of happily ever after. Not when the threat of his own divorce hung like an ominous cloud over his head.

Clearing his throat, Drake gestured with a tilt of his head toward the rest of the wedding crowd. "Looks like everyone is gravitating toward the food." Automatically, he brought his hand against the small of Hope's back. "Ready to eat?"

It suddenly dawned on Hope that Stevie wasn't with Drake. Her eyes met his. "Where's Stevie?"

"Dora and Jessie have set up a special room for the kids to have a little party of their own. He's probably playing games or eating right now."

The four of them began to move in the general direction of the dining room, where the reception would take place. As they walked along, R.J. asked Drake, "How is your little nephew adapting to being here in Austin without his parents?"

Like the flip of a switch, Drake's expression turned grim. "He hasn't once asked about Denise or Phillip. And I don't expect he will."

The other man cast a curious glance at Drake. "What's the matter, he doesn't get along with his parents?"

Drake let out a mocking snort. "The kid doesn't even know his parents. My sister and her husband are too busy globe-trotting and merrymaking to notice they have a son."

R.J. shared a knowing glance with his wife before he turned his gaze on Drake. "So it's like that," he said with regret.

"Yeah. Like that."

Thoughtful for a moment, R.J. reached over and slapped a friendly hand on Drake's shoulder. "Then maybe you should consider keeping the boy here with you, Drake."

At his friend's suggestion Drake's jaw visibly dropped. It was one thing to consider the idea in his private thoughts. But to hear his closest friend suggest he could be a father to Stevie in front of Hope was more than he wanted to contend with at the moment.

Drake glanced at Dana. "What have you done to this man?"

Dana's green eyes sparkled with a hint of mischief. "Married him. That's all."

"You must have done a hell of a lot more than that," Drake pointed out with a mocking smirk. "Me keep Stevie! I don't have any business trying to be the boy's father."

Disappointment sliced through Hope, but she carefully tried her best to keep it hidden. She wasn't going to be the one to tell Drake what he should or shouldn't do about Stevie. The child was his nephew. He would have to come to a decision on his own.

To Dana and R.J., Hope said, "Drake has only agreed to be a temporary father for Stevie. Just for Christmas."

A grin as big as Texas crossed R.J.'s face as he looked at Hope. "Well," he drawled with confidence, "the holidays have been known to work miracles. I have an idea Drake will be one of them this Christmas."

Drake glared at his friend. "I'm going to remember this, R.J." Turning a dark glance at Hope's pinched face, he added, "You put him up to this, didn't you? It's not enough for you to want me to feel like a selfish bastard, you want my friends to make me feel that way, too."

"Drake!" Dana gasped with shock.

Her face white, Hope glanced at her friend. "Sorry, Dana," she half whispered, then hurriedly turned and made her way out of the crowded room.

Thankfully everyone was headed for the dining room, leaving the garden at the back of the massive house empty except for the roses and a group of white wrought-iron furniture. Hope sat down on one of the benches.

Though she hadn't bothered to grab a wrap, the breeze whispering through the bare branches of the cottonwood trees was not unpleasant against her exposed arms.

*The roses are still in full bloom. You'll make one more.*

The corners of Hope's lips turned downward at the thought of Harold's romantic words. She hadn't felt like a rose in a long time. And Drake certainly hadn't thought of her as one. To him she was a conniving bitch, out to get a child from him at any cost.

Dear God, how was she going to get through the rest of this day. How was she going to go back inside, eat, dance and pretend she was ecstatically happy for Abby and her family?

"Hope, aren't you going to come in and eat? Besides, it's too cool for you to be out here without a wrap."

Hope glanced over her shoulder to see Dana's tall, slender form walking down the brick path to where she was sitting. A worried frown marred her friend's face, and Hope felt guilty for spoiling this day for Dana and R.J.

"I'm not the least bit cold or hungry. Don't worry about me, Dana. Please go back in and eat with R.J. You don't want to miss this time with him and your family."

Dana wrapped the velvet shawl more tightly around her shoulders as she eased down on the bench beside Hope. "I'll go back in a minute or two. Right now, I just want to make sure you're okay."

"Of course I'm okay," Hope insisted with a wan smile.

Dana's green eyes quietly surveyed Hope's face. "I don't think Drake meant to sound so nasty."

"Oh, yes he did," Hope replied with bitter resignation.

A sigh slipped from Dana as she reached for Hope's hand. "R.J. considers Drake a brother. He didn't mean to sound as though he were pushing his nose into your private life. Well, maybe he was a little," she added with a wry smile. "But only because he loves you both. So do I. And we don't like to see our friends unhappy."

Hope bit on her lip as she shook her head. "Thanks for your concern, Dana. But—it's just too complicated to explain."

It wasn't really, Hope thought. But she didn't want to get into it with Dana. Not today, on their friend Abby's first day as a married woman.

Dana started to make a reply when the sound of a

footstep caused both women to glance in the direction of the house. The moment Hope spotted Drake walking toward them, she groaned under her breath.

Quickly Dana jumped to her feet. "I'm going back in," she whispered hurriedly to Hope.

"Not without me," Hope vowed, practically leaping from the bench.

"No!" Dana whispered insistently. "You need to talk to him, Hope. Avoiding your husband isn't going to help matters."

Hope started to tell her that avoiding Drake was akin to trying to skirt a snarling dog, but she didn't have the opportunity. Before she could stop her, Dana scurried away, pausing on the walkway to speak with Drake for a few seconds, then hurrying toward the house.

As for Drake, his long, purposeful strides carried him straight to Hope. It took everything inside her to stand her ground and wait for him, when her heart was screaming for her to run and escape another volley of pain.

"Abby and Kyle have started eating. All her bridesmaids should be with her."

Rather than look at him, she kept her gaze firmly fixed on a brilliant cardinal perched on the ledge of a bird feeder. The bird was as red as her Christmas wedding dress, reminding her the holiday would soon be upon them. And after it had passed, she could only guess what Drake intended to do about both Stevie and their marriage.

"You're right. I should be getting back to the reception."

Swiftly she rose to her feet, only to have him catch her by the upper arm.

"Not yet," he said flatly. "I have something to say to you."

Anger flashed through her like the kick of a double-barreled shotgun. "Don't you think you've already said plenty?"

He scanned Hope's face, his expression sober. "I'm sorry about what happened inside, Hope."

The feeble attempt at an apology had little effect on Hope. "I'm not the one you should be apologizing to. I'm used to this sort of thing from you, Drake. It's R.J. and Dana who deserve an apology."

Regret welled inside Drake. Clearly, she didn't understand that hearing Abby and Kyle's vows of lifelong love had tortured him as he thought of their own vows and the impending threat of divorce. She couldn't know that R.J.'s simple suggestion that he be a father to Stevie had paralyzed him with fear. It was something he'd tried to explain to her in the past. He'd long given up hoping to make her understand. And perhaps a part of him didn't want to admit his fears to her; he had always wanted Hope to see him as a strong, capable man.

"I've already told them both I was out of line. They've accepted my apology. Anyway, I think they're more concerned about you."

Aware that his fingers had loosened their hold on her arm, Hope pulled free of him. "And I'm sure that irks you, doesn't it?"

Drake struggled to calm himself as his gaze traveled over her flushed cheeks. He had no right to be angry with her. But his blood was fired. In more ways than one. "What irks me is you childishly running out here to the garden."

Her mouth fell open. "It was childish of me to come outside for a breath of fresh air? Compared to your little outburst? I don't think so, Drake."

Determinedly, she stepped around him and started toward the house. Before she could take two steps, his fingers snagged her shoulder.

"Just a minute. I'm not through with you."

Outrage quivered through Hope as she whirled to him. "Oh, yes! You're through! We're through. But then, that's what you've wanted all along, isn't it?"

Drake's jaw clamped together, knotting the muscles in his cheeks and neck. "Damn it, Hope, you think you know me so well. But you don't. You don't even want to try!"

"Try!" she repeated incredulously. "I've been trying for months—no years—to understand what you really want from me. But I can't figure you. And I seriously doubt a psychiatrist could crack your hard shell!"

Drake couldn't stand it any longer. The first moment he'd seen Hope in that damned red dress, he'd felt as if his very breath had left him. He'd been trying like hell to forget just how good she looked. In and out of his bed. Now the sight of all that smooth, creamy skin was taunting him, making him forget he wasn't supposed to be wanting her.

Muttering an oath, he tugged her off the brick path and behind the massive trunk of an oak tree.

Her breasts heaved with exertion and outrage as his hands pinned both shoulders to the rough bark and his face dipped close to hers.

"One look at you and a psychiatrist would damn well know the hell I'm going through," Drake muttered.

"What are you—"

Suddenly his thumb and fingers were bracketing her jaw, drawing her face even closer to his. "Talking about?" he finished mockingly. "This."

Hope was totally unprepared for "this." Not since that reckless night in the kitchen when they'd forgotten themselves had he touched her or kissed her in a passionate way. Having his lips on hers again, feeling the rough skin of his fingers sliding against her face, her neck and down to her bosom were igniting a flash fire through the rest of her body.

With a helpless moan, she parted her lips, allowing his tongue access to her mouth. She welcomed the intimate invasion.

His long body pressed into hers, jamming her bare back and shoulders against the rough bark, but Hope was oblivious to the discomfort. All she could feel was a fire growing deep in her belly, begging her to mate with the man she loved.

Her skin was so soft, so perfect beneath his fingers that Drake hardly knew where it stopped and the red velvet began. Only the warmth of her flesh guided him, and soon his hand was deep inside the bodice, cupping the weight of one breast in his palm.

"You say I don't want you," he whispered against her lips. "But this is all I want, Hope. This. You. Just the two of us making love."

The warmth of his breath softly grazing her lips and cheeks was as seductive as the fingers against her budded nipple. She wanted nothing more than to give in to the mindless ecstasy he promised her, but his passion was only momentary. She couldn't count on it to last any more than she could their shaky marriage.

"You've gone crazy, Drake. One minute you're hissing at me, and now—"

Now all he could think about was how much he wanted her. "I told you I was sorry, Hope. Damn it, I know you didn't put R.J. up to saying any of that. But I—"

He didn't know how to explain what had come over

him a few minutes ago when R.J. began talking about Stevie needing a father. Throughout the wedding ceremony, he'd kept remembering back to when Hope had trustingly put her hand into his and vowed to love him forever. Memories both sweet and painful had jabbed at him from every direction, reminding him of all that the two of them had shared so happily and lost so painfully. Seeing Hope looking so damned beautiful hadn't helped matters, either. When R.J. had brought up the subject of Drake being a father, it had been too much for him to take.

"But you what?" she prompted.

His sigh was rough as his hand left her breast, then cupped the side of her face. "I don't know what else to say but I'm sorry."

*Why not, I love you, Hope. I don't ever want to hurt you. I want us to have a child together. I want us to be together for the rest of our lives.*

But of course, Hope knew she could stand here in the garden until it froze over, which might be once every ten years in Austin, before Drake would say those things to her and really mean them.

The realization was enough to cool her heated body and remind her she needed to make an appearance inside with the rest of the wedding party. Abby and Katie were probably wondering where she was. If Dana hadn't already told them, she thought grimly.

"I'm sorry, too, Drake. For a lot of things."

Drake could feel her stiffening, pulling away from him, and he knew these moments of holding her were over. He stepped back and immediately felt bereft at the loss of contact with her warm body.

Grimly, he said, "We can't let this affect the truce we made, Hope. For Stevie's sake."

Yes, for Stevie's sake, the two of them would go home and pretend the house was filled with love, she thought desperately. When in truth, all they were doing was playing out the end of a bad melodrama.

"I have no intentions of letting anything harm Stevie. Especially our problems," she said curtly, then, stepping from behind the tree and onto the brick path, she added, "Now I'd better get back inside."

His mood dark, Drake jammed his fists into his trouser pocket. "Yeah, I think it's time we both got back inside."

And back to reality, he thought.

...

# CHAPTER EIGHT

HOPE HAD OFTEN HEARD Christmas was the most common time for a person to get the blues, but she'd never
suffered such an affliction. The holidays had always been
her favorite time of the year. Until now. She'd never felt
so depressed in her life.

For the past week decorations had been going up all
over the clinic, and the sights and sounds of the holiday
were everywhere. Not just at Maitland Maternity, but all
over Austin. Shops, streets and homes were strung with
lights and evergreens. Angels, Santas, reindeer and nativ-
ity scenes filled lawns and store windows.

Today was Friday. Nearly a week had passed since
Abby and Kyle's wedding. From what Dana had told her,
the couple were on their honeymoon in Mexico, and each
time the newlyweds called home, Abby sounded on top
of the world.

At least two of her friends were happy, Hope thought.
Dana had R.J., the man she'd always wanted. And now
sweet Abby had found the love of her life.

"I'm back," Tess sang cheerfully.

Hope turned from the artificial spruce she was trying
to assemble to see her young assistant coming into the
gift shop by way of the back storage room.

"Please tell me you managed to find lights?" Hope
asked her.

Tess proudly held up a plastic shopping bag. "Two

strands of clear twinkling lights and I only had to go ten blocks away to find them. I hope you don't mind, but I bought a box of candy canes, too, while I was shopping.''

Hope waved away her words. ''I don't care what you put on this tree. Just so we do our part to look the season. What with all the messy publicity these past months, I'm sure Megan and the rest of the Maitlands want this place to be looking merry and bright.''

Tess placed the plastic bag on a nearby display counter, then joined Hope in assembling the small tree. ''I honestly don't think all this gossip about baby Cody has hurt the clinic's business. Women seem to be flocking through the doors in droves.''

Hope grimaced. ''That's the trouble. I don't think all those women are pregnant patients. From what I hear, some of them are women claiming to be the baby's mother.''

Tess rolled her eyes as she reached for a branch and attached it to the pole that would eventually become a spruce. ''Surely they know that just saying 'I'm the mother' isn't any sort of proof. Haven't any of them heard of DNA testing?''

Hope shook her head. ''This whole thing is bringing all sorts of women out of the woodwork. The only thing they're thinking about is a way to get some of the Maitland money.''

''How sad,'' Tess replied.

Hope watched a shadow pass across Tess's face and instinctively knew what the young woman was thinking. ''I'm sure if you could have the choice between having the baby you miscarried or a stack of money, you'd choose the child.''

''In a second,'' Tess said with a sigh, then as she reached for another branch, she glanced at Hope. ''But I wouldn't choose to have Robert back. He would have been—well, bad for me.''

The way Drake was bad for her, Hope thought. This past week they'd managed to put on a good front for Stevie. An outsider looking in would never have guessed there was any sort of strain between them. But at night, after Stevie went to bed, Hope felt the usual iceberg moving in. Drake either kept to himself in the study or disappeared to his workshop outside. If she tried to talk to him, he was polite, but curt and distant with his responses. For the past two days, she'd decided not to try to talk or communicate with him. After all, he'd pretty much made his feelings clear at the wedding. This whole setup with her and Stevie was nothing more than a temporary thing.

"So, we're finally getting into the Christmas spirit around here!"

At the sound of Katie's cheery voice Hope turned to see her favorite nurse entering the gift shop.

"Hi, Katie," Tess said.

Katie returned the young woman's greeting then looked at Hope. "I just got back in town and thought I'd come by the clinic and say hello to a few of my friends. Do you have time for a cup of coffee?"

Hope glanced doubtfully at Tess and the half-assembled tree. "Oh, Katie, I wish—" She gestured helplessly. "Tess and I are in the middle of this."

"Oh, go on, Hope! You rarely get to see Katie," Tess urged. "And you haven't taken a break all afternoon. I can do this."

Katie, dressed in her favorite attire of boots and jeans, grinned teasingly at Hope. "You found a gold mine when Tess walked into this place. Don't do anything to rile her," she warned with a wink. "You'd never find anyone to replace her."

Her face tinged with a pink blush, Tess laughed modestly. "Hope is the best boss I've ever had. I'm going to try my best to keep in her good graces." She waved a dismissive hand at the two women. "Please go on and have your coffee. I'll hold the fort down here."

The coffee shop was on the same floor as the gift shop. Inside the partially filled room, the two women carried their coffee to a small table that looked out on the main waiting area of the clinic.

"So how did your week go? I guess you're counting down the days now until you come back to Austin," Hope said as she stirred a packet of creamer into her coffee.

Katie tilted her head one way and then the other as though she wanted to say something, then decided against it. "I will be glad to get back. I've missed working at Maitland."

"Dana says Abby and Kyle are in Vera Cruz right now. Soaking up the sand and surf. Must be nice," Hope said with a wistful sigh.

"Yeah," Katie agreed as she carefully sipped her coffee. "I can't remember the last vacation I've had. I think it was when my brother had the flu and I offered to help out on the farm for a few days."

Hope's short laugh was full of disbelief. "That was a vacation?"

Katie wrinkled her nose. "As close as I could get to one."

In an effort to ease the tension knotting the back of her neck, Hope rotated her head. It had been a long week, but thinking of the weekend at home was even worse. She didn't know what to expect from Drake anymore.

"Hmm, well, I've had a few memorable vacations, but it's been a long time." Her eyes grew distant as she reached for her coffee. "Drake and I went to the mountains in Colorado for our honeymoon. It was almost spring, but snow was still deep on all the slopes. But we, uh, didn't do much skiing."

Through slanted lashes, Katie covertly studied Hope's strained features. "I'll bet you didn't."

Shaking away the bittersweet memory, Hope forced a cheery smile onto her face. "I didn't have a chance to ask you at the wedding, but how is your course going?"

"Mm, pretty well. I assisted heart surgery on a newborn three days ago. This morning before I left Houston, he'd already been moved to the regular nursery and his mother was holding him." A wistful smile tilted her lips. "That's what makes everything worth it."

For a long time after her miscarriage, it had been difficult for Hope to look at the newborns in the nursery window. For the few months she'd been pregnant, she'd envisioned her own baby there, swaddled tightly in a blanket, the Logan name fastened to the end of the bed. But Hope was past all that pain now. She wanted to see the babies. She needed to keep the hope of her dream for a family alive. It kept her going.

"I'm so glad things worked out for the baby. And I know one thing, if or when I get a child of my own, I want you to be his nurse."

"Thanks for your trust, Hope. Coming from you, it means a lot," Katie said. Slipping her fingers through her strawberry curls, she gazed toward the lobby and the huge Christmas tree displayed in the center. "So how is your little nephew, Stevie? Is he getting excited about Christmas?"

Hope smiled. These past two weeks the boy had been

her one bright spot as she'd watched him slowly opening up to the other kids at day care and to her and Drake. He was far from being a normal child, but slowly he was responding to her and Drake's attention.

"Stevie still doesn't talk much," Hope told her. "And I'm not sure if he got to do much celebrating of Christmas at home. I told him to make a list to give to Santa and he didn't know what I was talking about."

Katie's green eyes grew wide. "You're kidding. Right?"

Hope grimly shook her head. "From the little he's told me, I gather he usually receives two gifts at Christmas. One from each parent. No surprises from Santa."

Katie tilted her head as she considered an explanation for such behavior. "Maybe it's their religion. I can't think of any other reason parents would deliberately keep the joy and wonder of Santa from a child. It's...downright cruel."

Hope rolled her eyes. "Believe me, Katie, that's only one of the cruel things Denise and Phillip have done to Stevie. But...I'm trying not to think of all that. I want to make this Christmas a very special one for him."

"Do you have your tree up yet?"

Hope suppressed a sigh as she looked at the festive decorations in the waiting area. All week she'd been waiting, hoping Drake would suggest they get the decorations out of the attic and drive to a local discount store to pick out a tree to trim. It was a task they'd always enjoyed doing together. But so far he hadn't mentioned the holiday at all, much less offered to prepare for it. Hope had decided for Stevie's sake she would have to take the initiative and do it on her own.

"No. I haven't done anything in the way of decorating. But I plan to this weekend. What about you?"

Katie chuckled. "My apartment in Houston is tiny. But I managed to put an artificial tree on the coffee table, a red candle on the television and a sprig of mistletoe over the door."

Hope's brows lifted with wry humor. "Are you expecting to do some kissing this holiday?"

Katie grimaced and shook back her tousled red curls. "I doubt it. But a girl needs to be prepared. Just in case the right man walks through the door."

"Are you expecting him to?" Hope asked without mentioning any names. But both women knew she was talking about Ford Carrington.

Katie drummed her fingers on the tabletop. "Nope."

Hope wanted to tell her friend that she needed to get over this infatuation she had for Maitland Maternity's pediatric surgeon. It wasn't healthy, and Katie deserved a man who'd give her real and lasting love.

"Maybe you should hold some over Drake's head."

Katie's suggestion interrupted Hope's thoughts, and she quickly scoffed. "Ha! Kissing doesn't get Drake and me anywhere except to another big argument." The episode in the Maitlands' rose garden last Saturday had proved that.

Katie wrinkled her nose with disappointment. "I can't believe that, Hope. The way you look—I know you could seduce your husband if you really tried."

Hope pushed her half-empty coffee cup to one side. "That's just the trouble, Katie. I shouldn't have to try."

THE LIGHT TAP on Drake's office caused him to look up from the financial report spread in front of him.

"Yes, come in," he called.

Juanita, his secretary, stepped through the door. A light jacket was tossed over one arm and a shoulder bag swung at her side. A disapproving frown marred her otherwise pleasant features.

"I'm leaving. Aren't you ready to go home? It's an hour and a half past quitting time. The place is closing up," she pointed out.

"I have a key."

She ignored his sarcasm. "Don't tell me something I already know. This place is wasting money by sending a security guard in early to unlock the doors. You always beat him here."

He scowled at the older woman. "How do you know that?"

"Humph," Juanita snorted, jamming a hand against one side of her plumpish waist. "There's all sorts of little birds around here that talk."

Drake glowered. "That's the trouble with this place. There's too much talk and not enough work."

"Some of us do have lives other than work," Juanita reminded him.

Drake leaned back in his chair and rubbed his fingertips over his burning eyes. Along with R.J., Juanita was the only other person who talked to him so frankly. And he let her because he liked her. And because she could somehow see past his brusque business side to the human, needy part of him.

"I have too much to do to watch the clock, Juanita."

She continued to frown at him. "I'm sure your work will all be waiting for you when you get back here in the morning."

Sighing, he scrubbed his palms over his face. "It always is. And more."

She walked to her boss's desk and studied him with obvious concern. "You know, I think this whole thing about Cody has caused you more stress than anyone in this clinic. Including the Maitlands.''

Drake had to laugh at that idea. "You're wrong, Juanita. The Maitlands are weighted down by this thing. They just try to act as though everything is normal. That's the type of people they are.''

Juanita didn't appear convinced. "Maybe so. But you're the one dealing with the consequences of this thing. This place can't go without money.''

Drake leaned forward and closed the folder on his desk. "Things aren't that bleak yet, Juanita.''

"Good, then we can both forget work for tonight.''

"Okay, Juanita, you talked me into it. I'm going home.'' He stood and reached for his briefcase on the shelf behind him. "Do you need a lift to your place?''

"No. My hubby's coming by to pick me up. We're going to search out the stores for a Christmas tree. Have you already decorated your family tree yet?''

The question brought Drake up short. He hadn't thought about a tree. Even though the clinic was decked out in Christmas trim, the approaching holiday had seemed like something that was happening to other people, not him. Especially when his family was only temporary.

"No. Not yet.''

He leaned over and switched off a banker's lamp at one end of his desk, then gestured for Juanita to precede him out of the office.

Once in the hallway, he locked the office door then walked with his secretary to the elevators.

"I'll bet that little nephew of yours is getting excited about Christmas,'' she said. "My grandkids have been hounding us for the past week to put up a Christmas tree.

Their thinking is that a tree at their grandparents' equals more gifts for them,'' she said with a laugh.

Stevie. Drake felt a pang of regret as he thought of the boy. The quiet little guy hadn't spoken a word to him about Christmas or what sort of gifts he wanted.

*You haven't bothered to ask him, either,* a little voice came back at Drake. *You've been too busy thinking about yourself. Why you shouldn't make love to Hope and try to be a father.*

"Sounds like you've already got your Christmas bonus spent," Drake said to his secretary.

Juanita's smile was full of pride and affection. "The holiday would be terribly boring without my children and grandchildren. Now that you have little Stevie, you're going to see what I mean."

*Now that you have little Stevie.*

On the drive home Juanita's words rolled over and over in Drake's head. For the past two weeks or so, he hadn't allowed himself to think of Stevie as anything more than his nephew, a child who needed his care for this month and then would be gone from his life. But R.J., damn him, had spouted off at the wedding about him keeping Stevie on a permanent basis. Juanita's casual comment implied that Stevie belonged to him, too.

What was wrong with these people? he wondered. Couldn't they see he wasn't daddy material? Sure, the kid seemed to like him. But that didn't mean a heck of a lot. It sure didn't mean Drake would know how to steer the child in the right direction or raise him with the right moral values and priorities.

Drake tried to shake off the pestering thoughts as he pulled into the garage and parked beside Hope's sedan.

As long as Stevie was here, Hope would be, too. That was the only thing Drake could count on for the time being.

"WHAT DO YOU THINK about this angel, Stevie? Should we put her or a star on top of the tree?"

Stevie's small hands cradled the angel as he studied her closely. Although her white dress was getting a little tattered and her gold hair was a bit ratty, Hope couldn't bear to part with the ornament. The angel had graced the very first Christmas tree Drake and she had shared, and in a way she was a symbol of their marriage. Ragged but not entirely ruined. Yet.

"Her hair is falling out. But she's kinda pretty." He carefully handed the angel to Hope. "I think I like her better than a star."

Hope patted his shoulder. "So do I. We'll put her in with the rest of the ornaments we're going to use."

From the open doorway of the living room, Drake silently watched the exchange between Hope and Stevie as they sat on the floor, sifting through the contents of two cardboard boxes.

Apparently she'd gotten into the attic this evening and carried down the boxes of Christmas decorations. The fact that she hadn't waited and asked him for help cut Drake deeply. But then what did he expect, he asked himself. He hadn't made any offers to help her get things prepared for the holiday.

"Looks like you two are getting ready for a visit from Santa Claus," he said as he stepped into the room.

Both Hope and Stevie turned their heads in his direction. Stevie shot him an eager smile. Hope simply watched her husband's approach with a cautious expression.

"Aunt Hope says we need a tree for Santa to put gifts

under. Is that right, Uncle Drake?'' Stevie asked. ''Do you have to have a tree to get gifts from Santa?''

This evening the boy was dressed in jeans and tennis shoes and an orange T-shirt with a longhorn steer on the front. Hope had always been a Longhorn football fan. So had Drake. And normally they attended all the university's home games. Until this year. This year their lives had been anything but normal. For months he'd been angry about that. Angry that Hope was ruining their marriage, and their lives, with her incessant quest for a child. But now he was more sad than anything, and wondering if the fault might lie within himself.

''No,'' he said to Stevie, ''you don't have to have a tree. But I think it makes Santa a little happier to see one.'' Then, because he just had to, he bent and placed a kiss on top of Hope's head.

''Hello,'' he murmured to her.

Her head tilted, and her blue gaze connected with his. ''Hello.''

The wariness in her eyes spoke volumes. She didn't trust him. She believed every move he made was calculated. He hated that. Hated the stilted climate between them. He realized he was mostly to blame for it, but she'd forced him to the edge of a cliff. Now he was scared to reach out for her. Scared of what the consequences might mean. Getting her pregnant again could kill her. It almost had. If she died trying to have his child, he wouldn't want to live.

''I didn't plan on working so late this evening. Have you and Stevie eaten supper yet?''

He ruffled Stevie's brown hair.

''No,'' Hope answered. ''Stevie and I have been busy and I haven't taken the time to cook anything. I thought we'd have sandwiches if that's okay with you.''

"Actually, I'm glad you two haven't eaten because I thought we might go out to eat."

Hope's lips parted with surprise. "Go out?"

After the cool treatment he'd given her since the wedding, taking her out to eat would be quite a switch, Hope thought.

"Yeah," he answered casually. "I thought we might have some hamburgers, then pick up a Christmas tree. Or did you have something else planned for tonight?"

Hope had planned to take Stevie out to find a tree on their own. She'd given up on Drake. If it had been just herself involved, she would have told him to forget it, she didn't want the crumbs of his attention. But Stevie was involved, and the little boy desperately needed Drake.

"No," she answered. "Nothing else was planned."

Drake looked at Stevie, who was watching the two adults with a guarded expression. Did the child know there was something wrong between his aunt and uncle? Drake wondered. He wouldn't doubt it. Although Drake had been trying hard to make things appear normal in front of the child, he couldn't wipe the misery from Hope's face, and he was afraid Stevie might have picked up on her unhappiness, too.

"What about you, Stevie?" Drake asked him. "Would you like to go eat hamburgers, then find a Christmas tree?"

Stevie's eyes sparked with sudden excitement. "You mean I get to go, too?"

"Of course you get to go. You're going to be the designated tree picker this year."

Stevie scrambled to his feet and tilted his head to look up at Drake. "What's a tree picker? I don't know how to be a tree picker."

Chuckling, Drake tweaked him beneath the chin. "All you have to do is tell your aunt Hope and me which tree you think is the best, and that's the one we'll get. You can do that, can't you?"

"Yeah!"

The excitement in Stevie's voice was the most Hope had ever heard him display, and she glanced gratefully at Drake as she rose to her feet.

"If you're ready, I'll go get our sweatshirts," she told him.

"As soon as I change into jeans I'll meet you in the garage," he replied.

FIFTEEN MINUTES LATER, Drake parked in front of a fast-food restaurant. As the three of them left the car and started up the sidewalk, a puzzled look came over Stevie's face.

Seeing the child's confusion, Hope asked, "What's the matter, honey? Is something wrong?"

"I don't see any trees around here."

Drake glanced at Hope as though he couldn't believe the child hadn't recognized the popular franchise. "That's because this is a restaurant. It's where we're going to eat."

Hope paused on the sidewalk to look at the boy. "Haven't your parents ever taken you out to eat a hamburger or anything like that?"

Stevie shook his head. "I always eat at the big table in our house. Or in the cafeteria at boarding school. Mommy says hamburgers are bad for you."

Drake's brows rose at a mocking angle as he glanced once again at Hope. "I guess cocktails are on the nutritious list."

She nodded in agreement, and for the first time in days

she felt a connection with Drake. Even if Stevie was the reason, she felt foolishly grateful.

Once inside the restaurant they waited at the counter for their order, then found a booth near the front. To Hope's surprise, Drake slid in beside her and left Stevie to sit across from them.

The boy quickly dug into his food with obvious relish, making both Hope and Drake smile.

"I think he's finally found his appetite," Hope said to Drake. "Beth says he's gained a pound this week."

"He could stand to gain a few more," Drake commented, then glanced pointedly at Hope. "So could you."

Surprise crossed her face. "Me? There's nothing wrong with me."

"You've been eating like a bird lately."

Hope didn't know what she'd been eating these past few weeks. She simply put food in her mouth and forced herself to chew and swallow. Still, she found it hard to believe Drake had noticed her lack of appetite.

Her eyes gently roamed his face, searching for a sign that he might really care. But with Drake it was hard to tell exactly what he was thinking or feeling. He'd never worn his emotions on his sleeve. They were always carefully hidden. "I eat enough."

Drake glanced across the table at Stevie. The child had spotted the indoor playground connected to the front of the building and was engrossed watching the children climbing up ladders and through tunnels.

His eyes on Hope, Drake said, "I know this hasn't been easy for you, Hope."

She didn't know if he meant taking care of Stevie or their separation these past few months. Either way, the compassion she heard in his voice surprised her and she wondered what might have brought about the change. He seemed different somehow. As though he actually wanted to be closer.

The disturbing thought unsettled her. She purposely looked away from him and reached for a French fry. "I love having Stevie with us," she said.

"I understand that. But—"

When he didn't go on, she turned a questioning glance at him.

"I haven't exactly made things easy for you," he said.

His admission was the last thing she expected to hear from him, and though she told herself not to get excited, she felt her spirits ready to take flight.

"I haven't been perfect, either. I suppose our white flags have become rather tattered lately."

He smiled at that, and suddenly Hope was remembering all the times they'd gone out together in the past. Simple times like this. In a way, she'd taken all those years for granted. She'd believed the two of them would be together forever. Till death do they part. Now the parting would come as soon as Stevie headed back to Dallas.

"I'll try to hold mine up a little higher," he murmured to her, then turned his attention to Stevie. "Have you made a list for Santa yet, young man?"

Stevie swallowed the fries in his mouth before he spoke. "Aunt Hope says I'm supposed to write down all the things I want for Christmas on a list. But I can't think of anything I want."

"Surely there's something you would like that you don't have now. I'll bet if you think hard, it'll come to you."

Stevie tilted his head thoughtfully. "Well, I can think of one thing."

One thing. Most kids had dozens of things they

wanted, Drake thought. But then Stevie didn't really
know what Christmas was all about. The love and the
giving of gifts in honor of the holy child. He didn't expect Stevie knew much about being loved at all. He was
a little boy growing up in Drake's footsteps, and the idea
tore right through his heart.

"What is the thing you want?" Hope asked curiously.
"Drake and I need to know just in case we run into Santa
Claus so we can give him the message."

A faint, sheepish smile spread across Stevie's face. "I
want a pair of cowboy boots. Like Uncle Drake wears."

The two adults looked at each other, both surprised the
child had noticed the boots Drake often wore with his
suits to work.

"You like cowboy boots?" Drake asked him.

His head pumped up and down in an emphatic nod.
"I like horses, too."

Drake's looked a little taken aback, then he laughed.
"Well, a horse might be a little more difficult for Santa
to manage. But I'll bet the boots will find their way to
our house."

Stevie's brown eyes flew wide open. "Really? Santa
will really bring boots to our house?"

"Boots and a lot more things, if you're a good boy,"
Drake promised. "So eat up and we'll go find a tree."

Stevie didn't have to be prompted a second time. He
ate all of his meal, then finished an ice cream before they
left the restaurant. And because it seemed to make Drake
happy, Hope did her best to finish the food in front of
her, too.

FRESH CUT evergreen trees could be found all over the
city on street corners and stacked in front of various discount stores. Hope expected Drake to stop at the nearest

bunch of trees he could find, so when he headed toward the outskirts of town to a place where the two of them had always purchased their Christmas trees in the past, she was more than surprised. She'd figured the large greenhouse had totally slipped his mind. Apparently, she'd been wrong.

The night air was cool but not uncomfortable with the heavy sweatshirts she'd brought for herself and Stevie. Drake had thrown an old bomber jacket over his jeans and flannel shirt, and as she had often done in the past, she thought how different he looked in the casual clothes compared with the suits and ties he wore to the office. This Drake was more approachable, more human, more like the man she'd first fallen in love with.

Inside the busy greenhouse, a young man in his early twenties, wearing a red sock cap and carrying a large flashlight, offered to assist them. His name was Todd, and he quickly invited the three of them to follow him outside to the standing grove of evergreens.

As they walked through the rows of carefully tended trees, Stevie clung to Hope's hand and stared in wonder at the branches towering like dark mountains over his head.

"What sort of tree are you folks looking for?" Todd asked Drake. "Pine? Cedar? Spruce?"

Drake motioned toward Stevie. "You'll have to ask him. He's the boss."

Wide-eyed with doubt, Stevie looked at Drake. Immediately he gave the boy an encouraging smile.

"It's all right," he urged. "Pick out any tree you like. Just so it's not too big to get into the house."

Not quite convinced that he could or should follow Drake's instructions, Stevie glanced questioningly at Hope.

"Remember, Uncle Drake says you're the tree picker this year," she reminded him. "You'll do fine."

As if he'd suddenly spotted a rainbow, a smile spread across Stevie's face. Quickly, he turned to Todd. "I want a big one!"

The assistant grinned as though he'd heard that very same request several times this evening. "Then you'd better follow me down to the end of the grove."

The arc of the flashlight bobbed wildly as the young man attempted to keep up with Stevie, who raced enthusiastically from tree to tree. Hope and Drake followed at a more sedate pace, picking their way carefully over the dark, rough ground.

"One thing is for sure," Hope said to Drake. "Tonight we've learned Stevie is capable of getting excited."

Drake chuckled. "Who would have thought a trip to the tree farm would do it."

Suddenly Hope stumbled slightly as her toe came in contact with a loose rock. Drake caught her by the hand to right her, then continued to hold on to steady her as they walked.

The simple touch of his fingers wrapped around hers was both comforting and exciting. It had been a long time since he'd held her hand for any reason, and Hope realized she didn't want him to let go. Not tonight. Not ever.

Casting him a sidelong glance in the darkness, she said, "I was surprised you drove out here to Mendez's. I figured you…well, that you'd probably forgotten about the place."

He'd never forget anything they'd done together. Surely she knew that.

"How could I forget? We come out here every year."

A pang of regret touched a spot deep between her

breasts. "I know…but…this Christmas isn't exactly like the ones we've had in the past."

*Now that you have little Stevie, you'll see what I mean.*

For the second time this evening, Juanita's words drifted through Drake's mind. He hadn't expected the child to make a difference in his and Hope's life. But for the moment, Stevie was holding them together.

"You're right," he murmured, his fingers unconsciously tightening around hers. "This Christmas Stevie is with us."

## CHAPTER NINE

EVENTUALLY, Stevie chose a thick Virginia pine that stood at least nine feet tall. More than half of the tree hung over the edge of the car trunk, forcing Drake to tie down the lid with bungee cords.

All the way home, Stevie was in constant motion, twisting in the seat in an effort to look out the back window and assure himself the tree wasn't falling onto the street. Both Hope and Drake recognized it was the first time they'd seen Stevie squirming and wiggling like a typical little boy, and neither had the heart to order him to sit still.

Once they arrived home, Hope cleared a space for the tree in the living room near the picture window, while Drake allowed Stevie to help him secure the tree in a sturdy stand. When the pine was finally standing upright, the top came only a few inches from touching the ceiling.

"Wow! It's really big, Uncle Drake!" Stevie exclaimed as the three of them stepped back to take a look.

Drake chuckled. "It sure is. Santa ought to be mighty pleased with this tree."

For tonight, at least, Stevie's quiet, defiant nature had disappeared. He was smiling proudly, his eyes glowing with excitement. "You think he'll really look at our tree?"

"No doubt about it," Drake answered. "He might

even come by early and take a peek in the window, just so he can see how much room he has to put all the gifts."

For a man who'd never had visits from Santa when he was a child, Drake was doing a fine job playing out the fantasy with Stevie. Just knowing he wanted to make things special for the child gave Hope a warm feeling. And made her wonder, too, what this Christmas would have been like if their own child had been born. She had to believe they wouldn't have been headed for divorce.

"Gosh!" Stevie breathed in wonder. "I didn't know Santa was so nice. Why is he so nice to boys and girls?"

A wry smile on her face, Hope glanced at Drake, who quickly indicated that this was a question she could answer.

Placing her hand on Stevie's shoulder, she gave it an affectionate squeeze. "Because he thinks you and all the children in the world are very special. And he's right."

Stevie looked amazed. As though he'd never once thought of himself as special to anyone. Hope's eyes met Drake's, and she could see her husband was as disturbed by the sad notion as she was.

Quickly clearing his throat, Drake crossed to the couch, where the two boxes of decorations sat waiting. Rubbing his hands together, he said, "Well, I think it's time we all got to work."

At first Stevie wasn't sure he could do anything to help the two adults decorate the tree. From the anxious look on his face, Hope suspected he was worried about breaking something or inadvertently making a mess that might displease her or Drake.

She quickly tried to reassure him, then went on to show him how to attach the shiny glass bulbs to the branches of the tree. In no time at all, he was scurrying around the pine, hanging bulbs, red bows, candy canes and silver icicles.

From time to time, his excited giggles erupted in the living room like a bottle of bubbly champagne popping open. The sound brightened Hope's sad heart, and as the three of them worked to make the tree beautiful, she couldn't help but think how wonderful it would be if Drake really loved her and wanted the three of them to be a family for always. Each Christmas would be special. Each day of their lives would be precious, because they would be together.

After nearly an hour and a half, Hope and Drake stood back to view the brightly decorated tree. Wedged between the two adults, Stevie asked, "Is it finished now?"

Hope laughed softly. "It had better be. We've run out of decorations."

"Looks finished to me," Drake added.

"But there's one more thing we haven't put on the tree," Stevie pointed out.

Both Hope and Drake turned questioning looks on him. In answer, he raced over to the couch and picked up the angel he'd carefully placed to one side on a throw pillow.

"The angel," he said, handing the ornament to Drake. "Aunt Hope says she's supposed to go on top."

For a moment Drake stared at the golden-haired angel with her raggedy halo and tattered white robe. After all these years, he could still remember Hope purchasing the ornament for their first tree.

*She'll watch over us,* Hope had said to him. And every year thereafter, the same angel had perched on the top branch of a new Christmas tree to watch over their home through the holiday.

Suddenly Drake had to swallow before he could speak.

"That's right, Stevie. She's the most important thing. Hope and I shouldn't have forgotten her."

*The most important thing.* Would she be crazy to think he really meant that? Hope wondered. Or was this just a part of his continuing act for Stevie? Either way, she felt a sting of tears at the back of her eyes as she leaned down and kissed the boy's cheek.

"Thank you for reminding us, Stevie," she said. Then, encompassing both of them with a wide smile, she suggested, "I think it's time we had a snack after all this hard work. While you two put the angel in her place, I'll go to the kitchen and hunt up some goodies."

Drake winked at Stevie. "Sounds like we're in for a treat, so we'd better get our work finished."

A few minutes later, Hope returned to the living room carrying a tray loaded with mugs of hot cocoa and a plate filled with squares of fudge and sugar cookies baked in a variety of holiday shapes.

While she was in the kitchen, Drake had turned off the overhead lights to make the lights on the tree shine brighter. On the coffee table in front of the sofa, two fat white candles flickered in the semidarkness.

She placed the food between the candles, then took a seat on the couch. To her surprise, Drake ambled over and eased down on the cushion next to her.

"This is nice," he said quietly as he glanced around the room, which was filled with the tree and food and the two people who made up his family. "Maybe this is why some people say every day should be like Christmas."

"It is nice," Hope agreed softly. "Thank you, Drake, for making this evening so special for Stevie. I'm beginning to think the little boy is truly becoming happy here with us."

He glanced to where Stevie was still standing by the tree, staring in wonder at the glittery sight. For the past few days, Drake had seen the boy slowly relaxing and opening up. But tonight it was as if a switch had suddenly been flipped inside him. He was giggling, chattering, smiling and bouncing on his toes. It was obvious he was happy. And the fact tore a hole right through Drake's heart, because he knew it was a happiness that would be short-lived once Stevie returned to his parents in Dallas. How could he possibly send the child back to that sort of life? It would be cruel.

"You helped to make it special, too," Drake pointed out to her.

Her eyes locked with his. "Maybe. But...I couldn't have done it without you."

Without Drake, the light of excitement wouldn't be in Stevie's brown eyes. And she wouldn't be feeling the warm glow that was spreading through every part of her body.

Their gazes were still connected, still searching and questioning, when Stevie bounded over to the coffee table to get his share of the snacks. Hope was forced to tear her gaze away from Drake to assist the child. And afterward she was almost afraid to look back at him, afraid she would break down and beg him to love her. Even if it had to be on his terms.

After the big supper Stevie had consumed, Hope didn't expect him to eat much, so she was thoroughly surprised when he devoured several of the cookies and drank a whole mug of cocoa.

"I think we're going to have to buy bigger jeans for him," Hope said to Drake.

Drake glanced at the boy, who was sprawled on the

carpet beneath the Christmas tree. From the drowsy look on his face, he would be asleep in five minutes.

"He's not small-framed. He'd be a big boy if he—"

When his pause stretched into silence, she cast him a sidelong glance. "If he what?"

Drake grimaced, then tilted the mug to his lips. He was thinking like a damn fool. He was letting all this Christmas hoopla get to him. He couldn't be a full-time father to Stevie. No more than he could be a full-time father to a child of his own. He'd be a total failure. Or would he? So far Stevie had made progress. He wasn't withdrawing deeper into his shell. He was coming out of it. Drake had to be doing something right for the boy. But could he keep doing the right thing on a full-time basis? And if he did, would Hope see it as a sign he was ready to be a father to their own child?

The questions raged a silent war inside him.

"If he...stayed here with us a little longer." Drake finally made himself reply.

Hope's expression softened as she glanced across the room at Stevie. It gladdened her to think the boy's head was filled with amazing visions of Santa and a sleigh pulled by reindeer. So far in his young life, he'd experienced little or no childhood magic. He needed to see the world as a fun place.

"I wish that were possible," she said softly.

Drake glanced across the small space between them. The flickering candle glow bathed her face with soft light and shadows and turned her blond hair the color of dark, rich gold. Tonight she had pulled her hair casually up in a tousled mass at the back of her head. A few wisps had managed to escape the tortoiseshell clamp to fall heedlessly against her forehead and cheeks.

For the past few minutes, Drake had been fighting the

urge to reach over and push the wayward tendrils off her face, to tilt her chin up and taste her lips. But that was only a small part of all he'd been fighting this evening.

As he'd left the clinic with Juanita and she'd begun talking about Stevie and her own kids and Christmas, something strange had started twisting and turning in the middle of his chest. He'd tried to pass it off as hunger, but eating hadn't eased the uncomfortable state. And what was worse, the feeling intensified every time he looked at Hope and Stevie.

"I think Stevie has gone to sleep. I'd better carry him upstairs and put him to bed." He had to leave the couch before he did something crazy and reached for his wife.

Nodding, Hope rose along with him. "I'll help you with the bedcovers," she whispered.

Stevie was as limp as a rag doll when Drake picked him up and started for the stairs. Just a step behind him, Hope said in a hushed voice, "He's out like a light. I don't think there's any danger of us waking him."

"All the excitement wore him out," Drake agreed.

In Stevie's bedroom, a night-light dimly illuminated the bed. Hope moved ahead of Drake and quickly pulled down the covers.

Drake gently placed the boy on the bed, then carefully removed his tennis shoes and blue jeans. All the while, Stevie continued to sleep deeply.

"There's no need to bother taking his T-shirt off," Hope said. "It's clean and it won't bind him."

With a nod, Drake reached to pull the covers over the boy. Hope did the same thing, and for a moment their fingers tangled in the blanket.

Awareness sizzled through Drake, reminding him that his wife was only inches away and that his body had gone too long without her.

His head turned slightly toward her, and their eyes met in the semidarkness. The soft, hungry look she gave him sent a shaft of heat ripping through him. "I think you'd better do it," he murmured, then stepped to one side to give her more space.

For the past months Drake had made himself something of a stranger to Hope. But just now, she'd seen a look on her husband's face that was achingly familiar.

Her hands shaking at the thought, she quickly tucked the sheets and blankets around Stevie, then slowly turned away from the bed.

Drake was still standing a step behind her. His hands were jammed in the back pockets of his jeans, and his sandy hair fell in mussed waves across his broad forehead. Tonight he looked younger than his thirty-eight years, as though seeing the magic of the coming holiday through Stevie's eyes had banished the tension from his face.

Hope's heart squeezed with longing as she moved ever so slightly toward him. "I'm sure Stevie will be dreaming of Christmas trees tonight." *While I'll be dreaming of you,* she added silently.

"Hope—"

Whatever he'd been about to say started and ended with her name. The one word was wrapped in anguish and a desperate kind of yearning that echoed the need inside her.

Before Hope could stop herself, her hands were clutching his upper arms, her body pressing against his.

Instantly, Drake's long fingers curled tightly over her shoulders. Hope tilted her head to meet his hot gaze. His name was on her tongue, ready to be whispered, but it never got past her lips. Drake grasped her face between his hands, then roughly covered her mouth with his.

The sudden, intimate contact nearly buckled Hope's knees. Her fists tightly clenched folds of his flannel shirt as she fought to keep from sliding to the floor. Like cottonwood leaves in a dry creek bed, her senses were scattering, dancing this way and that in wild abandon. Up or down, she didn't know where he would lead her. She only knew the direction they took was all up to him. She was past the point of resisting. She wanted him. Needed him with a desperation that shook the deepest part of her.

Time ceased to exist as Drake continued to kiss her with hungry abandon. She didn't know if seconds had passed or long minutes when he finally eased his head back and bent slightly to slip his arms beneath the back of her thighs.

Her breath coming in rapid snatches, she felt him cradle her against his chest, much the same way he had Stevie. Then he began to walk with her, and she didn't have to question him to know he was taking her to their bed. Anticipation had her heart wildly thudding.

Unlike Stevie's bedroom, theirs was dark, the blinds closed tightly against any outside light. Drake eased her against the mattress, then quickly joined her.

Wrapping his arms tightly around her, he pulled her on top him, then tugged her face to his. As Hope found his lips, a sense of homecoming poured through her like a warm spring rain. This was the man she loved. The only man she would ever love. Her heart refused to believe it could be any other way.

"Oh, Drake," she whispered against his lips. "Let me undress you. Let me love you."

Desire tightened his throat, making his voice hoarse with need. "I couldn't stop you even if I wanted to."

Joy, sweet and heady, spun through her, numbing her with pleasure and blocking the pain and fear of the past few months from her mind. All she could think of was this moment and him.

Quickly her hands found the buttons on his shirt. They popped away from the soft fabric with little effort. As she pushed the material aside, her head dipped and her lips scattered moist kisses down his chest, along the same trail her fingers had taken.

The sharp intake of his breath told her how much she was affecting him, and her fingers trembled as she worked the buttons loose on his jeans, then slipped her hand inside his open fly.

His hard arousal told her he was aching to be inside her as much as she was aching to have him. In the past her hand would have lingered to please him in ways she knew he liked. But their separation had been too long and the need to be connected to him was too urgent to dally.

Reckless, she jerked off his boots, then tugged his jeans down and over his feet. But before she could go any further, Drake caught her by the waist and hauled her beside him on the mattress.

"It's my turn now," he whispered roughly.

Like her, he was in no mood to wait, and his hands made rapid work of removing her jeans and turtleneck, then the two lacy scraps of fabric that served as her underwear. As he pulled her tight against him, his hands savored the smooth satiny feel of her skin against his fingers, the taste of it as he nibbled a hungry path down her neck, across her shoulder, then lower to the sweet, hard bud at the center of her breast.

Need swiftly fired her loins, causing her to moan deeply and thrust her fingers against his scalp. It had been too long since her husband's hands had touched her with fire, too long since his warm mouth had teased her breast.

She wanted all this and more. And because she couldn't get it fast enough, her body was fairly humming with frustration.

The moment her legs wound around his and her fingers dug into his back, he lifted his head and drew in a ragged breath. For one split second, sanity tried to invade the fringes of Drake's brain. But then her soft hands were on his chest, gliding over him, down to his belly, then lower still to where his manhood throbbed to feel her velvet heat surround him.

Once she touched him, he was lost. It didn't matter why he was here in their bed or what tomorrow might bring. This was his wife. This was where she was supposed to be. Back in his arms. Back in his life.

He sank into her slowly, and as he did an overwhelming sense of homecoming tightened his chest and burned his throat and the back of his eyes.

"Oh, Hope! Hope! Do you know—how much—I need you?"

His voice was so thick and low she could hardly hear him. But she managed to catch his words. And even if she hadn't, his body was telling her everything and more. He wanted her. Nothing else mattered.

Their union was too explosive to last very long. Urgency drove them both to a swift release, and before Hope realized it, she was spiraling to earth to find Drake gripping her hips and whispering her name against her lips.

Drake's awareness was slow to return, but once it did, he realized the two of them were drenched in sweat and Hope was still trapped beneath the weight of his body.

He rolled to one side of her, but kept a hand possessively on the mound of one breast. Hope snuggled beside him, her head nestled against his broad shoulder. They remained that way for long minutes, each of them content to simply be touching, reliving the pleasure they'd just shared.

After a while, Drake murmured, "I haven't felt this weak since I ran that five K race two years ago."

Hope laughed softly. "You're not a runner. You suffered through that for charity."

Leaning on his elbow, he searched for her face in the darkness, but all he could make out was the faint line of her nose and lips. It was enough to know she was smiling. That was all he really needed to see.

"Well, I sure as hell didn't do this for charity." His lips nuzzled her cheek and the tender skin behind her ear. "And I wasn't suffering, either. I've tried to forget how good it is with us, Hope. But I couldn't blank you or this from my mind."

His admission thrilled her. Especially after all the weeks she'd believed his passion for her had died.

Sliding a hand across his chest, she paused between the flat nipples to tangle her fingers in the thatch of curly hair. "Neither could I," she murmured. "I've been trying to imagine another man making love to me. But I can't. It always winds up being you."

His thumb and forefinger closed firmly around her chin. "I'm not going to let you think about anyone or anything but me tonight."

His voice was rough with passion and the sound of it sent shivers of fresh desire rushing over her.

"I thought you said you were weak," she taunted.

The hold on her chin tightened, and because the room was so dark, she didn't know he'd lowered his head until his lips were on hers.

This time the reckless urgency was gone as his lips

made a slow, meandering search of hers. Hope felt herself melting, burning to make love to him once more.

"I'm not that weak," he promised against her parted lips.

Her hand slipped behind the back of his neck to tug him down over her. Drake went gladly, willingly, letting the soft pleasures of her body block out any thoughts of tomorrow.

THE NEXT MORNING, Hope woke groggily to the sound of the shower running. Rising on one elbow, she raked the tangles of blond hair from her forehead, then glanced at the disheveled bedcovers, some of which had slipped to the floor. Her jeans and top had been flung halfway across the room. Her pink lace bra and panties had landed on top of Drake's black boots.

The cobwebs of sleep instantly vanished as memory of the night before came rushing back to her. Her husband had done more than sleep with her last night. Drake had made love to her!

The joy of it bubbled inside her until she wanted to shout it to the world. He loved her, after all. He must. Otherwise, he would never have made love to her without the protection of birth control!

Their problems, the separation—everything was going to be over now. Why, she could even become pregnant in the next few days!

As she glanced at her naked body, a wide, glorious smile spread across her face. Drake hadn't just made love to her once. No, the two of them had spent most of the night trying to make up for the months of their separation.

A glance at the digital clock told her it was still too early for Stevie to be awake. She'd cook them all a big leisurely breakfast and then she was going to start on a Christmas list. She had gifts to buy and plans to make. The holiday was going to be glorious. Drake loved her. And for now they had Stevie.

Happiness surged through her like a burst of sunshine as she tossed back the sheet and reached for her robe. For the first time in ages, she was excited about living. And even though her body was stiff and sore from the unaccustomed lovemaking, she felt light as air.

She was hurriedly raking a brush through her hair when the door to their private bathroom opened and Drake stepped out wearing jeans and nothing else. His hair was wet, and though he hadn't shaved the shadow of beard from his face, she could smell the spicy scent he'd slapped on his jaws.

Turning from the dressing table, she shot him a provocative smile. "Good morning. Ready for breakfast?"

Drake couldn't look at her. He was afraid to. For the past ten minutes, he'd stood in the shower, wondering what in hell had come over him last night. Wondering, too, how he was going to find the strength to keep it from happening again.

"I'm not all that hungry. Cereal will be fine."

She laughed at his suggestion. "Cereal! After all the energy you used up last night? I was thinking more like pancakes and sausage. Or would you rather have biscuits and gravy? Stevie seems to like either one and I have plenty of time."

She was bubbling with happiness. A lilt was in her voice, and her face was glowing like a new rose on a spring morning. It amazed him that making love to her had done so much. After ten years of marriage, he'd feared their physical relationship had become routine to her and that she'd wanted a baby to make up for the lost sizzle.

*A baby.* Of course. He silently cursed himself for not being quicker to understand the drastic change in her attitude. She was happy because she'd had her way. She believed they'd started on a baby. And dear God, maybe they had. Last night he hadn't let himself think about birth control, and even this morning, he'd been more concerned about not repeating the reckless behavior than any possible consequences of their lovemaking. But one night might be enough to make Hope pregnant. The idea was so terrifying, his insides began to quiver.

Turning his back to her, he reached for his boots. The sexy pieces of underclothing draped over the tops were a sharp reminder of his weakness. He tossed the lace onto the mussed bedclothes.

"It doesn't matter to me. Fix what you want."

Oblivious to his mood, Hope secured her hair from her face with a silver barrette. "You know, Drake, I was thinking earlier while you were in the shower that I haven't done a bit of Christmas shopping yet. And it's already getting down to the wire. Everything's going to be picked over." She turned to look at him. "Do you think you might want to go out this afternoon and see what we can find in the way of gifts? I realize it's Saturday and the shoppers will be out in wild droves, but we don't have much time left."

She'd already said more to him this morning than she had in the past week. This was the Hope he'd married and loved for ten years. This was the woman he'd desperately wanted back. But, damn it, not on her terms.

Still careful to avoid her gaze, he eased down on the side of the mattress to pull on his socks and boots. "No. I don't want to go out today."

"Well, you're probably right," she said agreeably. "Tomorrow might be better. And that would give me longer to come up with gift ideas."

Smiling slyly, she left the dressing bench and stepped forward to slide her hands down the slope of his bare shoulders. "It would also give us more time for something else," she murmured.

He caught her wandering hands, but before he could protest further, she bent and pressed an affectionate kiss on his forehead. "It's so good to have you home, Drake. So good," she whispered.

Suddenly Drake had never felt so used or so scared in his life. She'd made love to him only because she wanted a baby. And now—if he'd made her pregnant again— dear God, he couldn't live through each day fearing the worst.

"So good now, you mean."

The curtness of his voice was like a slap to her face, and she stared at him in disbelief. "What—what do you mean?"

His throat was so tight his next words were forced, raspy. "Surely I don't have to explain."

Hope stepped back as though she expected him to coil up like a poisonous snake and strike her at any moment. "I'm afraid you do. I thought—" She broke off, shaking her head in bewilderment. "Is something wrong, Drake?"

For the past hour, since he'd woken up beside her, the consequences of what they'd done, what *he'd* done, were overwhelming him with a mix of emotions. He wanted his wife. He'd never stopped wanting her. And now his desire might eventually take her life.

Trying to hide the shudder rippling through him, he said, "Last night was a mistake, Hope. A big mistake."

# CHAPTER TEN

HOPE WATCHED HIM speak the words, but her mind refused to decipher them, as though he was using a language she couldn't translate.

"A mistake?" she repeated in a whisper. "You think—" She swallowed as a hot lump of pain suddenly filled her throat. All those kisses, the whispered words of passion, the urgent thrust of his body as he'd spilled himself inside her. None of it had meant anything to him. It had all been lust. Sex. And now he regretted sharing even that with her. "You think—last night was a mistake?"

His fear helped to block out the wounded pain in her voice. "I don't think. I *know* it was. You caught me at a weak moment. You purposely seduced me just so—"

Fury swamped her like a black wave of floodwater. "Since when should a wife *have* to seduce her husband?"

Crimson color seeped into his face. "Hope—"

"Don't answer," she swiftly interrupted. "As far as husbands go, you're not the norm. You couldn't know the answer to that one!"

He hadn't been angry before, but her misguided accusation was a taunt he couldn't bear. "I made it clear to you that I didn't want us to try to have another child. Yet you purposely enticed me to make love to you."

Blood throbbed furiously at her temples as she bit back

the urge to scream at him. "I didn't exactly see you try-ing to resist."

"I am human, Hope," he said tightly. "I do have blood pumping through my veins."

Her gaze was scathing as it traveled over his handsome face. "I'm not so sure you do. You'd have to have a heart for that. And so far I haven't seen any clues that you do."

He jerked on his boots, then stood before her, his jaw rigid. "I may not be the nicest guy in Austin, but at least I shoot straight from the hip."

Her breasts were heaving beneath the flimsy silk robe. "Meaning?"

"I think it was pretty damn low of you to use your sexual charms to trap me into doing something you wanted!"

Her finger jabbed the middle of his bare chest. "You're a big boy with a mind of your own. I didn't make you do anything. And what's more, you know it!"

The fact that she was right only made him more furious with her and himself. "If you wind up pregnant over this, I hope you'll be happy. Because I damn sure won't be."

His scathing words were like daggers plunging deep into her chest. There wasn't anything he could have said to hurt her more.

"I want you to get the hell out of my bed and stay out!" she said angrily between gritted teeth.

Surprise flickered in his eyes, then his lips flattened to a grim line. "What about Stevie and—"

"If you want to keep up appearances for Stevie's sake and sleep in the same room, then you'll have to do it on the floor!" She turned as if to go, then on second thought whirled to him. "And as far as me becoming pregnant, don't worry, Drake. A child of mine would have to be conceived with love, and I'm certainly not feeling any of that at the moment. Besides,'' she added resolutely, ''I wouldn't want you hanging around, being a father to a child you didn't want anyway. So why don't you go have a cup of coffee and breathe a big sigh of relief. You're off the hook. You'll never have to be a father and you sure as hell won't ever have to have sex with your wife again!''

THE NUMBERS began to blur, turning the column of figures into a fuzzy black streak. With a weary sigh, Drake closed his eyes and pinched the bridge of his nose.

Damn it, this was a great way to start his week, he thought. Ten o'clock Monday morning and he was already too tired to think.

What did he expect? he thought dourly. The makeshift cot he'd been trying to sleep on wasn't much better than the floor. But he wasn't about to crawl into bed with Hope. Even if she invited him. Being that close to her was far too tempting. And way too risky.

With a heavy sigh, Drake left his desk and crossed to a small table holding a coffeemaker and an assortment of snacks. Juanita had made fresh coffee less than thirty minutes ago. He poured himself a cup and carried it to the window looking down on the clinic's front entrance.

Rain had moved in sometime during the night. The streets were wet, and water dripped from the juniper bushes landscaping the parking lot. Among the rows of vehicles, he spotted a television news van. Drake didn't have to look twice to know it belonged to Chelsea Markum and her crew. More of her salacious gossip was just what he and this place needed, he thought sourly.

A light tap drew him out of his reverie. Turning from

the window, he called for the person to enter and was mildly surprised to see R.J. stepping into the office.

The other man closed the door behind him. "Got a few minutes, Drake?"

Drake gestured for his friend to take the leather chair in front of his desk.

"Sure. Want some coffee?"

"No. I've already had a gallon this morning." R.J. eased his lanky frame into the chair and crossed his ankles in front of him. "After the weekend it takes that much to get me started again."

Drake could see R.J. wasn't complaining. In fact, the smug look on his face said the extra time and energy spent with his wife was more than worth it. Drake was reminded once again that he'd lost his head this weekend when he'd made love to Hope. Now things between them were in a hell of a mess. He seriously doubted she would ever forgive him for the awful things he'd said to her. When Stevie wasn't around she was like an iceberg. Cold, silent, unyielding. He didn't think it would do any good to try to explain that all the things he'd said had been born out of fear. Hope had never understood that she was more important to him than a child.

Returning to his desk chair, Drake glanced at his friend. "I thought you and Megan were supposed to have a meeting with the emergency management people this morning."

"It's been rescheduled for this afternoon. I've been watching TV."

Drake looked at him with wry amusement. "TV? R.J., you're getting downright lazy in your old age."

R.J. snorted mockingly. "Believe me, Drake, it wasn't for personal entertainment. Someone called Mother and warned her to watch a report on *Tattle Today*."

"What now?" Drake groaned. "Something about Jake and his woman friend?"

With a weary sigh, R.J. wiped a hand over his rugged features. "I'm sure that's coming. But this episode had to do with money. The show will now pay one hundred thousand dollars for an exclusive interview with Cody's real mother. Providing, of course, that the woman will name the Maitland who fathered her child."

"Damn, damn," Drake cursed. Then, his voice heavy with concern, he said, "I hardly have to tell you what this means. Another wave of women will be flooding through the doors of the clinic."

"What do you mean will be?" R.J. demanded caustically. "Mother's already had to deal with five of them since the news report ran earlier this morning. It doesn't seem to matter that my ex-lover Tanya's claim to the baby was discredited and she was marked a fraud. Or that these women will have to agree to DNA testing. Until the real mother is found, I guess there's going to be plenty more women out there willing to take a chance on all that money."

Amazed by the situation, Drake shook his head. "I honestly don't know how your mother holds up under the stress."

R.J.'s expression was rueful. "Raising seven kids forced her to be strong. But I do worry about her, Drake. She hasn't been herself lately. Especially since that long-lost nephew of hers showed up."

"You're talking about Connor O'Hara now?" Drake asked, meaning the stranger who'd appeared at Maitland Clinic two months ago.

R.J. nodded. "Mother usually isn't this trusting with people. Especially those she's only just met. She sure as hell doesn't go around giving them money and setting them up in a family condo.''

"Well, he is supposed to be family, isn't he? A son of your uncle Jack and aunt Clarise?''

R.J.'s expression was skeptical to say the least. "Yes. But those two broke away from the family forty years or more ago. What the hell is he doing showing his face around here now? That's what I'd like to know. Mother keeps saying she's going to have the man checked out. But so far, she hasn't mentioned hiring an investigator.''

Drake had noticed that Megan seemed preoccupied lately, and uncharacteristically closemouthed. But maybe the woman figured at a time like this, the less said, the better.

"Well, I don't have any suggestions about dealing with your long-lost relative returning to the fold. But I do agree that something has to be done about this baby thing, R.J. I know we've said this before, but the problem is only intensifying. Just this morning I had to soothe one of our backers' feathers. God only knows how many more will be screaming after this new reward is offered.''

"I understand, Drake. Believe me, I do.''

"Yeah,'' Drake said regretfully. "I know you do. And I realize you can't come up with an instant solution to this thing. Not as long as we're in the dark about the baby's true parents.'' He cocked a speculative brow at R.J. "I take it you haven't gotten anything out of Jake yet?''

R.J. grunted in frustration. "No.''

"Why not?''

"My youngest brother isn't exactly a person who invites closeness. Ellie's talked to him. But apparently she didn't get any useful information from him.''

"Is there anyone he *will* talk to?" Drake wanted ·to know.

R.J.'s smile was more grim than anything. "Mother. But he'll only do that when he's good and ready. Right now, he's buried himself out at Garrett's ranch and isn't saying much of anything. Anyway, I'm not sure there's anything he could tell us about Cody— I just don't think he's the boy's father."

Drake's eyes narrowed perceptively. "Is he going to undergo buccal testing to rule himself out as the baby's father?"

R.J. shrugged. "I don't think he'll refuse, especially once he finds out both Mitch and I had it done. We'll tell him what a relief it is to be off the suspect list—it's the only way to end the speculation. But like I said, I don't believe Jake has anything to hide. Besides, he isn't a man to shirk his responsibilities."

"You sound pretty certain of a brother you rarely see or talk to," Drake countered.

"It's a feeling I have more than anything. This Camille, the woman he has with him—I get the idea she's important to him. And I just can't see him bringing her to Austin if there was a chance of Cody belonging to him. What woman in her right mind would want to get involved with such an obvious Lothario?"

"A woman out for money," Drake answered easily. "Specifically the Maitland money. From what little we know, Jake doesn't appear to live like a millionaire, but he is entitled to his share of the family wealth, isn't he? Maybe this Camille sees dollar signs for her and this baby she's carrying."

Frowning, R.J. rose from the chair and went to the coffeepot. "I'd really like a shot of bourbon this morning, but I guess I'll have to settle for more caffeine," he muttered as he poured the dark liquid into a foam cup. Glancing at Drake, he said, "If she's after the Maitland money, Jake will find it out. He's not a fool."

"Most men aren't," Drake said with a healthy measure of sarcasm. "Until a woman makes them one."

Coffee cup in hand, R.J. settled in his chair. "Is that how you see yourself? A fool over Hope?"

This past weekend he'd been a big one, Drake thought. But there wasn't any danger of that happening again. He'd made sure of it. Strange how the fact left a hollow feeling deep inside him.

"R.J., I'm not a stupid man, am I?"

His friend grinned. "If you are, you shouldn't be handling the clinic's finances."

Drake waved away his reasoning. "That's not what I mean. I'm good with money. How to manage it, invest and raise it. Generally, finances are easy to handle."

"So *you* say," R.J. replied with mild humor.

"It's—well, I think it's time I faced facts. I'm not the man Hope needs. I can't be what she wants. And the longer we refuse to accept that, the more miserable we both become."

"You're talking about trying for another child?"

Drake gave him one sober nod. "She won't give up the idea. And maybe I'm wrong for expecting her to."

R.J. was thoughtful for a moment, then he said, "Most women have a deep need to be a mother. They're born with it. Just because Hope wants a child doesn't mean she loves you any less."

"I don't have to tell you what happened the last time Hope was pregnant," Drake said tightly.

"Abby told you it's highly unlikely that will happen again."

And Abby was a brilliant doctor. Drake would be the

first one to admit that. But where Hope was concerned, love got in the way of logic.

Drake turned his gaze to the window, but he wasn't seeing the clouds or the rain. He was seeing Stevie's face as he'd stared in awe at the decorated Christmas tree. Stevie's hopeful eyes when he'd said he wanted a pair of cowboy boots. Fathering a child might not be as difficult as he'd once believed. But that was only a part of the issue.

"I don't want to lose Hope to a pregnancy gone wrong."

R.J. leveled a frank look at Drake. "I think you'd better wake up, old friend, because it looks like you're losing her anyway."

Long moments passed, but Drake didn't make a reply. He couldn't. He was too stung by the truth of his friend's words. R.J. stood and dropped the empty foam cup into the wastebasket beside Drake's desk.

"Are you leaving?" Drake finally managed to ask.

"Yeah. I'm going to see if Mother has cleared out the last of the fortune-seekers from her office." At the door, he paused to look at Drake. "By the way, what are you giving Hope this Christmas?"

What was he going to give Hope for Christmas? Drake asked himself. He couldn't imagine her accepting any sort of gift from him. And dear God, what she really wanted he might have already given her.

"That's something I'm still working on," Drake told him. Then he asked, "What about you? What are you giving Dana?"

The question brought a contented chuckle from R.J. As he stepped through the door, he tossed his reply over his shoulder. "Anything she wants."

AT THE SAME TIME, miles away from Maitland Maternity Clinic, another woman had baby Cody on her mind. The kid was going to be her ticket to a fortune and the life of luxury she'd always wanted.

For the past six days she'd been in the same town, laying low. But she was ready to get out of this place. Not that the hotel was a problem. It was plush, even swanky compared to the rattraps she'd been forced to stay in before Petey began to wire her money from Austin. But she was bored and restless, ready to move on. And anyway, moving would help insure no one could follow her trail. That is if anyone happened to be looking for her.

A smug smile tilted her pretty lips. Those idiot lawmen in Austin still didn't have a clue as to where the baby left on the Maitland Clinic steps had come from.

Now, if Petey could continue to hold up his part of the act, they'd soon be rolling in dough.

The idea made her chuckle with glee. Once the Maitland millions were in her hands, she'd go first class all the way. She'd have fancy clothes, cars and jewelry. Her home would be even fancier than this hotel, with plenty of maids to clean up after her. Anytime the urge hit her, she'd dine on prime cuts of beef, fresh shrimp and lobster, champagne and rich, gooey desserts that would melt in her mouth.

The thought of food reminded Janelle she hadn't eaten since early this morning. In a few minutes, she'd change into something nice and revealing and head downstairs to the restaurant. If luck was with her, some lonely businessman would spot her at the bar and be only too glad to buy her supper. And if he expected a little payment in return, that would be even better. A girl had to have some entertainment once in a while or she'd go stark raving mad.

But first she had to call Petey with the latest plans. A quick glance at her wristwatch told her it was two minutes away from the time she'd instructed him to be by the telephone. She hoped her dolt of a husband would already be waiting.

Sinking onto the edge of the king-size bed, she quickly punched in the number. Petey answered on the first ring, reassuring her that he was following her orders to the letter.

"Where are you?" he asked the moment he heard Janelle's voice.

"Damn it, Petey, I told you not to ask me stupid questions!" she snapped. "It doesn't matter where I am! Now tell me what's going on there. Has anything happened since we talked the other night?"

"Nothin' much. Just a bunch of stuff on the news," he said in a lazy voice.

Janelle gripped the phone and tried to keep from screaming with impatience. "What's happened? Megan hasn't discovered who you really are, has she?"

He heaved an indignant breath. "Don't get so excited. Megan isn't onto anything. I've got the old woman eating out of my hand."

With a roll of her eyes, she tossed her long brown hair. "Yeah, so you say. But what about the news, Petey. Get to the point," she ordered sharply.

"Okay. That newswoman—Chelsea Markum—came on TV this morning and announced the station would pay a hundred thousand dollars for the real mother to come forward. Megan isn't one bit happy about it. Neither are the rest of the Maitlands."

Janelle worriedly chewed her bottom lip. "Damn it, I

wished that reporter would keep her nose out of things. This could cause big problems."

"I don't get your thinking, Janelle. It's just a gossip show, not the real news," Petey countered.

"Think, Petey! With money like that up for grabs, women will be coming in from everywhere. It's a cinch the real mother is going to show up any day now!"

Petey made a scoffing noise. "When are you going to realize the real mother is dead? She can't show up."

Janelle reached for a cigarette. Her fingers trembled as she jabbed the cylinder of tobacco between her lips and lit it. "We don't know that for sure," Janelle argued after she'd sucked in a lungful of smoke. "I hit her pretty hard, but that doesn't mean I killed her."

"She's dead, Janelle, or she would have already come back for the baby."

"I hope to hell you're right, Petey. Because if she shows up, we'll have to get out of the country—and fast."

"You're gettin' paranoid, babe. Just calm down. Relax. Everything is going to go as planned. Just trust me on this."

Janelle could hear complacency threaded through his voice, and she knew if this whole plan was going to be carried out the way she intended, she had to keep him on his toes. Too bad her partner in crime had to be a man, she thought with disgust. They always got soft when you needed them the most.

After another long drag of the cigarette, she crooned, "Petey, honey, I do trust you. I just want you to be careful. We can't have any slipups."

"There won't be on this end," he promised. "So what now?"

Janelle's brown eyes gleamed with wicked pleasure as

she pictured the next step of their plan. "It's going to be your job to get Megan to the nursery window at twelve-thirty. That's the most obvious place a frantic mother would head for. I'll show up at the same time, desperately searching for my baby. With tears in my eyes of course," she added with a malicious chuckle.

"Megan's no fool," Petey warned. "You're gonna have to do some damn good acting to convince her that baby is yours. Hundreds of woman have already tried it."

Her confidence suddenly returning, Janelle laughed again. "Believe me, Petey darling, this will be the performance of my life. I'll just have to break down and explain how I had no other choice but to leave my little Chase in the safe hands of the Maitlands. Then when she wants proof, I'll be ready and waiting to give her the right answers."

BY THE END of the week, Abby had returned from her honeymoon and somehow cleared her schedule on Friday afternoon to invite her friends for an hour of conversation, drinks, festive food and an exchange of small gifts.

"You know we want to hear more about the honeymoon," Katie said to Abby as she nibbled on a finger sandwich stuffed with crab.

The private Christmas party was being held in Abby's office, and the four women were seated around the desk, their plates loaded with the catered food arranged by their hostess.

A dreamy smile curved Abby's lips. "You've already heard about every place we went to."

The other three women shared sly glances.

Dana, looking Christmasy in a green velvet pantsuit, waved her fork at her sister-in-law. "I don't believe that's what Katie really wants to hear."

Katie, who'd managed to drive in from Houston a little early for the weekend, was spreading her usual bubbly cheer around. At Dana's remark, her red head bobbed in agreement.

"You got that right, Dana. I can visit a travel guide and get the same information Abby's told us. We want to hear details!"

Abby's face flooded with color as her gaze encompassed her three friends. "Really! I throw this nice little party for us and you three expect me to supply X-rated entertainment!"

Katie leaned eagerly forward, her green eyes glittering with anticipation. "Hearing about it is the next best thing to doing it!"

The women hooted at Katie's remark, then as the laughter died away, Abby wagged her finger. "Sorry, girls. That part of the honeymoon is off-limits." She glanced beseechingly at Dana and Hope. "You two understand. It's—just too private to share. Even with your dearest friends."

Both Hope and Dana nodded, while Katie's expression sagged, then she shrugged good-naturedly.

"Oh, well, maybe one of these days I'll find out what a honeymoon is all about."

Dana turned a confident smile on Katie. "Sure you will. Good things always come to those who wait. I'm a prime example of that."

It was true, Hope thought. Dana had been in love with R.J., her boss, for a long time before he even noticed his secretary as anything but an employee. And it wasn't until the two of them married that he realized he loved her. Perseverance had definitely paid off for Dana in the long run, but as far as she and Drake were concerned,

Hope couldn't see that time was going to help solve their problems.

*You could be pregnant at this very moment, Hope.* The thought leaped through her head, sending a rush of mixed signals to the rest of her body. The woman in her would be euphoric if she was carrying Drake's child. Yet the sensible part of her knew a child not wanted by its father would ultimately suffer, no matter how hard she tried to love and protect it.

From behind her desk, Abby advised the lovelorn Katie. "You can't hurry love. Not the real kind."

For a brief moment a shadow crossed Katie's face, then just as suddenly she flashed a smile at Abby. "That's easy for you to say, Doc. Cupid's arrow came straight at you. Or should I say Kyle came straight at you."

Abby inclined her dark head in concession. "Yes. But—after many long years. Before Kyle came along I was content to be single."

Katie stabbed an olive on her plate. "Well, I'm the only one of us left single now. I feel like the odd duck."

"Don't worry, Katie." Hope spoke up. "You probably won't be the only single one of us for long."

All three women leveled looks of concern at Hope.

"Have you and Drake agreed to a divorce?" Abby asked.

"Not officially. But it's coming."

Dana shook her head with disapproval while Abby and Katie exchanged troubled glances.

Her appetite spoiled, Hope forgot the uneaten food on her plate. "I've been thinking I might move out of the house after Christmas. There's too many memories there. And I want to have a new start for the coming year."

Hope's announcement brought Katie to the edge of her

chair. "You're not going to move from Austin, are you? The clinic wouldn't be the same if I couldn't stop by the gift shop and dump my troubles on you."

Katie never dumped her troubles on Hope. In fact, Katie rarely complained about anything. Unless it was her secret frustration over Ford Carrington.

Rising from her chair, Hope tossed her plate into a nearby wastebasket. "No," she said, answering Katie's question. "I doubt I'll leave Austin. It's been my home for too long. And I don't want to give up my friends here." She couldn't add "family" to the friends part. Hope wasn't like Dana, Abby or Katie, who had plenty of relatives around for love and support.

Leaning back in her office chair, Abby studied Hope with shrewd blue eyes. "You know, Hope, you're a damn beautiful woman. There's probably a dozen men right here in the clinic that would fall over themselves to go out with you. Would you like us three to drop some hints that you're available?"

Hope looked at her sharply. "The divorce papers haven't even been drawn up yet. I can't go out with another man now!"

Abby raised her hands in defense. "Well, don't bite my head off. I'm only trying to help. And you are going to need a man to get the baby you want. Unless you're not planning on doing it the old-fashioned way."

Laughing lustily, Dana pushed a hand through her long blond hair. "What other way is there?"

The nurse in Katie blurted, "Artificial insemination! Now that's an idea, Hope." Her face brightened. "That could solve all your problems!"

As Hope had told Drake, a child of hers would have to be conceived in love. She couldn't imagine it any other way. "That's too cold and clinical for me, Katie. I'd rather wait and find a man who'll be glad to give me a child.''

"Men!'' Katie exclaimed with a groan. ''Just look at the trouble they cause. Some man out there is the father of Cody, but he's too much of a chicken—you-know-what to come forward and accept his responsibility. Now Abby and her family are paying the consequences.''

"Katie,'' Abby began placatingly, before her friend's Irish temper could get wound up, ''we don't know if the father realizes he has a child. The woman who gave birth to the baby might not have told the man.''

"That's right,'' Dana was quick to add. ''The man might be in the dark about this whole thing.''

Abby placed her empty plate to one side. ''And remember, girls, the man—whoever he is—is supposed to be a Maitland.''

"Supposed to be,'' Hope echoed curiously. ''Has something happened to make you think the baby might not really be a Maitland? The buccal tests your mother asked to have done—have there been any results turned in yet?''

"Fortunately both Mitch and R.J. have been eliminated as candidates. As far as my brothers go, that only leaves Jake.'' Abby shook her head. ''Even if he's cleared, Mother is convinced the child is a Maitland.''

"Sorry, Doc,'' Katie said through pursed lips. ''I guess I was talking rudely about one of your relatives.''

Abby's laugh was dry as she reached forward and picked up a square of fudge from a nearby plate. ''Save your breath with the apology, Katie. Everyone else is expressing their opinion about the whole thing.''

"R.J. is hoping Christmas might put Jake in a talkative mood,'' Dana said. ''At least enough to tell us more about Camille.''

Being home for Christmas had done more than put Drake in a talkative mood, Hope thought wryly. But their night of passion had only built a higher wall between them.

"Yeah," Katie agreed. "Christmas does unexpected things to people. And who knows, Cody's real mother might show up to collect the reward from *Tattle Today* and then the whole thing will be over."

*Over.* Hope figured her marriage to Drake would be over long before Cody's real parents were discovered. But she wouldn't let herself think about that right now. Christmas was coming. She couldn't fall apart and spoil it all for Stevie. Seeing her nephew happy was the only bright thing she had to look forward to.

# CHAPTER ELEVEN

UPSTAIRS, while the four women enjoyed the last of their
little party, a tall shadow crossed Juanita's computer
screen. The secretary glanced up from her work to see
Drake standing at the corner of her desk. A briefcase and
the jacket to his suit were crammed beneath one arm.

"Are you quitting for the day?" she asked in a
shocked tone.

"It's only an hour and a half early. Shut that thing off
and get your purse. I'm giving you the rest of the day
off, too."

Her mouth fell open as she stared at him. "Are you
sick? You didn't tell me you had a doctor's appointment
for today."

He grimaced. "I'm not ill, Juanita."

She glanced at her wristwatch and made a tsking noise
with her tongue. "You must be. I can't ever remember
you doing this."

In the past few weeks he'd done a lot of things that
he'd never done before, Drake thought. Was he going
crazy, he wondered, or just now coming to his senses?

"Don't try to figure me out, Juanita. Just thank me for
the time off." He started toward the door leading to the
corridor. "Before I change my mind and make you stay
here to finish those letters."

His assistant quickly switched off the computer and
grabbed her purse. "I still have plenty of last-minute

Christmas shopping to do, so I'm glad you've suddenly come down with some sort of fever.''

Fever? Maybe that's what was wrong with him. Maybe he was afflicted with some sort of fever that didn't cause chills or fatigue, but still affected the mind's ability to think clearly. Something sure as hell had come over him since he'd made love to Hope.

Nearly a week had passed since that fateful night, and he was no closer to getting Hope out of his mind. In fact, his misery had been compounded by the memories of those hours she'd been in his arms. All he could think about was her. The feel of her beneath him. Her lush breasts brushing his chest, the softness of her skin, the scent of her hair, the sweetness of her mouth against his. Dear God, how was he ever going to stop wanting her, he silently prayed.

Mentally shaking himself, he glanced at his secretary. ''Uh, Juanita, before you go, I wondered if you could give me some advice about buying a pair of boots.''

Juanita glanced at him as she pulled on a cardigan. ''Why ask me about boots? You wear beautiful boots. You buy them for yourself, don't you?''

''I'm not talking about boots for myself.''

The older woman smiled cheerfully as she came around from behind her desk. ''Oh, you're going to buy Hope a pair for Christmas? She'll love them! Get brown suede. That'll suit her perfectly. Trust me.''

He felt like a heel, although he wasn't sure why. He'd always taken great pains in choosing Hope special gifts for Christmas, yet this year he hadn't come up with anything. What his wife really wanted, he couldn't give.

''No. Not for Hope,'' he corrected her. ''For Stevie. I looked inside his shoes, so I know his size. But I'm not sure what type to get. All I know is that he wants cowboy boots.''

Juanita smiled assuredly. "When you were Stevie's age, didn't you want a pair of cowboy boots?"

When Drake was Stevie's age, he would have given his eyeteeth for boots. He'd wanted a pair just like the Range Rider or Hopalong Cassidy had worn back in the heyday of Western movies. Instead he'd had to wear conservative oxfords.

"You mean get him a pair just like I wanted?" Drake asked doubtfully. "But those kind might not be popular nowadays."

Juanita laughed. "Believe me, Drake, a kid his age wants lots of color and fancy stitching. Not conservative ropers."

He considered her suggestion. "All right, Juanita. You've had six kids. You must know what they like."

A wan smile crossed her face as she followed her boss out the door. "I know about women, too, Drake. Get Hope brown suede."

Drake had never allowed himself to get close to people. Other than Hope, he didn't consider himself close to anyone, except for R.J. There were many people on staff here at the clinic that he admired and respected. Some he even liked. Particularly the Maitlands. But as Juanita waited to walk with him to the elevator, it dawned on him that she was more than a damn good secretary. Down through the years she'd become his friend in spite of his determination to remain distant and strictly professional.

"I'm afraid it's going to take more than a pair of boots to make Hope happy again, Juanita."

Juanita studied the sadness reflected in his eyes. "Do you want to make her happy, Drake?"

The question caused him to draw in a deep breath, then

let it out slowly. "More than anything, Juanita. But so much has happened. After she lost the baby—everything seemed to go downhill."

She touched his arm with gentle reassurance. "Hills are meant to be climbed. A second time if necessary."

Not wanting to dampen Juanita's Christmas spirit, he smiled and tried to joke. "I sit behind a desk all day, Juanita. What makes you think I'm in good enough shape to climb a hill?"

Laughing, she patted his arm. "You have way more in you than you think, Drake. You can climb any hill. If you want to badly enough."

Drake wanted to believe Juanita was right. But what his secretary didn't know was that he'd already cut his bridges with his wife. And he doubted they could ever be mended again.

It had been dark more than an hour before Drake made it home from his shopping excursion. When he quietly stepped into the kitchen, he found it dark and empty. Apparently Hope and Stevie had already eaten the evening meal without him. Thankfully the living room was vacant, too, and he was able to place the wrapped boxes under the tree without anyone seeing him.

Upstairs, he found Hope in Stevie's room. She was sitting on the bed, her back resting against the headboard. Stevie was curled up beside her, his head propped on a pillow so that he had a perfect view of the book Hope was reading.

Drake paused just inside the door, listening, waiting for the story to end before he interrupted them with his presence.

After Hope closed the book, Stevie scrambled off the bed to gather another one from a stack on a nearby desk.

Drake took advantage of the moment to step forward to join them.

"I want to hear about the reindeer—"

Stevie's words trailed away as he turned and spotted Drake. Without a word, the boy raced straight to him and flung his arms around Drake's legs.

The unexpected greeting brought a thick lump to Drake's throat, and for a moment all he could manage was to ruffle the top of Stevie's brown hair.

From her seat on the bed, Hope said, "I didn't hear you come in."

Drake looked at her, and as their eyes met, his heart winced with pain. The blue orbs staring back at him were full of sadness and cold resentment. And the hell of it was, he could no longer blame her for feeling the way she did. He'd more or less asked for it. He'd been afraid to do anything else.

"I called down to the gift shop to let you know I'd be late, but Tess said you were out," he told her.

Her eyes purposely slid away from him to focus on some insignificant point across the room. "Abby was having a little Christmas party in her office." She swung her legs over the side of the bed and shoved her feet into a pair of leather loafers. "I'll go find you something to eat."

"No. Don't bother. I'll get myself something later."

Stevie leaned his head back to look up at Drake. "We ate pizza, Uncle Drake. It had olives and some other funny-looking things on the top."

Drake arched a questioning brow at Hope.

"Mushrooms," she answered.

Drake's gaze returned to Stevie, and he smiled at the boy. "Did you like it?"

Stevie's head bobbed. "It was really good. Aunt Hope sprinkled white stuff all over it. And I ate three pieces!"

"Wow! If I don't watch out, you're going to be as big as I am pretty soon."

Stevie grinned proudly. "Aunt Hope says I'm gonna be a big man like you someday. Do you think I will be, Uncle Drake?"

Maybe Drake was a big man in stature, but he didn't feel that way inside. Where it counted the most. As he looked at Stevie's trusting little face, it dawned on him that he'd come to love this child. He wanted to give him more than a special Christmas. He wanted to see that his whole future was happy and secure. How he planned to do that, he didn't know yet. He just knew Stevie had become a part of his life that he couldn't let go.

"I think—you're going to be a much bigger man than your uncle Drake." He ruffled the boy's hair again, then glanced at Hope, who had risen to her feet. "How long have you two been upstairs?"

She shrugged in a noncommittal way. "Thirty or forty minutes. I'm not sure. Why?"

"Because I think Santa has made an early visit. I thought I saw a new gift under the Christmas tree." He glanced at Stevie. "Do you think we ought to go check? He might have sneaked in the house and you two didn't know a thing about it."

Stevie's eyes popped wide open, and he looked to his aunt for her opinion. But Hope was too busy staring at Drake as if she were seeing a stranger.

"It's still a few days until Christmas," she said doubtfully. "I don't think Santa will come until then."

Drake grinned smugly. "He might have had too much to deliver in just one night, so he made an extra stop tonight. I think we should go see."

"Yeah!" Stevie exclaimed. "We should go see, Aunt Hope! Maybe he brought you something, too!"

It was only too obvious that Hope was forcing herself to smile for Stevie's sake. Drake could also see she looked pale. A part of him wanted to ask her if she was feeling well, but he didn't. She would only think he was worried about her becoming pregnant. And he was. Wasn't he?

"I didn't send a list to Santa this year," Hope explained to Stevie, "but we'll go look just the same."

The three of them headed down the stairs with Stevie in the lead. As soon as they approached the twinkling tree, the boy spotted the big boot box propped among the few gifts Hope had already wrapped and placed there.

Racing over, he dropped to his knees for a closer inspection. "This one is new!" he shouted excitedly. "It wasn't here before, was it, Aunt Hope?"

Once again she glanced suspiciously at Drake. Her attitude only reminded him what a Scrooge she considered him. Not with his money, but with his heart. And that was far, far worse.

"No," she answered Stevie. "See if you can read the name tag."

Quickly, he pulled the box closer. "It has my name on it! See, it says Stevie! And something else."

In spite of her dejected spirits, the child's bubbling excitement put a smile on Hope's face. She squatted on her heels to help him read the rest of the name tag. "It says that Santa wants you to open this gift early."

Stevie's wide eyes darted back and forth between the two adults as though he couldn't believe anything this special could happen to him.

"Well, you know what that means, Hope," Drake said. "I guess we'll have to let him open the box now. Otherwise, we'll have Santa mad at us for not following his orders.''

"That's what it looks like," Hope agreed, rising to her full height.

For a moment Stevie stared in awe at the box, then without further prompting began to rip away the red foil paper.

As he watched Stevie tear into the gift, Drake found himself inching closer to Hope, wanting and needing to share this moment with her. Before he could stop it, his arm went around her shoulders, his hand settling on her upper arm.

It was the first time he'd touched her since the two of them had made love. Drake half expected her to move away, but she didn't. He figured she was allowing him the closeness because of Stevie. Maybe he was a fool, but he didn't really care why she was enduring his arm around her. He needed to feel her warmth, needed to know she was here with him. At least for now.

"Oh, boy! Boots! Just like a real cowboy wears!"

Hope's eyes grew misty as she watched Stevie inspect the boots. They were black with intricate red and white designs inserted on the tall tops. Fancy stitching decorated the toe while the heels were high enough to dig into trail dirt. In her wildest dreams, she'd never expected Drake to do something so special for the boy, and her heart ached with gladness. Yet it was a bittersweet joy she felt. This time with Stevie would soon be coming to an end. Along with her marriage.

"Try them on, Stevie. See if they fit," Drake instructed. He knelt to help the boy.

"I wonder if Santa knew what size to get?" Hope asked.

"I'll bet while Stevie was sleeping he looked inside

his shoes to find his size. Santa does sneaky things like that. Or so I've heard.''

Once again Hope was amazed that Drake was so easily falling in with the magic of Santa. Especially when she knew he'd been robbed of such things during his childhood. But perhaps missing out on so much had made Drake understand even better just what Stevie needed. And if he could understand that, then perhaps he could see he'd make a wonderful father.

*No,* she quickly shouted at herself. *Don't start doing that again. Don't start hoping and wishing that things could be different.* Hardly a week had passed since Drake had told her their lovemaking had been a big mistake.

With that grim reminder, she stepped away from the two of them. ''I'll go fix us something hot to drink,'' she said, then quickly headed out of the room before either of them could spot her tears.

Ten minutes later, she returned to the living room with coffee for her and Drake and a mug of hot chocolate for Stevie.

To her surprise Stevie was sitting on Drake's lap, his booted feet dangling to one side of Drake's knees. The sight made her realize just how much the two of them had changed since that long-ago morning when Stevie had arrived at the airport. The child was learning how to be a normal little boy. And Drake—well, he still didn't want to be a father, but at least he'd grown close to his nephew. She had to be thankful for that much.

''Aunt Hope! I'm gonna go to a real ranch and ride a horse! Uncle Drake is gonna take me!''

Her eyes flew to Drake for an explanation.

''Tomorrow is Saturday. I thought I'd take him out to the Lord ranch. I haven't talked to Garrett in a while, but he's always given me a standing invitation to use his horses. I don't think he'll mind if Stevie and I borrow a pair for an hour or two.''

''Jake will think you're out there snooping, trying to find out what you can about him,'' Hope commented as she set the tray on the coffee table.

Drake grunted cynically. ''I'm sure I won't see the man. Besides, I'm not a detective for the Maitlands. I just handle their money.''

She passed Drake a cup, then placed Stevie's hot chocolate at the end of the coffee table. The boy scooted off Drake's lap and sat on the floor to carefully sip the drink.

''Are you gonna go to the ranch, too, Aunt Hope?'' Stevie asked.

Hope didn't glance at Drake as she took a seat in a nearby armchair. ''No, honey, I'd better stay here. You and Drake will have a good time together.''

Stevie scrunched his nose with disappointment as he tilted his head first one way and then the other. ''But Drake won't care if you come with us, too.''

For several nights running, Hope had lain awake in the queen-size bed, knowing her husband was sleeping only a few feet away on a narrow camp cot. He'd rather be there, or anywhere, just so long as he wasn't with her. Stevie was right in one respect: Drake didn't care. Not about her.

Careful to keep her eyes off Drake, she smiled gently at Stevie. ''I'll leave the riding to you two men this time. Okay?''

For long moments Stevie considered her words. Then he mumbled, ''Okay. I guess. But I don't want you to be lonely without us.''

It was all Hope could do to keep from bursting into tears. Desperately, she cleared her throat, then sipped her coffee. Finally, she managed to speak. "Don't worry about me, Stevie honey, I'll be fine."

Someday, she thought sadly. Someday.

LATER THAT NIGHT Hope was still awake when she heard the click of the door to the bedroom as it opened, then closed. The last time she'd glanced at the digital clock on the nightstand the time had already slipped past midnight. So far she hadn't slept a wink. But that was nothing new. Sleep had been a fleeting thing since Drake had come home to live with her and Stevie. And after the night they'd made love, she'd been lucky to sleep at all.

Each night this past week, after Stevie went to bed, Drake had been disappearing into his workshop. Hope hadn't bothered to ask him what, if anything, he was building. It was obvious he was using the place to escape from her.

Turning onto her back, she stared into the darkness and listened to Drake's quiet movements as he undressed. The clunk of his boots, the raspy whisper of denim as it slid down his long legs. A few days ago, she'd removed his clothing for him. Now she couldn't touch him.

The sound of her sigh must have been audible to him because the creaking of the cot springs stopped abruptly.

"Hope?"

Her breath froze in her throat. Since he'd moved out of their bed, he'd never once tried to talk to her while they were alone. She couldn't imagine why he would be doing it now. Unless he wanted to make divorce plans without the chance of Stevie interrupting.

When she failed to reply, he asked, "Are you awake?"

She swallowed, glad the room was too dark for him to see her.

"Yes."

There was a pause, then he said, "I've been thinking and...I just wanted to...well, if you'd like to go with me and Stevie to the Lord ranch...it's okay with me."

Dear God, just how much suffering did he think she could take, she wondered. The more time she spent with him, the more she anguished over all that she was losing.

"No. I think it's better the two of you have the time alone."

"The boy loves you, too."

Hope was forced to swallow again as a searing knot filled her throat. "Yes. But this was your plan. I'll...do something special with him later."

There was a long pause and Hope sensed, rather than saw, that he was looking in her direction. But what he was thinking was impossible to figure out. After ten years of marriage, she'd believed she'd known him inside and out. She'd believed his heart had been big enough to welcome a child into their lives. She'd been desperately wrong. She had to face the fact that she hadn't understood her husband at all.

"He seemed to really like the boots," Drake said quietly.

"He loved them. I'm...very glad you went to all the trouble. Thank you, Drake."

There was another pregnant pause, then he said, "Hope, I—"

Hope's heart thundered heavily in her chest as she waited for him to continue.

"You what?" she asked quietly.

"Nothing. Forget it."

For one wild moment, something in his voice had hinted that he wanted to make some sort of amends. But then Hope was feeling so desperate she was probably hearing things that weren't really there.

The cot creaked as he stretched out on the thin mattress, and Hope realized she was in for another long night without him.

*You told him to get out of your bed. This is what you asked for, Hope. This is what you wanted.*

She grimaced as the little voice sounded in her head. Drake had given her no choice. He considered making love to her a failing, a default of the worst kind. It didn't make sense that she could still love him while knowing how he felt. But she did. And it disgusted her that she couldn't turn off her emotions and accept the inevitable end of their marriage.

Her heart heavy, she turned onto her side and slid her hand over the empty spot beside her. She didn't know which was worse—having Drake in bed with her, hanging on to the edge of the mattress, determined not to touch her. Or having him a few feet away. Out of reach. But nowhere near out of mind.

## CHAPTER TWELVE

SATURDAY DAWNED CLEAR, and by early afternoon the temperature had warmed to light jacket weather. Once Drake had maneuvered out of city traffic, he drove the remaining miles to the ranch slowly to allow Stevie a leisurely look at the cattle and horses and open countryside. Something the child didn't have a chance to experience in boarding school.

At the ranch, one of Garrett's hands, who remembered Drake from a past visit, assured him they could spare two horses. As the cowhand guided them to a small corral at the back of the barn to pick their mounts, Drake told him, "Stevie doesn't know how to ride, so you'd better make his mount gentle."

The older man chuckled as he eyed Stevie. The boy was duded up in jeans, new boots and an old straw hat that Drake had found in the garage. He'd stuffed the lining with newspaper until he'd thought it was small enough to fit his head. Apparently he should have used a bit more paper, Drake thought with amusement. The hat was resting atop Stevie's ears. But he wasn't about to ask the boy to part with it. Stevie considered the hat nearly as grand as the boots.

"I got just the thing for you, young man. A little dun pony called Lightning. Think you can ride 'im?"

Stevie's mouth fell open as he stared at the grizzled old cowboy, and Drake realized the boy had never seen real chaps or spurs or a jaw full of tobacco. As far as that went, he figured the child had never seen a real horse, much less ridden one.

"Sure he'll be able to." Drake spoke. "I'll lead Lightning. All Stevie will have to do is hang on."

Thirty minutes later, Lightning and another horse called Rounder were saddled and ready to go. After many careful instructions, Drake positioned Stevie in the saddle, then mounted the bay gelding he was to ride.

The land was made up of rolling hills with only a few trees dotting the range, so the riding was easy. Drake kept the pace purposely slow as the two of them rode west, away from the ranch.

Surprisingly, Stevie was the first to make conversation. "Where are we going, Uncle Drake?"

"We're going to follow a cattle trail until we reach a windmill. Do you know what a windmill is?"

Stevie shook his head. "Is it a place where the wind blows?"

The question brought a patient smile to Drake's face. "Well, you're partly right. The wind has to blow to make it work and pump water out of the ground, so the cows and horses can get a drink when they're thirsty. But it's a long ways from here. Think you can ride that far?"

The beaming grin on Stevie's face said he could ride for hours. "Yeah! This is fun! Really fun!"

"Okay. Hold on tight. We're on our way."

Forty minutes later, the old wooden derrick of the windmill came into view. Spotting it, Stevie let out an excited squeal.

"There it is, Uncle Drake! Look at all those cows!"

A herd of mixed breeds was milling about the huge round watering tank. Catching the sound of the riders' approach, many of the animals lifted their heads to look in that direction.

As he and Stevie grew closer, Drake could see it was a herd of steers rather than cows. But he'd teach Stevie the difference at a later date, when the two of them took another ride.

The thought suddenly brought Drake up short. What the hell was he thinking? Stevie would be leaving in a few days. There would be no more rides together. No more chances to give the boy a taste of normal life. His time with Stevie was coming to an end. Just like his marriage to Hope. Unless he did something to stop it.

"We'll ride up to that little knoll." Drake pointed to a nearby slope of hill looking down on the cattle. "And we'll have our snack there, okay?"

Stevie nodded, but his expression had suddenly turned glum. "Do we have to hurry?"

Drake didn't have to ask the child what was going through his mind. He could remember the first time he'd gotten the chance to ride a horse on a real ranch. He'd been just about Stevie's age and by some miracle his parents, who'd been going out of town, had allowed him to stay the weekend with his best buddy. Drake hadn't wanted that special time to end for any reason.

"Don't worry, Stevie. We're not going to hurry. We'll spend all the rest of the day here."

Drake's promise seemed to appease Stevie somewhat. By the time the two of them had ridden to the top of the hill, the boy's excitement had returned.

Along with several kinds of cheese, crackers and fruit, Hope had packed them a thermos of cold water and one of hot cider. As Drake placed the little meal onto a square of red handkerchief material, he wondered what she was doing this afternoon. Last night when he'd mentioned her making this ride with them, he hadn't realized just how much he'd wanted her to come along until she'd refused his invitation.

Hope had always liked horses and riding, so he knew she'd stayed at home because of him. She didn't want to be near him for any reason.

Shaking away the dismal thought, he turned his attention to Stevie, who'd found a seat on a weathered log. From his nearby position on a large rock, Drake handed the boy a drink and two crackers wedged with cheese.

"Is this the first time you've ever been on a ranch, Stevie?"

The boy nodded, making his loose hat bob backward and forward. "I saw pictures in books at the library. And sometimes I see cowboys on TV. But I didn't get to watch TV that much back at boarding school."

"What about when you're home?"

His lips pursed and he shook his head. "Mostly I just stay in my room and draw pictures of things I'd like to do and see."

Out of sight, out of mind, Drake thought with disgust. As far as his sister and brother-in-law were concerned, they didn't have a child.

Drake could remember a time when he'd been very young and forced to create his own little world. Early on, he'd learned that no one cared what he thought or wanted. When he was home, he'd lived in a lonely, private place inside his head.

"What do you want to be when you grow up?" Drake asked Stevie.

The question seemed to surprise the boy. Clearly he didn't expect anyone to care or wonder about his dreams. After a moment, he shrugged and ducked his head.

"I really would like you to tell me," Drake gently urged.

Stevie peeped at him through long lashes, then his lips tightened as though he was desperately trying to hold something back. "You'll laugh at me," he said in a low, accusing voice.

Resting his elbows on his knees, Drake leaned earnestly toward the troubled child. "I would never laugh at you, Stevie. Knowing what you like is important to me."

After much consideration, Stevie lifted his chin to a point that almost made Drake break his promise and laugh. "I want to be a cowboy. I want to have cows and horses and barns with lots of hay. And green pastures where they can eat."

Even though it was obvious that Stevie was currently enamored with boots and horses and Garrett's ranch, Drake had not been expecting this answer from the child.

"I understand you're enjoying today, Stevie. But I'm talking about when you grow up big, like me. Surely you've thought about what you want to be. A doctor maybe. A fireman or policeman? Something like that?"

Stevie shook his head with resolution as he bit off a bite of cracker. "I told you, Uncle Drake. I want to be a cowboy."

"Since when?" Drake persisted. "Since today? Since you came to Austin?"

He frowned because Drake wasn't readily believing him. "Uh-uh. Since a long time ago. When I was little."

Stevie's last remark made Drake want to smile. "What do your mommy and daddy think about you wanting to be a cowboy?"

The little boy's eyes were suddenly defiant. "They

don't ask me. And I don't tell them. Besides, that will be when I'm big and I won't live with them anymore."

At least Stevie knew his life would be his own once he reached a certain age, Drake thought. Too bad he hadn't felt that independence himself early on in his childhood. He might have been a different man today. A better man.

"You know what, Stevie," Drake said after a moment. "I wanted to be a cowboy, too."

Drake's revelation brought a look of wonder to Stevie's face. "Really? How come you're not one now?"

Drake's brow wrinkled in wry contemplation. "That's a good question, Stevie. I'm not sure I can answer it."

Stevie crammed the rest of the cracker into his mouth and reached for another. "You figured you wanted to be something else. But I won't. I'm gonna be a cowboy. I'm gonna keep eatin' so I'll get big and strong and I won't be afraid to do anything. Aunt Hope says I'm gettin' bigger and braver every day. You think she's right, Uncle Drake?"

Stevie wasn't just filling out with flesh and muscles, Drake decided. The boy was growing mentally stronger. He was building confidence with each day that passed. He was no longer afraid of the outdoors or his peers. He'd learned he wasn't different or strange. He knew he was loved and accepted by his uncle and Hope.

"I think your aunt Hope is very right, Stevie."

As he bit into a crisp apple, Drake gazed at the herd of cattle. Years ago, a place like this was all he'd wanted. Cattle, horses and a spread to raise them had been his deepest dream. But none of that had been good enough for the child of a Logan, he thought bitterly.

"Has your mother ever talked to you about your grandparents?" Drake asked Stevie.

"Mommy showed me pictures once," Stevie answered. "They were rich and lived in a big, fancy house like the Maitlands."

Drake smiled cynically. "Not exactly like the Maitlands. But it was a big house," Drake agreed. "Did you know your grandfather was once a cattle baron?"

The boy didn't answer immediately, and a quick glance at Stevie's puzzled face told Drake he didn't understand the word.

"What's that?" Stevie wanted to know.

Old memories rushed up to taunt Drake, and he sighed. "That means he was a rancher. He owned lots of land and cattle."

Stevie was thoroughly impressed. "You mean he was a real cowboy?"

Drake's short laugh was mocking. "Hardly. He never touched a horse or cow. He hired men to do it for him."

Stevie's face drooped with disappointment. "That wouldn't be any fun."

"No. Not in my opinion."

For a moment Stevie studied Drake with open curiosity. "Did you get to see the cows and horses? Did you have a pony of your own and ride the range?"

Drake shook his head. Not until this very moment had he realized how much that time in his life had affected him. Harris Logan's ranch had been in west Texas, where the dust was as common as horned toads and sidewinders. His mother, Lilah, had despised the place, but she'd put up with it because her husband had been an affluent man with his hand in all sorts of enterprising ventures. Then oil had been discovered on the Logan ranch, and money began to pour in like floodwater on the plains.

"No. My parents—your grandparents—didn't want me

doing such things. They didn't want me to be a cowboy or to be near any of the men who worked the ranch.''

"Did that make you sad?"

It had made him more than sad, Drake thought. The fact that his parents believed his dreams were unworthy and beneath his dignity had squashed his self-confidence.

"Pretty sad," Drake answered. "But then oil was discovered on the ranch. That made your grandparents even richer and they moved to Dallas.''

Harris had sold off the land and cattle, but kept the mineral rights to the oil wells. It was his parents' way of making sure Drake lost all chance of inheriting the ranch without losing any of the money they had so coveted.

After the move to Dallas, Drake had continued with boarding school and then college. He'd thrown himself into his studies, determined to be a success once he graduated. Because his parents were so driven by finance, Drake had chosen the field to make his own living. In his parents' eyes, handling money was a far more respectable job than handling a lariat or branding iron.

"Did you have to go with them, Uncle Drake? What happened?''

Stevie's questions interrupted his somber reverie, and he glanced at the boy's fresh, innocent face. Dear God, he'd been so wrong all these years, he thought. He couldn't let the same thing happen to Stevie. This time he wasn't going to allow the same mistakes to repeat themselves. He had to do something to stop it.

Heavy memories weighted down his sigh. "Yes, Stevie, I had to move to Dallas, too. But I had already been living most of my life there at boarding school, anyway, like you do. After that, I went to college and got a job.''

Stevie wrinkled his nose with distaste. "How come?''

Drake's lips curved into a wry smile. "Because we have to get our education, Stevie. It's very important for all of us to learn—no matter what we plan to do in life."

Stevie shook his head. "No. I mean, how come you didn't be a cowboy when you got big and out of school?"

How come? Drake repeated the simple question to himself. Why hadn't he done what was really in his heart, rather than what his parents had wanted?

For a long time he'd told himself he'd made the choice to become a financier because it was the sensible thing to do. He was an intelligent man, and working with his head would be far easier than toiling with his hands outside in all sorts of wicked weather. Not to mention that a career in finance would make him financially secure.

Hell, who had he been kidding, Drake wondered bitterly. Only himself. Everything he'd done in his young life had been for his parents, to gain their love and admiration. What he hadn't realized was that they'd been two people incapable of caring for anyone but themselves. In the end it wouldn't have mattered what he'd done or where he'd lived, because neither of them had ever understood the meaning of love.

"I made a mistake, Stevie. A big mistake. Sometimes people do that." With a sudden smile, he leaned over and patted the boy beneath the chin. "But you know what, son? I'm not going to let you mess up like I did. I'm going to make sure you get to do just what you want to do."

Stevie grinned, and Drake noticed that being outside these past few weeks had produced even more freckles across the boy's nose and cheeks.

"I like staying with you and Aunt Hope," Stevie confessed. "She makes good things to eat and she's nice to me. Really nice. Do you think she'll come riding with us next time, Uncle Drake?''

Next time? Would he ever have a next time with Hope? Drake wondered. He probably didn't deserve it, he thought ruefully. These past months he'd done nothing right. He'd hurt her in so many stupid ways.

Hope had given him ten years of love. Without her, he would have been an empty man. And he'd repaid all of that by refusing to give her—them—another chance at having a child. He'd been so blinded with fear of losing her, and he'd been incapable of seeing beyond his own terrible childhood.

The whole notion had him silently groaning with shame and regret. His parents were in their graves and had been for a few years now. He'd been wrong to let them dictate his life while they were alive. He'd be even more wrong if he allowed them to keep imposing on his dreams. In spite of their materialistic values, he'd grown up to be a good man. And he could be a good father, too. The time he'd spent with Stevie, the happiness that was clearly on the child's face had proved it to him.

Maybe it would be a risk for Hope to get pregnant again. But he realized it was a risk he had to allow her to take. It wasn't right for him to put conditions on their marriage any more than it had been for his parents to put demands on him.

Drake realized his thoughts had kept him occupied far too long for Stevie's liking when he heard the boy repeating his question.

''You haven't answered, Uncle Drake! Will Aunt Hope come riding with us next time?''

He glanced at the boy, and suddenly his heart was filled with all the things he wanted to do for this child and, he hoped, children of his own.

"I don't know, son, but I'll try my best to change her mind."

He had to, Drake thought desperately, because he couldn't live without her. But how was he going to convince her that he'd changed? Words would never be enough. Right now, he wasn't sure there was anything he could say or do that would help him win his wife back.

LATER THAT EVENING Hope returned home from a shopping trip with her friends to find Drake and Stevie back from their ride.

"Hi, Aunt Hope!" Stevie sang from his seat at the kitchen table. "Uncle Drake is making chicken noodle soup. Want some with us?"

She went over to the boy and placed a kiss on top of his head. "If there's enough."

After placing her packages in a nearby closet, she walked to the stove, where Drake was stirring the saucepan of soup with a wooden spoon. So far he hadn't bothered to look in her direction.

"Sorry I wasn't here," she said stiffly. "If you'd like, I could thaw out steaks or something."

He turned his head in her direction, and Hope was surprised to see a smile on his face. Especially when she could find no mockery behind it.

"That's okay. Don't worry about it. The soup will be plenty. I'll put in another can for you."

"How did the ride go?" she asked.

"It was good." He glanced away from her and reached into the cabinet for a second can of soup. "Really good. Maybe you should have Stevie tell you about it."

Naturally, she thought. He didn't want to have to talk to her any more than he had to.

She walked to the small kitchen table and took a seat

next to Stevie. "Did you have fun out at the Lord ranch?"

Before she could get the question out, Stevie was bouncing on his seat, eager to tell her about their adventure.

"Yeah! It was the best time I ever had! My pony was named Lightning and he was pretty! He had a long mane and tail just like the color of your hair."

With a doubtful laugh, Hope touched a hand to her hair. "Well, I guess it's a compliment to be compared to a horse."

"Coming from Stevie it is," Drake observed from the stove.

"We rode for a long, long way," Stevie continued without further prompting. "All the way to a windmill. The tank was full of water and Drake said if it was in the summertime I could have went swimming in it. I told him I didn't know how to swim. But he says he's gonna teach me and that you will, too!"

Hope glanced at Drake, but his back was to her. "Really?" she asked with slow thoughtfulness. "What else did you do?"

"We ate all the crackers and stuff you gave us. And on the way back to the ranch, Drake let me hold the reins and ride Lightning all by myself!"

She looked at the child and was amazed at the joy she saw shining in his brown eyes. Apparently Drake had done and said all the right things. Just like any devoted father, she thought sadly. If only he could see himself through Stevie's eyes.

"Did you like that?"

"It was great, Aunt Hope! Lightning didn't buck or jump or do anything bad, and Uncle Drake said I was gonna be a natural cowboy. He's gonna ask Santa to get me a lariat and a pair of spurs, and next time I might even get to rope a calf!''

''That sounds like real fun, Stevie,'' Hope murmured. But inwardly she was wondering what all these future plans meant for the boy. Drake should know better than to make promises he couldn't keep.

Throughout the simple meal, Stevie chattered about the horses, the cows, the dogs and all the things he'd seen on the ranch. But mostly he talked about his uncle Drake and what the two of them were planning to do together.

When the boy finally left the table to go watch television, Hope couldn't hide her concern any longer.

She turned a troubled look on Drake. ''I'm very happy that Stevie had such a good time today. But he—''

Drake frowned. ''But what?'' he asked. ''The boy is finally getting to do the things he's only dreamed about before. What's wrong with that?''

''Nothing.'' She spread her hands in a helpless gesture. ''It's all these things he's talking about doing in the future that concern me.''

His expression turned deceptively smooth as he rose from his chair and began to gather the dirty dishes from the table. ''The child has to have something to look forward to, Hope. We all do.''

No one had to remind her of that. These past few months, her future had looked black. She understood what it was like not to see any sort of light at the end of the tunnel. Her light of hope had been extinguished a long time ago.

''I just don't want him to be disappointed, Drake. His spirits are so high now. I hate to think how low they'll sink once he's away from us and back in Denise's hands.''

He opened the dishwasher and put in the dirty bowls.

"Just trust me about this, Hope. I know what I'm doing. Stevie isn't going to be disappointed. And I don't intend to let him turn back into the timid, lonely child we picked up at the airport."

Surprise parted her lips, and she started to ask him how he planned to stop such a thing from happening, but before she could, he closed the dishwasher and reached for his jacket on the back of the chair.

"Would you clean up what's left here, Hope? I have some work to do out in the shop."

She stood and stepped away from the table to intercept his passage. "Drake, why…"

Only inches separated their bodies. Heat infused Hope as she felt his eyes wander slowly over her face. She'd seen that same wondrous light in his eyes when he studied a piece of precious artwork or a beautiful rose in the Maitlands' garden. It didn't make sense. But then nothing between them made sense anymore.

Reaching out, he patted her cheek. "Stevie really missed you today. Why don't you read him an extra couple of stories tonight before he goes to sleep."

"But, Drake—"

"Are you feeling all right?"

The unexpected question put a puzzled wrinkle on her brow. "Why do you ask?"

One side of his lips lifted in a cautious grin. "You look pale."

In a curt voice she said, "I told you not to worry about that, Drake."

*That* meaning her being pregnant, Drake realized. Would she even tell him if she was? he wondered sadly. "I just don't want you to be ill. Especially at Christmastime."

He sounded so sincere, she almost felt ashamed for being short with him.

"I'm fine," she said, aware of the wobble in her voice.

"Good. And don't worry, Hope. Stevie is going to be fine, too."

Not giving her a chance to say more, he stepped around her and hurried out the back door.

She stared after him, her mind whirling, her heart heavy. She could follow him to the shop, demand that he give her some sort of answers about Stevie and this strange new attitude of his. But why bother, she asked herself. He didn't care enough about her to share his plans with her. He didn't even want to spend the rest of the evening under the same roof with her.

Red or black lingerie. What a joke, she thought as she suddenly remembered the packages she'd left in the broom closet. She wasn't going to bother wrapping the gifts her friends had talked her into buying for Drake. She'd give the sensual nightwear to Abby and Dana. Their honeymoons were still going strong. Hers and Drake's had died a long time ago.

## CHAPTER THIRTEEN

"I CAN'T BELIEVE it's finally Christmas Eve and we're going home. The past couple of hours have been murder."

Hope glanced at Tess, who let out a weary sigh. With the rapid approach of Christmas Eve, the gift shop had become far busier than usual, keeping the two of them hopping from one customer to the next. Both women were exhausted from the long day. For once, Drake had left the clinic before her and had picked up Stevie from day care before heading home.

"Well, at least we'll have a few days off before we have to come back to work," Hope said. "Are you staying here in Austin for Christmas?" she asked as she reached for her light jacket. A few minutes before, she'd locked the front door to the gift shop and shut off the lights. Tess had already pulled on her coat and was waiting for Hope to follow her out the back entrance.

"No. I'm going home to Port Lavaca. My folks are expecting me."

Tess didn't sound all that enthusiastic. Apparently her assistant was going into the holiday with a heart as heavy as Hope's own.

"But you don't want to go?" she asked gently.

The two women stepped outside the building before Tess answered. "I always want to be home for Christmas. But I'm afraid this year it just ·von't be the same. You see—things have been rather strained with my father since—well, since my ordeal with Robert. I've disappointed him terribly.''

After making certain the door was locked, Hope pulled the key, then turned and patted Tess on the arm. "He'll get over it, Tess. And you will, too, in time."

The young woman gave Hope a lopsided grin. "I guess neither one of us plans on having a grand Christmas this year."

Hope shrugged. "Maybe we need to stop and remind ourselves things could be worse."

As far as her own life was concerned, Hope didn't see how it could get any more dismal, but she kept the thought to herself. There was no need to heap her problems on Tess's squashed spirits.

In the parking lot, the two women wished each other a merry Christmas, then with a last goodbye headed to their separate cars.

Before Hope pulled out of the parking lot, she noticed Drake's car was gone, but Megan's and R.J.'s vehicles were still parked in their personal slots.

The Maitlands weren't exactly having smooth sailing this holiday, either, Hope thought. Not with all the gossip about Cody tearing at the very foundation Maitland Maternity Clinic was built on.

Even with today being Christmas Eve, the baby story was still the main source of interest at the clinic. Snippets of news, whether true or not, had been carried into the gift shop today.

Drake hadn't said much more about how the negative publicity was affecting clinic funds. But then he hadn't said much about anything since he and Stevie had visited the Lord ranch.

Frankly, Hope was growing more and more puzzled

over his behavior. He wasn't exactly cool or distant with her anymore. In fact, most of the time, even when Stevie was out of earshot, he was agreeable, almost to the point of being warm. Yet, he was still avoiding her, escaping to his workshop as soon as he got up from the supper table.

In spite of the change in him, Hope had been very careful to keep her guard up and maintain a safe distance from him. She wasn't about to give him any reason to accuse her of trying to seduce him a second time. Once had given her enough pain and humiliation to last a lifetime.

On her way home, she stopped at a nearby grocery market to pick up the last-minute items she needed for Christmas dinner. By the time she parked in the garage next to Drake's car, it was well after dark.

With a grocery sack in each arm, she entered the door leading from the garage into the kitchen. Except for a small light glowing beneath the hood over the gas range, the room was quiet and dark.

Hope eased the sacks down on the cabinet counter, then flipped on the overhead light. Immediately, she noticed the note pinned to the refrigerator door and crossed to the room to read it.

Stevie and I have work to do this evening, so we won't be back in the house until much later. Don't bother about supper. The two of us have already eaten.

Drake

Biting back a sigh, she turned to the groceries and slowly began to put everything away in its proper place. So much for a nice Christmas Eve with the family, she thought ruefully. Drake hadn't only taken himself out of her life, he'd taken Stevie along with him.

A few minutes later, she made herself a sandwich, and even though she wasn't hungry, she forced herself to eat the major part of it. After the simple meal, she carried her coffee into the living room and switched on the television.

Across the room, the Christmas tree twinkled against the dark backdrop of the picture window. Apparently Drake had plugged the lights in sometime after he'd gotten home from work.

Her gaze drifted to the packages beneath the heavy green boughs of the tree. After Dana and Katie had talked her into getting something for Drake, she'd gone all out and purchased him a pair of expensive field glasses. Occasionally, he went on hunting trips to Colorado and New Mexico with R.J. and he'd mentioned needing a stronger pair for scanning the wide-open ranges.

She didn't know how he would view the gift. He'd probably see it as one more way to soften him into her way of thinking. If he did, she couldn't help it. Moreover, she didn't care. She was tired of worrying and arguing. And she was especially tired of hurting over a husband who didn't love her.

After an hour of television she gave up trying to concentrate on programs mainly geared toward the holiday. Her heart just wasn't in it.

She switched off the TV and went to the kitchen. After rinsing her dirty coffee mug, she walked over to stand at the door leading out to the small porch and backyard beyond. Through the window she could see the faint light in Drake's workshop, slanting across the dead winter grass.

Before their separation, Hope had often gone out to

the small building to share in her husband's hobby. Sometimes, she'd helped him hold boards or take measurements. But mainly, she'd simply watched him work and shared the quiet time with him.

Hope had always encouraged him to make time for his hobby. Especially when he was so talented at crafting wood into beautiful objects. Not to mention in need of a break from the long hours he put in at the clinic. But back then, Drake had never neglected her because of the hobby, or chosen to spend more time with it than with her.

*Nothing is the same now, Hope,* she told herself. *Your life together, your marriage are ending because you want a baby.*

Dear God, why was she being punished for something so natural, so necessary to a woman? she prayed. Maybe if she knew the answer, she could accept the loss.

A chilling draft seemed to fill the kitchen. Hope hugged her arms to her chest as she turned away from the door. She could go out to the workshop and join Drake and Stevie. It wasn't as though he'd banned her from the place. But she hadn't been invited, and she'd feel like an intruder.

Besides, Stevie needed the time alone with Drake. Just like all little boys needed special time alone with their fathers. Only in this case, Drake wasn't Stevie's father, and their time together would soon be over. No, she wouldn't impose on them tonight. Not even to keep from spending Christmas Eve alone.

HOPE HAD BEEN ASLEEP for nearly two hours when the sound of Drake's low voice woke her.

Disoriented, she raised herself up on one elbow and

rubbed a hand over her eyes. "What's wrong?" she murmured huskily.

"Nothing. I'm sorry I had to wake you. But I wanted to make sure all Stevie's Santa Claus gifts were in the pantry."

By now all the cobwebs of sleep had cleared away, and she could see he was standing beside her bed. The fact that he was so close sent her foolish heart into overdrive.

"That's everything. Have you already put them under the tree and in his stocking?"

"Yes. It's after midnight. Stevie's in bed asleep."

"I put out cookies and milk on the coffee table for Santa. Did you explain all that to Stevie?"

"Well, actually we ate them. But we put out more for Santa. I made sure they were gone after Stevie went to bed."

The room was too dark to see his face, but she could hear a big smile in his voice and wondered how he could be so happy. Was it because this month of living with her was finally coming to an end? The thought left a crushing weight in her chest.

"Just so he understood what the little snack was for," Hope said. "I don't want him to miss out on anything. God only knows what his next Christmas will be like."

To her surprise he eased down on the edge of the mattress. "Hope, I told you not to be worrying about Stevie," he said gently.

"How can I not worry, Drake? When I think of him with Denise and Phillip, I—well, I can hardly bear the thought."

"I'm going to make sure things are different with Stevie. I told you that."

"But how? With him in Dallas—"

"Don't ask me how. Just trust me, okay?"

There was no anger or frustration in his voice, only a tender sort of promise, and suddenly Hope forgot all about Stevie and why her husband was sitting beside her on the bed.

The faint scent of his cologne mingled with the smells of wood dust and the bayberry candle she'd left burning on the coffee table. Without touching him, she could feel the warmth of his body radiating to her. She wanted to touch him so badly, she was weak with it.

"Okay. I trust you to take care of Stevie."

He sighed, and the soft sound of relief sent a rush of longing through every part of her.

"I'm—I hope you didn't mind being alone this evening. Stevie wanted to help me and I couldn't say no. I guess I'm learning what it's like to spoil a child."

His admission surprised her, not to mention tugged at her heart. "I don't believe Stevie could be spoiled. Not in a bad way. He's too good a child."

He didn't say anything to that, and after a moment she realized the soft sound she was hearing was his palms rubbing up and down the denim covering his thighs.

The gesture puzzled Hope. Drake was never nervous about anything, and even if he was, he would never show it outwardly.

"Tomorrow's Christmas," he said, as though the two of them needed to be reminded.

"Yes."

He turned ever so slightly toward her, and her heart pounded so hard she was certain he would hear the same thundering sound that was beating in her ears.

"Hope, I—I know I've picked a hell of a time, but—"

He didn't go on. And Hope didn't prompt him. She was suddenly afraid to urge him to say anything. She couldn't bear to hear him ask for a divorce tonight. Not on Christmas Eve.

He rose to his feet, and Hope's pent-up breath left her in ragged jerks.

"I just wanted to say Merry Christmas."

The wild beating of her heart stopped altogether as she tried to focus on his face in the darkness. He sounded so tender, so sincere, she told herself she must be dreaming.

"Merry Christmas, Drake." *I love you,* her heart added, but her lips couldn't form the words. And when she heard him move to the cot where he'd been sleeping, she knew she'd been right to keep them to herself.

THE NEXT MORNING Stevie was the first one up. His excited squeals carried all the way upstairs, waking both Hope and Drake. While she pulled on a robe, Drake jerked on a pair of jeans and followed her to the living room.

Still in his pajamas, Stevie was standing near the tree, his wide eyes trying to encompass all the gifts that had been placed there while he slept.

"Santa really did come last night! And he ate all the cookies left for him!" He whirled toward the two adults. "Gosh! He carried all this stuff in here without making a noise. Do you think his reindeer were outside, too?"

"That's the only way Santa travels," Drake said with a sly wink at Hope. "If we search hard enough we might find some deer tracks on the front lawn. But right now it looks like you'd better get to opening all those gifts before it's time for breakfast."

Stevie blinked with confusion as he surveyed the pile of packages. "I can't," he said sullenly.

Hope and Drake exchanged a sharp glance of concern.

"What do you mean, you can't?" Drake prompted him to explain.

The boy's head twisted to the two adults, and Hope felt close to tears at the torn look on his face.

"'Cause I only get two gifts for Christmas—from my mommy and daddy. Santa doesn't bring me things. Mommy says rich kids aren't supposed to ask Santa for toys or anything."

Hope couldn't prevent the soft gasp rushing past her lips. Beside her, Drake groaned, then reached for Stevie and gently drew him into the circle of his arm.

"Stevie, why didn't you tell us about this when Hope and I asked you to make a list for Santa?" Drake questioned him.

The child's bottom lip quivered and his head hung dejectedly. "'Cause I didn't want to. And anyway, I didn't think Santa would come like you and Aunt Hope said he would."

Drake's gaze slipped to Hope, and the tears shimmering in her eyes reflected his own pain. On the other hand he was suddenly very happy that Stevie had come into his life. From now on, Stevie was going to be loved. Very loved.

Patting the child's cheek, Drake said, "But he did, didn't he?"

Stevie glanced over his shoulder at the stacks of presents, then nodded.

"So now you know he wants you to have gifts, too. Just like the other kids. And he'd be sad if you didn't open them."

Doubtful brown eyes vacillated between Drake and Hope. "Do you think so?"

"Oh, he'd be awfully sad," Hope assured him.

Once more Stevie turned a skeptical look at the piles of gifts. "Are you sure they're for me?"

"Sure as sure can be," Drake answered. "Why don't you go open them and see? You can start with your stocking."

Stevie didn't have to be prompted a second time. Grabbing his stocking from the fireplace, he began to empty the bulging sack.

Drake and Hope took seats on the couch to watch his reaction while he discovered the gifts both of them had taken pains to choose for the boy. Within seconds they realized their efforts had been worth it. Stevie's little round face became a mirror of amazement and joy. Before long, he was racing back and forth between the pile of gifts and the adults on the couch, eager to show them his newly acquired treasures.

Neither Drake nor Hope was surprised to learn his favorite gifts were the cowboy items he'd asked for after the visit to the Lord ranch. Hope tried not to think what Denise might do with the boy's spurs, chaps and lariat. It would break Stevie's heart to part with them. But then Drake had told her not to worry, so she tried her best to push the thought out of her mind and concentrate on his present happiness.

Once all of Stevie's packages were opened and he'd settled on the floor to play, Drake left the couch to fetch one of the boxes still under the tree.

"I think Santa brought you something, too," he said to Hope.

Her eyes met his as she accepted the gift from his outstretched hands. With a tiny ache in her heart, she said, "I didn't expect Santa to remember me this year."

His face shadowed with regret, he sank down beside her. "How could I not remember, Hope?" he said softly.

The poignant question filled Hope's eyes with stinging moisture, forcing her to look away from him.

"I guess old habits die hard," she said, forcing the words through her tight throat.

"Some habits never die," he replied.

Her gaze flew to his face, and when she recognized the look in his eyes, shock parted her lips. He was going to kiss her!

The thought was zinging through her brain at the same time that his face was leaning into hers. In unwitting response, her lashes fluttered down, and her breathing slowed.

The warm pressure of his lips against hers was heady, evoking memories too sweet to bear. For long moments after he'd eased away from her, she was loath to open her eyes and break the spell.

"Open your gift. See if you like it."

Swallowing hard, she tried to gather her scattered senses, but her fingers continued to tremble as she worked to remove the red foil paper from the box on her lap.

"Oh!"

The one word was all she could manage as she gazed at the boots nestled in tissue paper. They were dress boots made of the softest suede she'd ever seen and would be a perfect accessory to her winter skirts and dresses. Hope hadn't been expecting anything so expensive or personal from him. But then the boots weren't nearly as personal as that kiss had been, she thought.

*Don't make any more out of the kiss or the gift than is really there, Hope. This is all just a show for Stevie, part of the plan to make this a special Christmas for him.*

"You like the boots?"

The question brought her gaze to his face. "Very much."

Drake would have to remember to thank Juanita. But right now, he wished his wife wasn't looking at him so cautiously. She obviously considered his gift and his kiss to be connected to some dark, ulterior motive. He could only hope that what he had planned for later would erase the doubts veiling her blue eyes.

He watched her set the boots to one side, then leave her seat to search among the few gifts remaining under the tree. After a moment she walked over and extended a package to him.

"It seems Santa didn't forget you, either," she said.

His brows arched with surprise as he accepted the small box, then he chuckled as he turned it over once, then again. "Should I take this in the other room before I open it?"

A wry smile curved her lips. "It's not going to spray you with paint or shower you with confetti. I'm not that mean."

There wasn't a mean bone in her body. Or a selfish one. In all the years they'd been married, she'd done nothing but give to him. Now it was his time to start giving back. If only she would let him.

He quickly ripped into the package, expecting to find a couple of ties or a bottle of cologne. After all, he knew the gift was simply for the sake of appearances, not given with true Christmas spirit.

When he spotted the binoculars resting beneath a layer of tissue paper, he was totally taken aback. She'd even remembered the wide-angle lens and the particular brand he'd wanted.

"This is—really something, Hope," he said with quiet amazement.

"Are they anything like you wanted?"

He lifted his head, and as he looked into her blue eyes, he couldn't stop the forward motion of his body. Leaning toward her, he pressed his lips against hers once again.

Drake had never had to struggle so hard to keep from wrapping his arms around her and deepening the kiss. Somehow he managed to ease himself away, though there was a telltale raggedness to his breathing when he did finally speak.

"They're exactly what I wanted. Thank you, Hope."

Awkward, Hope rose to her feet and wiped her damp palms down the sides of her robe. "I'd better go cook breakfast."

Before Drake could make any sort of reply, she walked away. On her way out of the room, she bent over and kissed Stevie on the top of his head.

"Merry Christmas, honey," she said to him.

The child looked up from his play to give her a lop-sided grin. "You know what, Aunt Hope?"

She smiled at him. "No. What?"

"I think the angel on the tree done a good job watching over us. Can we put her on the tree next Christmas, too?"

Next Christmas. Right now Hope didn't want to think where the three of them might be in the coming year. In three different places? With no family for any of them?

She patted his cheek, wondering if the ache in her chest would ever go away. "She's getting pretty fragile. If we can keep her from falling apart, we'll use her again next year," she promised.

## CHAPTER FOURTEEN

BECAUSE BREAKFAST was so late, Hope made the suggestion to Drake that they have their big Christmas meal that evening instead of earlier.

"That suits me just dandy," he said as he swallowed the last swig of his coffee. "I still have some work to finish out in the shop."

Hope turned away from the kitchen sink to stare at him in disbelief. "You're going out there to work? Today? It's Christmas, Drake. Or have you already forgotten?"

Rather than being peeved, he appeared to be amused at her outburst. "I haven't forgotten anything. It's just that I have a little left to finish and I want to get it done today."

She walked over to where he was shrugging a worn jacket over his jeans and black sweatshirt.

"Finish what? What could be so important that you have to work on it today?"

He glanced away from her and focused his attention on buttoning his jacket.

"Just something I've needed to make for a long time. I'll show you later," he added offhandedly. Walking to the open doorway that lead toward the living room, he called to Stevie.

"I'm going to work out in the shop, Stevie. Want to come with me?"

"Yeah! Can I wear my chaps and spurs?" Stevie eagerly called as he loped down the hallway to the kitchen.

"Sure," Drake answered as the boy skidded to a halt in front of him. "And get your jacket, too. It's a little cool out there today."

Stevie raced away, only to return moments later, dressed and bouncing on his toes in his eagerness to go.

Great, Hope muttered to herself as she watched the two of them head out the back door, chattering between themselves. Christmas day and they were leaving her alone again.

By late afternoon, she was bored to distraction. A couple of times she considered calling Abby or Dana, but she knew both of them would be at the Maitland mansion celebrating the holiday with all the family, and she didn't want to intrude. The same went for Katie. The nurse was from a big family that thrived on get-togethers. Katie would be in the thick of eating and drinking and merrymaking.

Once again Hope was reminded of just how alone she would be once Drake was out of her life. She rarely ever heard from her vagabond mother, and other than Georgia, she had no family to speak of. Only very distant relatives who lived hundreds of miles away. And now two of her friends were married and would soon be making families of their own.

*Face it, Hope,* she told herself, *you're going to have to get used to the quietness. The loneliness.* These few hours Drake had been spending in his workshop would be nothing compared with what her life was going to be like once they divorced.

Determined not to feel sorry for herself, she popped Christmas music into the tape player and went to work in the kitchen.

A half hour later, she was placing a pumpkin pie in the oven to bake when the front doorbell rang. Wiping her hands on a dish towel, she hurried to the living room, wondering who in the world would be coming by to visit on Christmas evening. She didn't remember extending invitations to anyone.

Swinging back the door, she was shocked to see Katie Topper standing on the other side of the threshold.

"Katie! What a surprise! Come in!"

Stepping into the small foyer, the nurse glanced regretfully at her friend. "I'm sorry to be bothering you like this, Hope. But I—I didn't know who else to turn to."

The distress in Katie's voice had Hope taking a second look at her friend. Usually her strawberry blond curls were shiny and bouncy, but this evening they lay dull and limp against her head. Red, puffy crescents lay beneath her green eyes, and the rest of her skin resembled the pasty color of pie dough.

"Don't be silly. You're not bothering me—but, Katie, what's wrong? You look awful."

Releasing a ragged breath, Katie touched her fingertips to her face. "I didn't bother to put on makeup. I know I look a mess."

"You look ill," Hope corrected, then grabbed her by the arm and led her toward the kitchen. "Come on and I'll get you something to eat."

Katie groaned sickly. "Lord, no! I couldn't eat a bite."

Hope glanced at her sharply. "I'll make you some coffee, then. Maybe that will help."

In the kitchen, Katie took a seat at the small dining table. Hope went to work putting fresh coffee on to brew.

"Something's cooking," Katie said with a sniff, then pressing a palm to her midsection added, "if I jump up and suddenly run out of here, don't be offended. My stomach feels like a roller coaster right at the moment.''

"I'm cooking turkey and pie for our Christmas dinner," Hope told her. "I'd ask you to join us, but it sounds as though you're not going to be able to eat.''

Katie shook her head with regret. "Thanks for the invitation, but I won't be staying that long, Hope. Besides, I wouldn't dare intrude on your Christmas dinner. I really just came by to—'' She glanced around her as though it just dawned on her that someone else might be in the room with them. "Are we alone?''

Hope nodded as she took a seat opposite Katie. "Drake and Stevie are out in Drake's workshop. They won't be coming back in for a while.''

"Oh.''

When she didn't go on, Hope reached across the table and squeezed her hand. "Katie, have you had a row with your family or something? I thought you'd be celebrating the holiday with them today.''

Katie closed her red, puffy eyes. "I haven't seen my family since—well since I got back to Austin yesterday. I called them to say I'd be coming by later today, but I can't go over there and see them—like this.''

"What do you mean like this?" Hope asked. "Is something wrong?''

Katie peeked at her with one eye. "Trust me, Hope, it's a long story that I just can't—well, like Abby said the other day, some things are just too private to share. All I can say is that it wasn't intended. None of it.''

Hope decided not to ask what "it" was. Instead she gave her friend a brief smile. "We're all entitled to have a mess-up now and then, Katie. It's nothing to beat yourself up about.''

Katie pressed her lips together, but they quivered anyway. Her eyes were wet with tears as she looked across the table at Hope. "This nausea will eventually go away. But I'm not so sure—about—about anything else."

Suddenly Hope looked worried. "Is something wrong with your health?"

A short burst of mocking laughter erupted from Katie, causing Hope to stare at her in puzzlement.

"No. There's nothing wrong with me, except that I'm pregnant."

Hope gasped. The word *pregnant* was the last thing she'd expected to come out of Katie's mouth. "Katie! Are you sure?"

The other woman nodded grimly. "I don't know why—I've been putting it off for a long time—but I decided to have a blood test run yesterday. I'm nearly three months pregnant."

"Three months! Katie, why haven't you said anything before now?"

Katie's fingers were trembling as she passed them over her forehead. "Because I—the father doesn't know yet. Neither does Papa. You're the only one I've told."

Although Hope had some suspicion who the father was, now wasn't the time to ask. She rose from her seat and went to fetch the coffee.

Behind her, Katie whispered with anguish, "Oh, Hope, I dread like hell telling him. He's not going to be happy about it. I'm sure of that."

Hurrying to the table, Hope placed the coffee in front of Katie, then curled a comforting arm around her shoulders. "First of all, you're going to quit worrying."

"Quit worrying? Are you crazy? I've gotten myself into a heck of a mess."

Hope gave Katie's shoulders another gentle squeeze. "No, my dear friend, if you're going to have a baby, I don't see it as a heck of a mess. I see you as one of the luckiest women in the world.''

With a tiny sob, Katie looked at her. ''Somehow I knew you'd say that. Dana and Abby wouldn't understand how I feel. They're too happy, too rich to understand women like me and you. That's why I had to see you, Hope.''

Touched that Katie had sought her out before anyone else, Hope pushed the limp curls off her friend's pale forehead in a gesture meant to soothe. ''Come on and drink your coffee. And maybe in a little while you'll feel like driving over to see your folks.''

After a bit more coaxing, Hope finally managed to persuade Katie to try a sip of the coffee. Halfway through the cup, she fetched Katie a few saltine crackers and ordered her to eat them.

By the time the two women walked to the front door, Katie was feeling somewhat better, but she was still clearly frazzled. Such a state was totally out of character for the normally unflappable nurse. In fact, it was difficult for Hope to imagine Katie putting herself into such a compromising situation with a man. But then men had a knack for making women behave foolishly, she thought grimly. She was a prime example of that.

''Hope? Where are you?''

As Drake stepped through the back door, his voice carried to Katie. ''That's Drake,'' Katie said in a rush. ''I'm going. I don't want him to see me like this!''

Katie hurried down the sidewalk to her car, and Hope called after her, ''Bye, honey. Merry Christmas!''

Katie turned and gave her a little wave, then quickly slipped behind the wheel and drove away.

Hope shut the door, then turned to see Drake had entered the living room. "That was Katie leaving," she explained. "She just stopped by for a few minutes."

He smiled. "Why didn't you have her stay for dinner? The more the merrier."

His suggestion took her by surprise. Drake had always encouraged her to have friends, but he'd never been the dinner party type.

"Katie was...she had to be leaving. She couldn't stay."

"That's too bad," he said, then stepping closer, he searched her troubled face. "What's wrong? You look like you're going to burst into tears."

She took a deep breath, but it didn't help. Hot moisture welled in her eyes and spilled onto her cheeks.

His fingertips reached to softly touch her face. "Hope, tell me what's wrong," he urged in a husky voice. "You shouldn't be crying. It's Christmas."

She sniffed. "Nothing is wrong. Nothing except that Katie is pregnant. She's worried about telling—the father."

Instead of a sarcastic retort, Hope was surprised to see concern flicker across his face. "And what did you tell her?"

She drew in another deep breath and let it out slowly. "I told her she shouldn't be worried about anything. That if she was going to have a baby...she was the luckiest woman alive."

A rueful smile twisted his lips, then suddenly his hand was on her hair, stroking the silken strands away from her face.

"My poor darling. I'm so ashamed of what I've done to you."

Tilting her head, she looked at him, her features scrunched with bewilderment. "Drake, what are you—"

Before she could put the question together, he took her by the hand and began to tug her along after him.

"It's time I showed you something. It'll answer all your questions. At least I hope it will."

Her heart pounding with anticipation, she allowed him to lead her out of the living room and down the short hallway to the kitchen.

"I don't understand, Drake. Are you trying to say—"

She stopped in midsentence as the two of them entered the room. The scent of roasting turkey and pumpkin pie now mingled with fumes of varnish.

Then she spotted it, and her heart nearly stopped. There in the middle of the floor, not far from the dining table, was a wooden crib with a big red bow tied around it. A baby crib!

Gasping, she rushed forward, then stopped to look at Drake to make sure she wasn't dreaming. He was smiling and nodding in answer to the question on her face.

"That's your real Christmas present this year, Hope. All this week I've been working like crazy, trying to get it finished. I wasn't sure I was going to have it ready by today. But Stevie was a big help. Without him I don't think I could have managed."

It was then Hope realized Stevie was sitting in one of the chairs at the dining table. The boy was smiling proudly, eagerly waiting for her reaction.

"How do you like your gift, Aunt Hope? I helped Uncle Drake sand the wood and then we rubbed stain on it. And today we put that shiny stuff over it."

"It—it's beautiful, Stevie," she said in a choked voice. "I love the crib. So very much."

Drake was suddenly standing beside her, and as his arm slid around her back, she began to cry in earnest.

"I built it from pecan wood. Isn't the grain beautiful?

The varnish isn't quite dry enough to touch yet. But the heat here in the house will do the trick. I'll move it upstairs so the fumes won't interfere with supper." He pulled a handkerchief from the back pocket of his jeans and handed it to her. "Here. It sounds like you need this."

She took the white square of fabric and dabbed the tears from her eyes. "I've never seen anything so beautiful, Drake. You must have worked so terribly hard on it."

The head- and footboards were carved in a scalloped design. The legs, along with the spokes that made up the sides of the bed, were intricately carved and spaced close enough together so that there was no danger of a baby's head or foot being lodged between them.

"It was a labor of love. I hope you believe that, darling."

Suddenly all the terrible weight of the past months melted away from her heart, and she flung herself against his chest. "Oh, Drake, I love you!" she sobbed with happiness.

Gathering her close, he bent his head and whispered against her ear. "I love you, too, Hope. So very much. Forgive me, darling. Please forgive me."

He held her tightly for long, long moments, then tilted her head and kissed her softly on the lips.

Grinning at her, he murmured, "I think Stevie deserves a hug of appreciation, too. Don't you?"

Laughing, Hope turned in his arms and motioned for Stevie. The boy scrambled off the chair to join the two adults.

Hope quickly knelt and gathered the child in her embrace. "Thank you, Stevie. You're the most wonderful boy anybody could ever have."

He tilted his head to one side as he studied her tearful face. "But why are you crying, Aunt Hope? You're supposed to be happy."

Hope laughed again, and Drake realized it was the most precious sound he could ever hear.

"She is happy, son. Women just do that sometimes."

Satisfied that his aunt wasn't sad after all, Stevie grinned broadly at Hope. "When will you have a baby to put in the crib, Aunt Hope? Will it take a long time to get one?"

Unsure of how to answer the boy's question, Hope glanced at Drake for help. The sly little smile on his face sent a thrill rushing all the way from her head to her toes.

"Not long if I have anything to do with it," Drake said.

Stevie jumped up and down. "Oh, boy! When he grows up, can he be a cowboy, too?"

Both Hope and Drake laughed with pure joy.

"Only if he wants to, Stevie," Drake answered. "But I have a feeling he just might want to be your sidekick."

MUCH LATER that night, after the three of them were stuffed with turkey and all the trimmings and Stevie was sound asleep in his bed, Hope lay on her side, her head pillowed on Drake's shoulder.

Contentment purred deep in her throat as his hand slid over the bare mound of her hip. "All this time I thought you wanted a divorce," she confessed.

Since the two of them had just now caught their breath from making urgent, desperate love, the idea of a divorce seemed ludicrous, making Drake chuckle.

Then in a sober voice, he said, "I've been mixed up for a long time, Hope. But deep down, I never wanted a divorce. Thank God, I never lost all my senses. I still had enough to know I could never live without you."

She pressed a kiss against his cheek, then three more along his jaw. "And all this time I've been wondering how I could possibly survive without you."

He groaned with regret. "I hate myself for putting you through this agony. For putting both of us through it. But I was...I guess I was like a blind man, Hope. All I could see was my past...my parents. The very idea that I would be the same sort of father filled me with sick fear. And the fact that Denise had turned out to be such a horrible mother justified my thinking. Like brother, like sister. Like father, like son."

Shaking her head, she cradled her palm against the side of his face. "You've never been like your parents or Denise. It just isn't in you. That's why I kept thinking if you agreed to stay here with me and Stevie for the month, you might see yourself in a different light."

He looked at her, his eyes full of love. "I thank God for Stevie. Without him I might never have realized what I was missing. All the wonderful things I was throwing away by denying you a child. *Us* a child."

Her hand slipped from his face to glide across his damp chest. "What did finally make you change your mind, Drake?"

One corner of his mouth lifted in a lopsided grin. "The day I took Stevie riding, the two of us had a long talk. I told him all about how his grandparents sold the ranch so that I could never work it, and that they expected me to do only the things they wanted." He shook his head as though he couldn't believe he'd been so misguided for so many years. "You know, Hope, I discovered that seeing life through the eyes of a child will open your own eyes to a lot of things. My parents never loved me. They didn't know how. And they damn sure didn't deserve all the sacrifices I made in an effort to gain their love and respect. I suddenly realized I didn't want the same thing to happen to Stevie. Not now or ever. And that I would never treat a child of my own as they treated me. I also understood it was wrong of me to put conditions on our marriage. Forbidding you to get pregnant was making me just the same—no, even worse than my dictating parents."

Tears of pain and joy filled Hope's heart. Pain for all the awful years of his childhood. Joy that he'd finally broken free of those invisible chains his parents had bound around him. "Oh, Drake, I understand you have fears—"

He placed a gentle finger against her lips. "If you're brave enough to try again, then I have to be brave enough to let you."

Her eyes misted over. "Things will go right for us this time, Drake. Abby says I can have plenty of babies. And I know in my heart I will. But, Drake, why didn't you tell me your feelings had changed? All this week—I've been in agony!"

He turned to her, his cheek finding the smooth curve of her neck. "I didn't say anything because—well, I knew I'd hurt you so badly that you were probably hating me. I knew it was going to take a lot more than words to prove to you that I'd changed. That I really did want us to have children. That's why I was working so feverishly on the crib. Building it was the only way I could think of to show you what was really in my heart."

"Oh, Drake, I do believe you. I love you so much, my darling." She went suddenly still as she realized what he'd said. "Children? Would you really like more than one?"

He chuckled as his mouth searched for hers in the darkness. "We're not about to have just one."

She sighed blissfully against his lips. "What about Stevie?"

"The boy is like me, Hope. He's already beginning to feel like my son. When Denise returns from Europe I'm going to have a long talk with her. I think I can convince her that Stevie belongs with us."

Hope wasn't too surprised. These past few days, she could see a bond growing stronger and stronger between her husband and his nephew. "Is that what you want?"

He smiled, then nodded. "What about you?"

She slipped her arms around his neck. "Yes, very much," she whispered happily, then as he began to nuzzle kisses down one breast, another thought struck her and she began to giggle.

"What's the matter? Are my whiskers tickling you?"

"No. I just remembered I have another gift for you. It's hidden downstairs in the kitchen broom closet. Should I go get it?"

"Hmm. I can't imagine anything better than having you in my arms."

"Well, I'd decided not to give them to you, anyway. At the time I bought them, I didn't think it would help our sorry state of affairs. But Dana and Katie talked me into it."

Curious, he lifted his head. "What is it? Handcuffs and a whip?"

She laughed. "Nothing that kinky. Just sexy lingerie to tempt you with."

His hands cupped her breasts, his fingers kneading their warm fullness. "I've got all the temptation I can stand right now."

To prove it, he lowered his body over hers and slowly began to make love to her again.

"Didn't we already do this a few minutes ago?" her husky voice teased.

"We're not counting tonight. Besides, I want to make sure we conceive a Christmas baby."

"Oh, I see. Just another labor of love."

"Exactly."

"You could be wasting your time. I could already be pregnant," she reminded him with a throaty whisper.

His hips thrust deeper, driving home the fact of how much he needed her and the family they would surely have.

"Then this will just be added insurance, my darling."

# *EPILOGUE*

DRAKE CALMLY REACHED for the burning cigarette on the edge of the ashtray and squashed it with a vengeance.

Across the kitchen table, Denise's thin, angular face said she was clearly annoyed with her brother. "Why, Drake, what's the matter with you?"

Her offended wail grated on his nerves, just as everything else about his sister rubbed him the wrong way. Her too bleached hair, showy jewelry, and clothing were more suited to a high-priced call girl than a mother in her early thirties. Denise's taste in clothing had never matched her bank balance. But if that had been her only fault, Drake could have easily overlooked it.

In fact, when the two of them had been young, he'd wanted to be close to her, needed her companionship. But early on, he could see she was too much like their parents, too full of herself to be a loving sister. As for a mother, he'd seen alley cats demonstrate more affection for their young.

Denise had arrived only ten minutes ago, yet after a pat on the head and a few questions about his Christmas, she'd dismissed Stevie, ordering him upstairs to get his things ready to leave.

"This is my house, Denise. Not yours. I don't want it smelling like a bar. Besides, you've already had too many of those damn things."

Outrage popped her mouth open even wider. "I've only been here a few minutes!"

He leveled a dry look at her. "That ought to tell you something."

"Well," she huffed, "it's a good thing I've already called for a taxi to be here in an hour."

Drake hadn't been expecting her to leave so quickly. This was going to force him to get straight to the issue. "There's no need for you to rush, Denise."

Somewhat mollified by his words, she waved a hand through the air. "I'm attending a New Year's party back in Dallas tonight, anyway. So I've booked a quick turn-around flight."

Drake drummed his fingers against the tabletop. He'd been dreading this day, this moment for some time. Denise was unpredictable and prone to hysterics. He didn't want Stevie subjected to one of her tantrums. But then the boy was probably already used to his mother's moods, he thought grimly.

"I told Hope not to bother packing Stevie's things," he said bluntly.

Denise's glossed lips parted, and her eyes went blank. "What did you say?"

"Hope isn't helping Stevie pack his things. She's reading a story to him."

"Why the hell not? You mean nothing has been packed?"

Rising from the chair, Drake moved across the room, away from his sister. Gazing somberly out the bay window, he said, "I don't think Stevie should go back to Dallas with you."

Instead of the instant outburst he'd expected from her, she was silent for long moments. Drake glanced over his shoulder to see her glowering at him.

"Just where do you think he should go, big know-it-all brother? You want to put him in boarding school here in Austin?"

Folding his arms against his chest, Drake turned slightly toward her. "No. The boy doesn't need to be in boarding school, period."

This floored Denise, and she jumped to her feet and crossed the room to confront him. "What's with you, Drake? Boarding school is a tradition in our family. You and I both went to boarding school and we both got a good education and good care."

His lip curled at her comment. "Oh, yeah. We got care, all right. But we didn't get what we needed the most. Like a family. A home that was really a home."

Anger tightened her features. "Are you implying I haven't given Stevie a good home? Why, he has the best—"

"Best what?" Drake swiftly interrupted. "Best clothes? Best house?"

"Are you saying those things aren't important?" she demanded, jamming her hands on either side of her slender hips.

Denise was a petite woman, and as Drake looked at her, the notion struck him that she was more child than anything else. And as a child, her own needs came first and foremost.

Frustration sent his fingers slicing through his hair. "Of course they're important, Denise. But there's a damn sight more that he needs than material things. Like a mother and father at home every morning and night to give him love and attention, to teach him things little boys need to know to become men."

Her lips thinned, and she darted a glance toward the entryway of the kitchen as though she expected Hope to appear any moment. "I should have never confided in Hope and told her that Phillip was neglecting Stevie. Now you have the wrong idea—"

"Denise! A blind person could see the man hasn't spent any time with his son."

Denise rolled her eyes and slashed her hand helplessly through the air. "It isn't my fault! I've tried to make Phillip be more attentive, Drake. But he never wanted kids in the first place. He's just not the father type. And anyway, we have enough problems without me hounding him about Stevie!"

Drake's eyes narrowed. "What's going on with you and Phillip, anyway?"

She mouthed a few curse words he hadn't heard since his locker-room days. "We cut our trip short. We're getting a divorce. Phillip has already moved out of the house. And good riddance to the bastard is all I can say."

Drake breathed an inward sigh of relief. "It sounds as though he doesn't care what you do with Stevie."

The laugh Denise gave was like bubbling acid. "Care? That's a joke. The man doesn't even care about me, much less his kid." Then her eyes narrowed with suspicion. "What are you getting at, anyway, Drake? You say Stevie doesn't belong in boarding school, so what the hell do you expect me to do with him?"

If Drake had had any misgivings about making Stevie his own child, Denise had just crushed them. She honestly didn't have a clue what being a mother really meant.

"Leave him here with me and Hope," he said frankly. "We want to adopt him as our own son."

Her brown eyes widened, then narrowed as a surly smile twisted her lips. "You can't have a kid of your own, so now you want mine."

It took all Drake's effort to hold on to his temper.

"Hope and I are going to have children of our own. That's just a matter of time. But this thing with Stevie has nothing to do with any children we might have in the future. We love him. We want him to be a part of our family. And we believe he feels the same way."

Furious at the idea of Stevie choosing Drake over her, Denise whirled on her heel. "I'll just go see about this!"

Before she could take two steps out of the room, Drake caught her by the shoulder. "I'm warning you, Denise, don't go upstairs and upset that boy in any way. If you do, you'll have me to answer to. And I think you know I'm not the soft pushover Phillip is."

Even though he'd dropped his hold on her, the dark threat in his voice was enough to set Denise back on her heels. "What do you think I am, Drake? Some sort of bitch who'd just turn her child over to someone else?"

His stony expression didn't waver. "You've been doing it for more than six years, haven't you?"

She was silent for a moment, and then her shoulders sagged as though his question had knocked the air from her. "You know how to punch low, don't you?"

"I only want you to think about Stevie. For once in your life."

She turned her back to him, then shook her head in defeat. "I know I'm a rotten mother, Drake," she mumbled. "I admit he'd be better off with you and Hope."

Stepping forward, Drake put his hand gently on her shoulder. "Then you'll agree to have adoption papers drawn up?"

She made an indecisive gesture with her hand. "You're going too fast, Drake. Give me time to think this thing over. He is my son, after all. I can't just give him away without a thought. Still…"

"Look, as long as Stevie stays here, I'm willing to

deal with the legal part of things later. But in the meantime, what about Phillip? Do you think he'll give you any problems about Stevie living here?''

She shrugged. ''I can't be certain. But he's asking for a big divorce settlement. Mostly money. I seriously doubt he'll rock the boat by fighting me over Stevie.''

Drake squeezed her shoulder. ''Do you want to go upstairs and tell him? Or shall I?''

She glanced back at him and for the first time he could ever remember, Drake saw a mist of tears in her eyes. ''I'll do it. He deserves that much from me.''

SEVERAL MINUTES LATER, Hope was sitting beside Drake on the living room sofa when Stevie descended the stairs followed by Denise.

A lump of emotion lodged in Hope's throat as the boy came to stand quietly in front of them. His chin sagged against his chest as he mumbled, ''Mommy says I'm to stay here.''

Drake pulled the boy between his knees and circled one arm around his back. ''Stevie, Hope and I really would like to be your new mommy and daddy. But the important thing is, would you like it, too?''

The boy's brown eyes flickered with mistrust as he looked from Drake to Hope and back again. ''Would I get to stay here all the time? I wouldn't have to leave? Or go to boarding school?''

Smiling, Hope shook her head at him. Next to her Drake said, ''This will be your home, Stevie. You won't ever have to leave. But you'll probably want to when you grow to be a big man and get that ranch you want.''

Still not quite convinced he was truly wanted, he gazed skeptically at Drake. ''What about when Hope has a baby? You might not want me here then.''

Drake chuckled softly while Hope had to blink back tears. ''Don't you worry about that, son. It won't make any difference how many babies Hope has. We'll always want you, too. The only difference will be that you'll have to share your toys with your brothers and sisters. Okay?''

For an answer, he flung his arms around Drake's neck and hung on tight.

Across the room, Denise picked up her bag and stepped out the door to the waiting taxi.

## MAITLAND MATERNITY

*continues with*
*Diagnosis: Daddy*
*by*
*Jule McBride*

*Ford Carrington and Katie Topper had worked together to save the lives of hundreds of babies... And now they'd made one of their own! Ford wanted marriage, but Katie wanted love. Would they manage to find both, or would their differences tear them apart?*

*Coming up next*
*Here's a preview!*

# CHAPTER ONE

KATIE STOMPED her foot on the pavement, fisting her hands. "Yes, Ford! Yes, it's true! I'm pregnant! I'm pregnant!"

When Ford drew air into his lungs again, he started to suggest they get in her car, so they could run the heater while they talked, but he couldn't risk being in such a small, enclosed space with her. In close proximity, he'd either throttle her or do what he shouldn't, wouldn't allow himself to do before this was settled—make love to her.

Katie had paled, her translucent skin turning the color of paper. "Uh...how did you guess?"

Images were still filling his mind, of watching her belly become rounder, of holding the baby in his hands. "I'm surrounded by pregnant women sixty hours a week, just as you are." And yet it was more than that, as if he were simply in tune with Katie.

She nodded, suddenly looking small and strangely miserable. "I...I'm sorry. I should have called."

*No kidding.* "You're sure it's mine?"

As the remaining color drained from her face, he realized he didn't feel as guilty as he should have about wounding her pride, not when she hadn't even bothered to call him. Her voice was a near whisper. "Of course it is, Ford."

He forced himself not to acknowledge his relief. "But I didn't rate a phone call?"

"I'm here, aren't I?"

"Only because you were called in for an emergency," he pointed out, barely able to believe her silence or the fact that he was going to be a father. "For all I know, you were considering taking that job in Houston."

"No. I'm staying here." She stared at him for a second. "At least I think so."

As if he'd force her to leave. "Were you going to tell me?"

Her lips parted with shock. "Yes. Of course."

A stranger seemed to get hold of him, one with less pride than Ford usually possessed. Or more anger. "But you *didn't* tell me, did you, Katie?"

"You're not making this easy, Ford."

"I don't intend to."

"I was nervous," she explained and as she stepped defensively back, he reached out, wrapped a hand around her upper arm and drew her toward him. Too late, he realized he'd brought her just inches away. For an instant, Ford almost forgot the conversation. It took everything he had not to kiss her, but he could never allow himself the pleasure, not when she hadn't even called him. She wanted him to kiss her, though. That was the hell of it. Her mouth puckered. Her lips parted. And as pleased as he was to see desire spark in those come-hither green eyes, it threatened to gentle his emotions, so he loosened his hold.

She wrenched away, rubbing her upper arm as if he'd done real damage, which he hadn't. "Never grab me like that."

"I'll never touch you again. I promise."

He immediately wished he hadn't spoken. Not that it

mattered. Her eyes said she knew it was a lie. "I was going to call from Houston," she told him. "But this seemed like news I should deliver face to face."

"Yeah," he muttered. "You could have driven to my place." He glanced away, fighting emotions he couldn't even begin to untangle. They'd been together only one night, he'd desperately wanted her back in his bed for months, but now they'd be tied together for life. Life was a long time. Even with a woman whose body he craved as much as Katie's.

# MAITLAND MATERNITY

**Silhouette®**
**HARLEQUIN®**

If you've enjoyed getting to know the Maitland family,
Harlequin® and Silhouette® invite you to come back and
visit the Maitland Maternity clinic! Just collect three (3)
proofs-of-purchase from the backs of three (3) different
MAITLAND MATERNITY titles and receive a free
MAITLAND MATERNITY book that's
not available in retail outlets!

Just complete the order form and send it, along
with three (3) proofs-of-purchse from three (3)
different MAITLAND MATERNITY titles, to:
MAITLAND MATERNITY, P.O. Box 9057, Buffalo, NY
14269-9057 or P.O. Box 622, Fort Erie, Ontario, L2A 5X3.

Name: _____

Address: _____ City: _____

State/Prov.: _____ Zip/Postal Code: _____

Please specify which title(s) you would like to receive:

☐ 0-373-65074-4   **Baby 101** by Marisa Carroll
☐ 0-373-65075-2   **Adopt-a-Dad** by Marion Lennox
☐ 0-373-65076-0   **The Trouble with Twins** by Jo Leigh
☐ 0-373-65077-9   **Fugitive Fiancée** by Kristin Gabriel

**Remember—for each title selected,
you must send three (3) proofs-of-purchase!**

(Please allow 4-6 weeks for delivery. Offer expires October 31, 2001.)

**093 KIF CSAS**
PHMMPOP

ONE
PROOF-OF-PURCHASE
MM-POP

# You're not going to believe this offer!

**In October and November 2000, buy any two Harlequin or Silhouette books and save $10.00 off future purchases, or buy any three and save $20.00 off future purchases!**

Just fill out this form and attach 2 proofs of purchase (cash register receipts) from October and November 2000 books and Harlequin will send you a coupon booklet worth a total savings of $10.00 off future purchases of Harlequin and Silhouette books in 2001. Send us 3 proofs of purchase and we will send you a coupon booklet worth a total savings of $20.00 off future purchases.

*Saving money has never been this easy.*

---

## I accept your offer! Please send me a coupon booklet:

Name: _____

Address: _____ City: _____

State/Prov.: _____ Zip/Postal Code: _____

---

### Optional Survey!

In a typical month, how many Harlequin or Silhouette books would you buy new at retail stores?

☐ Less than 1    ☐ 1    ☐ 2    ☐ 3 to 4    ☐ 5+

Which of the following statements best describes how you buy Harlequin or Silhouette books? Choose one answer only that best describes you.

☐ I am a regular buyer and reader
☐ I am a regular reader but buy only occasionally
☐ I only buy and read for specific times of the year, e.g. vacations
☐ I subscribe through Reader Service but also buy at retail stores
☐ I mainly borrow and buy only occasionally
☐ I am an occasional buyer and reader

Which of the following statements best describes how you choose the Harlequin and Silhouette series books you buy new at retail stores? By "series," we mean books within a particular line, such as *Harlequin PRESENTS* or *Silhouette SPECIAL EDITION*. Choose one answer only that best describes you.

☐ I only buy books from my favorite series
☐ I generally buy books from my favorite series but also buy books from other series on occasion
☐ I buy some books from my favorite series but also buy from many other series regularly
☐ I buy all types of books depending on my mood and what I find interesting and have no favorite series

---

Please send this form, along with your cash register receipts as proofs of purchase, to:
**In the U.S.:** Harlequin Books, P.O. Box 9057, Buffalo, NY 14269
**In Canada:** Harlequin Books, P.O. Box 622, Fort Erie, Ontario L2A 5X3
(Allow 4-6 weeks for delivery) Offer expires December 31, 2000.

PHQ4002

# MAITLAND MATERNITY

**Where the luckiest babies are born!**

### If you missed the first three books in the MAITLAND MATERNITY series, here's your chance to order your copies today!

## MAITLAND MATERNITY

| | | | |
|---|---|---|---|
| #65062 | **DAD BY CHOICE** by Marie Ferrarella | $4.50 U.S.☐ | $5.25 CAN.☐ |
| #65063 | **CASSIDY'S KIDS** by Tara Taylor Quinn | $4.50 U.S.☐ | $5.25 CAN.☐ |
| #65064 | **MARRIED TO THE BOSS** by Lori Foster | $4.50 U.S.☐ | $5.25 CAN.☐ |

*(limited quantities available)*

| | |
|---|---|
| **TOTAL AMOUNT** | $ |
| **POSTAGE & HANDLING** | $ |
| ($1.00 for one book, 50¢ for each additional) | |
| **APPLICABLE TAXES*** | $ _____ |
| **TOTAL PAYABLE** | $ _____ |

(check or money order—please do not send cash)

---

To order, complete this form and send it, along with a check or money order for the total above, payable to Maitland Maternity, to: **In the U.S.:** 3010 Walden Avenue, P.O. Box 9077, Buffalo, NY 14269-9077; **In Canada:** P.O. Box 636, Fort Erie, Ontario L2A 5X3.

Name: _____

Address: _____ City: _____

State/Prov.: _____ Zip/Postal Code: _____

Account # (if applicable): _____ 075 CSAS

*New York residents remit applicable sales taxes.
 Canadian residents remit applicable GST and provincial taxes.

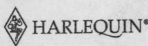 

Visit us at www.eHarlequin.com

MAITBACK4